On The Rocks

Jared Paakaula

For my Aunty Denise, our beautiful butterfly.

This book is also dedicated to my Hawaiian people,
my local Hawaii people and my people of the LGBT+
community all over the world.

Acknowledgments

First of all, I have to thank my partner in this life, my love, Drexten. Thank you for being so patient with me through this long journey of writing my first book. I thank the Universe for you every single day.

Thank you to my mom, who has supported me through my craziest of ideas and dreams, especially this one. Your edits in this book were the final touches needed to truly feel complete.

Thank you to my cousin, Michelle, my first best friend and my continued support system in this strange thing we call LIFE.

Thank you to my friend, Malia Tippets, for taking time out of your busy schedule and offering me some great edits and suggestions.

Thank you to my grammar genius, Cortney Silva, who I would text at all hours of the day and night, just to see if a sentence needed a comma or a word needed to be capitalized.

Thank you to my book cover creator/designer, pixelstudio. Thank you for your amazing creation.
(Find them at: www.fiverr.com/pixelstudio)

Thank you to Amazon KDP, for without which, this story would never have been able to truly come alive and get out into the real world. I am so grateful for the ease and thought put into your process for first time self-publishers.

Finally, thank you to YOU! Thank you for picking up this book and giving a little Hawaiian boy a chance. I hope this story resonates with you no matter where in the world you may be from.

Table of Contents

On

The

Rocks

1. Bloody Mary

- 1 1/2 oz Vodka
- 2 oz Tomato Juice
- 1 tsp Worcestershire Sauce
- 3 dashes Tabasco
- 1 pinch Salt
- 1 dash Black Pepper
- 1/4 tsp Lemon Juice
- 1 stalk Celery

The sun has just set on a Friday night in Hawaii, marking the beginning of the weekend. There's a little bit of pink left in the sky and rush hour traffic, while still present, is finally thinning out. Businessmen and executive women head home to their families as the day comes to a close, while others get ready for their night shifts.

In a bedroom, an alarm blares from a cell phone on a nightstand. It has been going off for thirty minutes. On the bed, Kaleo (pronounced Ka-LAY-ō) sleeps naked, flat on his stomach, with his nice plump butt facing the heavens. His dirty black hair is a mess and his naturally tanned skin was glowing just before the sun went down.

Still single and having just turned thirty, Kaleo has been questioning himself as to why his dreams are still just that, dreams. He questions why he's still a bartender and not the owner of his own bar. Feeling frustrated and lonely, Kaleo drinks to drown the heaviness of reality.

The alarm has now been going off for thirty-four minutes. When he is finally conscious enough to hear the alarm, Kaleo's head starts to throb immediately. He grunts with irritation. He reaches for his phone with what looks like a possessed left arm, while the rest of his body is in the exact same position. Once he finds his phone on the nightstand, he snoozes his alarm and lies in bed half awake.

He opens his right eye to peek and see where he is; he had one hell of a night last night. He realizes that he is home and he's proud of himself for that. Based on his almost dark room, Kaleo's brain registers that it's after dusk. Instantly he thinks, *What time is it?!* He sits up in a panic, scrambles around looking for a clock, then finally finds his phone which displays 7:14pm.

"SHIT!" Kaleo shouts. He's late for work. Other than the owner, Kaleo is the only one with a key to *Violet*, Honolulu's hottest and trendiest gay nightclub. Being the lead bartender, it's his responsibility to open the club and organize the staff's duties for the night.

"Shit, shit, shit, shit…" Kaleo keeps muttering as he runs around the room trying to find clean clothes. He's still a bit dizzy from the shots he took last night. He runs into the bathroom, gargles some mouthwash and splashes some water on his face. He looks at himself in the mirror and says, "You're in deep shit" and thinks to himself, *God, I look like shit.*

He runs back to the bedroom, grabs his keys and his phone off the nightstand, then runs out the door, completely unaware that he has forgotten his wallet.

2. Hello Kitty

- 3/4 oz Watermelon Puckers
- 3/4 oz Sour Apple Puckers
- 1/2 oz Cranberry Juice
- Float of Bacardi 151
    *Shake and serve as a shot

In the bathroom, Ashley studies herself in the mirror. She's a small, local Hawaiian girl, with a little bit of chub left on her mid-region from having two kids. Just about ready to go, she makes sure every hair is in place and her C-cup boobs are pushed up nice and tight giving the illusion that they're D-cups. She applies her favorite strawberry flavored lip gloss to her full lips as her five year old daughter, Zaysha, runs into the bathroom.

"Mommy, I can't sleep," Zaysha says in a whiny, but cute voice. She's wearing her pink Hello Kitty pajamas that's one size too big.

"Go back to bed, baby," Ashley encourages gently.

"But it's Friday, why do I have to go to bed so early?" Zaysha asks, while seating herself on the closed toilet seat lid. She's still small enough that her legs hang like she's on a swing set, never touching the floor.

"Because you have a big day tomorrow, remember?" Ashley replies.

"No, my performance is next week, remember?" Zaysha counters mockingly.

"Yeah, but you have a rehearsal tomorrow morning, remember? Plus, Grandma doesn't wanna hang out with you!"

"Yes she does! She always lets me watch TV with her 'til I fall asleep," Zaysha accidentally admits.

"Oooh she does, does she?" The kids know that once the sun is down, it's time to brush their teeth, head to bed and absolutely no TV. "Well, I'm gonna have to have a talk with Grandma now, aren't I?"

Zaysha's eyes widen realizing that she just got her grandma into trouble. "Oops." For a second, she stares at her mom with her big doe eyes and then runs laughingly into the kitchen where her Grandma is making herself something to eat.

Ashley chases Zaysha to the kitchen in a fun cat-mouse kind of way. In a tattle-tale type of voice, Ashley mocks "I'm gonna tell Grandma you told on her…"

In the Kitchen, Ashley's mom, Grace, is making two plates of shoyu chicken and rice; one for herself and one for her husband. Zaysha runs up to her grandma and hugs her legs, trying to hide from her mom, who is just on her tail.

"So I hear somebody is letting Zaysha stay up past her bedtime when I go to work?" Ashley says sarcastically as she walks up to her mother, raising one eyebrow.

Grace looks down at Zaysha, who is looking up at her. Hugging her legs even tighter now, Zaysha lips the word "Sorry."

Grace smiles at her granddaughter and then looks sharply at Ashley. Her smile instantly vanishes, "Eh! You live in *my* house, you live by *my* rules!" Grace says sternly, then with an easier tone responds, "Plus, she doesn't even last an hour."

Ashley smiles. She knows her mom is right. *Count your blessings, Ash*, she thinks to herself. With prices in Hawaii constantly on the rise, living with parents or other relatives can often seem like the only affordable way to stay in the islands. While Ashley has been fortunate enough, some other Hawaiian families have not had such luck. Having been priced out of their own native land, many locals have had to move away to seek cheaper costs of living.

"Thanks for watching the kids, Mom." Ashley kisses her mom on the cheek.

"Of course baby. I love my grandchildren! And, it's only easy anyway. She'll be passed out in a bit and your son is already in la-la land, so my job is basically done."

In the Living Room, Ashley's dad, Bruce, and her boyfriend, Malu (pronounced MUH-loo), sit on the couch watching a UFC fight on TV; both with their shirts off, both with a bottle of Heineken in their hand. Her son, Zaysten, is cuddled up next to Ashley's dad, completely knocked out as if he just got K.O.-ed in the UFC fight himself.

"BABE!" Ashley exclaims.

"What?" Malu replies and looks up at Ashley confused.

"We have to leave! You said that you were ready!" Ashley stares down the father of her children.

"I AM ready! Watch this…" Malu puts down his beer and puts on his shirt in one swift move. "See. TADA! Ready." Ever the jokester, Malu smiles and flashes his eyebrows at his girlfriend.

Ashley rolls her eyes and then smiles slightly. As much as he annoys her at times, she knows that his boyish charm is why she fell in love with him in the first place. "HURRY UP! Before you sleep on that damn couch tonight!" She threatens her boyfriend as she walks out to the car.

"Oh, you better get going, boy!" Ashley's dad says to Malu with a joking undertone. "Just like her maddah. FEISTY!"

"Just how we like 'em!" Malu comes back with. The two men share a laugh and shake hands to say goodbye. "K, Pop." They've created a fun, friendly bond over the years and Malu knows that he couldn't have asked for better In-Laws.

Malu kisses his sleeping son, then exits through the kitchen kissing his daughter and Ashley's mom on the way out. "Love you guys!" Malu throws up a shaka as he leaves the house.

3. Scooby Snack

- 3/4 oz Malibu Coconut Rum
- 3/4 oz Midori Melon Liqueur
- 1/2 oz Pineapple Juice
     *Shake and serve as a shot, then top with whipped cream

Parker and Momi (pronounced MŌ-mee) walk hand-in-hand on their way to work. Passing an ice cream shop on the way, Momi lets go of her boyfriend's hand and uses the big glass window pane to check herself out.

While adjusting her boobs and fixing her hair, she notices a cute, white Yorkshire Terrier sitting on the inside of the window ledge. Conveniently placed next to its owner, the dog looks up at her through the glass. Momi starts to play with the dog from the outside, while Parker's eyes are locked on the owner of the dog; a cute brunette with big tits.

Completely unaware of Parker and Momi's presence, the brunette sits alone working on her laptop. Her empty paper cup with a plastic spoon suggests that she has already finished her scoop of ice cream. Parker nudges Momi to stop playing mime with the puppy and direct her attention toward the owner's *chest puppies*. Momi is intrigued.

Parker is a Norwegian-type of tall with a strong swimmer's build from playing water polo back in college. His light brown hair has streaks of blonde from the sun and his naturally fair skin is now bronzed from surfing for hours on end. His beautiful hazel eyes and long eyelashes make him a modeling agency's dream.

Momi is an average height female, with an above-average sized rack. She is part-Hawaiian and tanned like a golden goddess. Her hair is short, done up high into a fashionable punk rock pixie cut and her full lips leave nothing to the imagination. Women and men alike lust after these two and make people question their own sexual identity.

Both beautiful and easy-going, these two are seen as the "It Couple" of O`ahu and have been together for a solid three years. When prompted with the eventual question: "How do you keep your relationship alive?" Their reply is always the same. "We're honest, we communicate, and we fuck whoever we want."

Being the *kind* people that Parker and Momi are, they often *help* people explore and figure out their sexual orientation, either separately or together. They agree that an open-relationship, with open communication is what works best for them. Their mentality is, "If it isn't broken, don't fix it," and three years later, they can attest to that. Their only rule is… no sex with close friends.

The couple enter the ice cream shop and both give a flirtatious look toward the dog owner. The brunette notices their gaze, instantly realizes how beautiful they both are, then quickly looks back to her computer out of inferiority. The couple chuckle. The ground has been laid and their mission has officially begun.

Parker and Momi head straight to the counter and order from a 19-year old boy who is obviously in awe of Momi.

"Hi! Can I get a single scoop of the Raspberry Cheesecake Gelato please?" Momi asks kindly.

"And can I get a double scoop of the Salted Caramel please? I like my ice cream like I like my women: Tanned and Salty, you know what I mean?" Parker jokes with the 19-year old boy. Momi slaps his arm playfully.

Still in awe of Momi's voluptuous body, the 19-year old boy swallows hard, trying to rid the lump in his throat. With only enough courage to shakily muster up the words "Uh, sure," he scoops the correct flavors, but hands them the wrong cup.

Quickly realizing his mistake, he tries to switch his hands, but his arms get tangled. "Uh, oops… sorry."

"No worries, babe," Momi says with a smile. She takes her cup of gelato and winks at the 19-year old boy, before walking away.

"They're real." Parker messes with the 19-year old, implying that Momi's boobs aren't implants. Parker pays for the tab and gestures for him to keep the change. *Alright, back to business*, Parker thinks to himself. Getting ice cream was just a cover for what they really came to do.

While there are many empty tables, Momi has already strategically placed herself at the table right next to the dog owner. Parker joins her and sits at the table as well. Pretending nothing of it at first, they soon engage the brunette in small talk.

"Your puppy is so cute," Momi says to start the conversation.

"Oh, thanks. He's actually 6 years old," the brunette says with a smile. She looks to the dog and says in a baby voice, "Not so much of a puppy anymore, are you my boy," and pets under his chin.

"You from around here?" Parker asks nosily.

"Uh, yeah. I live a couple of blocks away."

"Oh cool, we're bartenders at Violet, the gay club just around the corner from here." Momi licks her spoon sexually. "Have you been?"

"Oh, no. I'm not a lesb… I mean… I don't usually…" The brunette trips over her words. Trying to imply that she's not a lesbian without being offensive, she sighs and then continues nervously, "I'm kinda new in town and I don't really have any friends to go with, so…" She starts to feel uncomfortable, but the attention of these two beautiful beings keep her present.

"Well, now you know us, so you should swing by and we'll hook you up," Parker suggests. "You can even bring Mr…" he looks to the dog and waits to hear his name.

"Casper. His name is Casper," the brunette answers. "I'm Simone, by the way."

"Momi."

"Parker. Very nice to meet you," Parker says with a smile.

"Well, why don't I give you my phone number, so you can text me when you get to the door tonight and we'll get you in for free. Sound good?" Momi aggressively offers, then winks her signature wink.

Without hesitation and before Simone can resist, Momi grabs Simone's iPhone right off of her table. Before a full ten seconds have even passed, Momi manages to save her cell number into Simone's phone. She's obviously done this before.

In a voice used to talk to babies, Parker says to Casper, "We'll see you tonight, my Casper boy!" Casper licks his hand and smiles. "Oh see! You HAVE to come now. You'll break Casper's heart if you don't come. You'll break my heart too," Parker playfully guilt-trips Simone.

Momi smiles and hands Simone her phone. "We'll see you tonight," she says, then in a quick jolt, grabs Parker's arm and drags him toward the exit.

Parker gives Simone one last up-and-down look, smiles and then gets pulled out the door. Once outside and out of Simone's view, the couple high-five each other and head to work. The seed has been planted.

Simone sits at her table confused and weirdly aroused. *Those are some really friendly bartenders*, she thinks to herself, *and fucking gorgeous too!* She's unsure of what exactly just happened, but she knows that she's in no place to turn down new friends. She sits and contemplates her next move. *Should I go? What am I talking about? Two strangers come up to me and say 'come to this barely lit night club.' Sounds like a scary movie waiting to happen. Two BEAUTIFUL strangers though...*

I mean... one drink wouldn't hurt, right?

4. Part-Time Lover

- 1 1/2 oz. Blanco Tequila
- 1/2 oz. Aperol
- 1/2 oz. Elderflower Liqueur
- 3/4 oz. Fresh Lemon Juice
- 2 dashes Angostura Bitters

Lopaka (pronounced Lō-PAH-ka) gets out of the shower with his naked body still dripping wet. From his full-head of hair, water droplets make their way down his well-defined physique caressing every ripple along the way. His arms are pumped and his abs are tight from hitting the gym just before he got home.

Grabbing a towel off the rack, he begins to wipe himself down. Now mostly dry, he wraps the towel around his waist and looks to his iPhone sitting on the bathroom counter. He presses the button that activates his home screen, only to reveal that no one has left him any messages.

"What the fuck!" Lopaka quietly whispers to himself.

Lopaka is a handsome Hawaiian male, naturally tanned from always being outdoors. He sits at a comfortable 5'8", with an uncomfortably thick 8.5" dick. Having joined CrossFit a year ago, his ripped muscles and all-around athletic body help contribute to making him one of Violet's top male go-go dancers.

About six months ago, Lopaka started hooking up with another go-go dancer named Ryan, a good-looking local white boy with the body of a Greek God. Having spent half a year working together, working-out together and working each other's prostate, it was only a matter of time before feelings arose. Living in a society where *No Labels* has become the trend, the two boys followed suit. Never fully committing to each other as boyfriends, but wanting to be more than just fuck-buddies, the lines and boundaries lie vague and blurry. Tonight is no exception.

Having agreed upon dinner plans the day before, Lopaka waits patiently to hear from his 'boyfriend/not-boyfriend,' Ryan. However, with no surprise, Ryan is, once again, M.I.A. Frustrated and tired of Ryan's constant flakiness, Lopaka wonders why he continually puts himself in this situation.

Staring at his reflection in the mirror, Lopaka looks into his own light brown eyes. The mirror could shatter with how intense his gaze is. He looks to the ceiling and closes his eyes before exhaling vehemently.

"I'm so over this," Lopaka says looking back at the mirror and speaking to his reflection as if it were another person in the room. His mood quickly changes from irritated to determined. He grabs his cell phone off the counter, walks into the bedroom and throws his iPhone into his duffel bag.

On the TV, a commercial for the ever-popular, reality competition show entitled *America's Next Top Drag Queen* catches Lopaka's eye. He focuses in as he puts on his clothes, never letting his eyes leave the screen.

Last year's winner, Tara Way, appears on screen and speaks directly to the camera. "Do you think you have what it takes to *drag* yourself to the top? Then, go to 'ANTDQ.com' and submit your video application today! You could be the winner of a $100,000! Who will carry on the legacy and *tear*…" She tears away her outer costume, to reveal another costume underneath, "down the competition? Are you that bitch?"

Lopaka watches the commercial and thinks to himself, *I wouldn't mind trying drag*, then immediately retracts his thought and thinks, *Shit, what am I thinking? Ryan would hate that. He said he doesn't date femmes.*

He turns the TV off, grabs his duffel bag and heads out the door to get something to eat… alone.

5. Old Fashioned

- 1 1/2 oz Bourbon or Rye Whiskey
- 2 dashes Angostura Bitters
- 1 sugar cube
- Few dashes of plain water

Robin sits in the office of Violet wearing her favorite butterfly print blouse. She's the only one in the club. At her desk, she stares blankly at a letter that states "Second Notice." She threw away the first notice hoping that it would magically disappear. *Out of sight, out of mind*, she thought. That is, of course, until it shows up in your mailbox again like a guy in your DMs after ignoring him the first time.

She's been staring at this letter for the past five minutes. This month's payment to the building owners is overdue and her rent for the upcoming month is due by the end of the week. With no money and no plan, Robin sighs a defeated sigh.

Robin, a transgender Hawaiian woman in her mid 50s, is the owner of 'Violet Nightclub' and has been the owner since day one. She's tall with broad shoulders and with her hair up in a bun, she makes "The Rock" look like a pebble. Her frivolous spending throughout the years and flippant attitude toward hiring a financial advisor has turned the once lucrative nightclub into a blackhole for green dollar signs.

"Hey," a familiar voice says from the doorway behind her. Robin turns around to discover it's her best friend Chyna.

Chyna is also a transgender woman. She's a similar height to Robin and just a year younger. Their friendship extends back to high school, when Robin was a senior and Chyna was a junior. They knew every cheerleading routine, even though they weren't on the cheerleading team. Of course back then, they

14

went by 'Robbie' and 'Chuckie,' short for Robert and Charles.

Coming from a strict, traditional Korean family, Chyna's family disowned her when she decided to transition from male to female. Having nowhere else to go and with the grace of her best friend, Chyna moved in with Robin into her tiny studio apartment. The two friends, both at the beginning of their transition journeys, decided at that moment to make a promise to each other: nothing and no one in this life would ever stand in their way again.

"How did you get in here?" Robin says slightly startled, but masking it with anger. She quickly throws the letter back into the envelope in which it came.

"Girl, how long have we been friends? I know you leave the back door open during the day for deliveries. If you ask me, you should leave the front door open too, if you know what I mean. Two for one special." She notices Robin putting away the letter. "What's that?"

"Oh it's nothing. Just a doctor's bill from my last check up. Gotta keep the poop chute still shooting, right?" Robin lies and jokes to change the subject.

"Which reminds me… Have you seen the new movie 'Constipated?' Oh wait, it hasn't come out yet." China spits the one-liner at Robin. They both scream dramatically and laugh hysterically.

"No, but I did see 'Diarrhea.' It leaked, so they had to release it early." Robin wittily comes back with. They scream again and continue cackling.

"Seriously though, how is your health?" Chyna asks, changing the mood.

"I'm good, girl. For real. Don't worry about me. You couldn't get rid of me if you tried," Robin jokes to calm her friend's mind.

Chyna is one of the few people who know that Robin is

HIV-positive. Not wanting everyone to constantly worry and check up on her, she keeps this information a secret. Her lack of protection during sex in her former years led her to the three letters every queer person fears: HIV. While there have been medical advances in recent years, there is still no cure for HIV. Again, with no money and no plan, Robin's hope and health are dwindling.

"Let's get out of here. Do you want to get some Mexican?" Robin asks.

"Always. As long as he doesn't give me the runs."

"Runs where? Across the border?" Robin one-ups.

"Yeah, girl. Let 'em! I love Latin men," Chyna expresses. "Seriously though, girl, that Mexican place we had last time gave me the runs. Let's not go there again." They head out the back door, locking the club on the way out.

6. POG Mimosa

- 2 1/2 oz Champagne
- 2 1/2 oz Passion fruit-Orange-Guava Juice

Ashley and Malu turn the corner in their slightly beat-up white SUV. Having left the kids at home with Ashley's parents, they rush over to work thinking that they're late, but realize that they're actually pretty early.

They pull right up to the entrance of 'Violet,' where the sign states *No Parking 24 hours*. Malu realized awhile ago that as the doorman, he's in the perfect position to watch their car and make sure no one tows it. This stall has become his very own VIP parking.

Malu is 5'11" and a proud Hawaiian. He's big-boned and thick. Not fat at all, but instead a solid mass of man. Having wrestled back in high school, his stature can come off as intimidating, but his class clown personality makes him lovable. Often being misread for flirting with other girls, his playful, fun-loving ways can cause tension between him and Ashley,

As Ashley is getting out of the passenger side of their car, she hears a "Good Mooooooorning!" Knowing that it's obviously not morning, Ashley gathers straightaway that it has to be an employee of Violet, but who?

'Good Morning' has become the greeting of the entire staff of Violet. Having started as a joke further back than anyone can or cares to remember, it has since caught on and stuck like E6000.

Ashley looks over her shoulder to see Parker and Momi walking hand in hand toward her. They've both got a devious smile on their face. "Uh-oh. Here comes trouble," Ashley says with a sarcastic tone, loud enough for them to hear.

Parker and Momi giggle, throw their empty ice cream cups into the nearby trash can and meet Ashley at her side of the car. "Hi cousin," Momi greets.

"Hi cuz," Ashley says back. The two girls hug.

Momi's dad and Ashley's dad are brothers. Although the girls are first cousins, Momi and Ashley grew up more like sisters. This is the case in many close, tight-knit Hawaiian families.

"Hey Ashley," Parker says with a warm smile on his face.

"Good Morning, babes," Ashley responds and kisses Parker on the cheek.

"HOOOOOOOOOOOOO YOU FUCKAHSSS!!!" Malu yells out of Ashley's open passenger door, still sitting in the driver's seat. Sounding like someone ready to fight, the opposite is actually true. "Fuckah" in many cases is a term of endearment and a common way for Hawaii boys to greet each other.

"SUP YOU FUCKAH!" Parker yells back and then heads to Malu's side of the car. Malu gets out of the driver's seat and the boys do the bro hug: hand shake first, keeping their first between them and hugging with the other arm. They start in their own conversation.

The two girls look at each other and roll their eyes. "That's *your* husband," Momi says sarcastically.

"He ain't my husband," Ashley replies. "Do you see a ring on this hand?" She flashes her bare left hand. "GUESS HE DIDN'T LIKE IT, CAUSE HE DIDN'T PUT A RING ON IT!" Hoping that Malu would overhear, she looks in his direction. Completely engulfed in his own conversation, Malu is unaware of her last statement. "Ugh. He's been irritating me recently," Ashley admits.

"You guys are always so up and down. If there was a rollercoaster in Hawaii, it would be called the 'Ashley and

Malu.'" Momi says while laughing.

"Shut up!" Ashley responds angrily, all the while knowing it's probably true. She playfully hits Momi on the arm. "Anyway, what were you guys just up to?"

"Oh nothing. We just got some ice cream from the shop around the block," Momi says nonchalantly, not making eye contact with her cousin.

"And…" Ashley replies as to infer that there's more to the story than she's saying.

"And what?" Momi responds, playing dumb and continuing to avoid eye contact.

"Cousin, I know you. And I know when you're not telling me something." Ashley is adamant. "Look, you can't even look me in the eye!"

After a very labored pause, "Ok fiiiiiine," Momi says pretending she doesn't want to spill the truth, but secretly hoping someone would ask. "We met this girl…"

"Let me guess… three-way?" Ashley interjects and jumps to the point.

Momi pauses and acts shocked, "You really do know me."

Ashley shakes her head, but with a smile on her face.

"What? Don't judge! You guys should try it. Maybe then you guys wouldn't fight as much." Momi offers her cousin some advice.

"Yeah, I'm sure *he* would love that," Ashley replies, referring to Malu. "Girl, you know my ass is too jealous. That girl would be dead before he even laid a hand on her. And we are not having a threesome with a corpse." The two girls share a laugh.

Ashley and Momi look back at their boyfriends. In the time that they've been talking, they hadn't noticed that Sam joined the other two boys.

Sam is the other doorman. They call him "Sam the

Samoan." He and Malu are like two peas in a pod, Tweedle Dee and Tweedle Dum. Being a 300 lbs Samoan, his size and mean face help keep people from getting rowdy in the club, but also hinder him from making friends and finding a special woman to call his own.

Sam makes eye contact with the girls and throws up a shaka to say hello. The two girls say "Good Morning, Sam" in unison and wave back.

"Sam's such a teddy bear," Momi says at a volume only Ashley can hear.

"No, he's not," Ashley disagrees quickly. She, then, changes her tone, "Don't get me wrong, I love the guy, he's like a brother to Malu, but he's such a hopeless romantic. He falls in love with every girl he sees in line. Did you know last week he let twelve girls in for free… TWELVE! And that was all in the same night! He ruins my count!"

Ashley works the door, collecting entrance fees and counting the number of people walking into the club to ensure the club doesn't go over maximum capacity.

"Big Softie," Momi responds.

"More like big for nothing," Ashley exhales.

7. STP (Sweet Tight Pussy)

- 3/4 oz Malibu Coconut Rum
- 3/4 oz Midori Melon Liqueur
- 1/2 oz Pineapple juice
- Splash of 7-Up
   *Shake and serve as a shot

A couple of blocks from Violet, at a Mexican restaurant named 'Taco Hell,' known for its fiery hot sauces, Lopaka sits alone at a table near the window. His burrito is cold and barely touched and he's scrolling aimlessly through Instagram. *He still hasn't texted me*, he thinks to himself, hoping that at that very moment, a text from Ryan would pop up magically with a wonderfully descriptive and viable reason as to why he couldn't make it to dinner… but this is not the case. Tired of the constant disappointment, he puts his phone face down on the table and decides to people-watch.

To Lopaka's Surprise, Robin and Chyna walk right past him on the outside of the big glass window pane. Chyna reaches for the door to the Mexican restaurant and holds it open, so Robin can enter first.

"Thanks, love." Robin thanks Chyna for her kind gesture.

"It's '*Miss* Love' to you! Thank you very much," Chyna responds sassily.

"Miss? Uh, don't you mean '*Mrs.* Love?'" Robin tries to remind her friend.

"Sssshhh. Shut up. I have clientele around here." Chyna tries to hush Robin. Although she is not technically married, Chyna hides the fact that she has a 'husband' for *business* sake.

"Oh, that's right. Forgive me…" Robin starts and then continues loudly and sarcastically, "Thank you so much, MRS.

Chyna Make Love of the Waianae Mountains; wife of the ever-missing and ever-fat, Larry Love, and resident whore of downtown Honolulu." Robin looks at Chyna and raises her eyebrows as to say *Don't test me, bitch.*

Chyna is, what they call in the LGBT world, a pre-op (short for pre-operation) transgender woman. While she has breast implants, her other private region is still of the male variety. Back in their late twenties, Chyna and Robin made the decision to transition from male to female, in hopes that their outer body would match their inner persona. With the lack of care and understanding from the world at large, help for transgender people from medical insurance companies, at that time, was poor to non-existent. Having found no other option as to pay for the expensive procedures that were to come, Chyna and Robin turned to prostituting.

Having saved up enough money to fully transition, the two friends began the process. After many years of ups and downs, Robin accomplished her lifelong dream of becoming a post-op transgender woman. Chyna, however, was a different story.

Having found that there is a niche market for pre-op transgender women in the escort service and also liking the easy money that comes from hooking, Chyna decided not to fully transition. This is a decision that she is proud of and will stick by 'til her dying day. Although her need for the money has now passed, Chyna continues to sell her 'goodies.' Her clientele leave happy and she now has regulars that take care of her very well. Her 'husband' was one of those regulars and he was the very one, who nicknamed her 'Chyna.' With skin as smooth and milky as porcelain chinaware, Chyna liked the name and adopted it.

As the two friends are bickering and just about to reach the register in Taco Hell, they here a "Huuuiii" come from behind them. (*Hui* is a common greeting call in Hawaii in order to get

22

someone's attention.) The ladies turn around perfectly in sync, as if it were a planned dance move, and find Lopaka looking at them shaking his head with a smirk on his face.

"Boy, what did I tell you about yelling at a woman like that?" Robin marches over to Lopaka, with Chyna two steps behind her.

"Sorry, *Mother*!" Lopaka jokes.

"Oh shut up, *daughter*!" Robin comes back just as sarcastically.

"What are you doing here all by yourself?" Chyna asks. Lopaka looks up at Chyna with eyes that say *Don't ask*.

"Again?!" Robin exclaims, assuming she already knows the situation. Without an invitation, she seats herself at Lopaka's table directly across from him. Chyna pulls up a chair from the next table over and joins them. "Why do you keep wasting your time with him?"

"Yeah, there's plenty of fish in the sea, honey," Chyna chimes in, but her focus is elsewhere. She's made eye contact with a Honolulu businessman on another table and she's trying to feel out if he is a potential "customer."

"Listen, life is short. Trust me, I would know." Robin refers to her illness. Lopaka, not knowing that Robin is HIV-positive, just assumes she's talking about her age. "You can't be spending your days waiting around for things to change. YOU have to be the change in your own life!" Robin delivers the last line looking directly into Lopaka's eyes.

"Yeah... yeah... Change your whole life," Chyna wrongly repeats Robin's last words. She has one ear on the conversation and two eyes on the businessman.

Robin slaps Chyna's arm to get her to snap out of it and focus back on the conversation. She gives her a wide-eyed glare as to say *Pay Attention*! Chyna returns Robin's glare and shrugs her shoulders pretending as if she had been paying attention the whole time. She looks over at Lopaka and realizes she has to make this speech quick, if she wants to make some money tonight.

"Look kid, you wanna know the truth? Ready or not, here it comes… If he wanted to be with you, he would be with you. That's it, nothing more. None of this, 'I'll text you,' 'keep you hanging,' 'making you doubt your own worth' shit. Nuh-uh. You're settling and you know what the saddest part is… you know you are." Chyna puts Lopaka in his place then looks back over at the businessman, but he's gone. "Oh great, Robin, see what you did? He could've been my future husband," Chyna fumes. Now pouting, she slumps in her chair and crosses her arms over her chest.

"You have a past and present husband. I think you'll be alright," Robin reminds her friend.

Lopaka chuckles slightly. The two ladies stop their bickering and look over at him. "Ohhhh, there he is," Chyna starts. "There's that handsome Hawaiian boy that we've all been missing." She starts physically poking him, making trouble and trying to get him to lighten up. "Alright, I'm starving. Who wants tacos? What day is it? Taco Tuesday?" Chyna gets up and heads toward the register.

"It's Friday," Robin corrects her friend.

"Well, it's Taco Tuesday somewhere, right?" Chyna responds without waiting for an answer.

"It's not like Happy Hour. That's not how it works," Robin shouts, but realizes Chyna is already ordering. She redirects her focus back on Lopaka. Touching his cheek gently, she says, "You'll be alright, babe."

8. Trash Can

- 1 oz. (30ml) Vodka
- 1 oz. (30ml) Gin
- 1 oz. (30ml) Rum
- 1 oz. (30ml) Triple Sec
- 1 oz. (30ml) Blue Curaçao
- 1/2 oz. (15ml) Peach Schnapps
- 1 can Energy Drink

Back outside the locked entrance of Violet Nightclub, two more bartenders, Beau and Chico, round the corner and walk toward the slowly-growing group of Violet employees. Each gnawing on a slice of pizza, the two boys flash the 'shaka' sign with their free hand to the other boys chatting on one side of the car. Ashley and Momi continue to have their own private conversation on the other side of the car.

Beau, the self-proclaimed "Straight Cheyenne Jackson," has the bone structure of a young Johnny Depp. His dark brown hair falls perfectly to one side and his light blue eyes are the color of a community swimming pool the first day after cleaning. He's a similar height to Parker, but slimmer like a 'Gap' model.

Ashley notices the two boys first and says sarcastically to Momi, "Here comes your *favorite*."

Momi glances over her shoulder to see who Ashley is speaking of and immediately regrets looking. Beau catches Momi's glance and puckers his lips in a kissy way. She quickly turns back to Ashley and says "Ugh, I can't stand him." Momi rolls her eyes.

"Who? Chico?" Ashley plays dumb, all the while knowing Momi is talking about Beau.

"No, Beau!" Momi proclaims with intense eyes.

Ashley laughs then says, "I know, I know. I'm just 'making.' Hey, you're the one who dated him!"

"I did NOT date him!" Momi defends herself. "We slept together one time... ONCE!" She uses her index finger to indicate how many times. "Everybody thinks he's so cool, he's so hot..."

"Especially himself," Ashley adds.

"Okay?!" Momi concurs. "And the truth is, he's not even that good in bed."

"Ooop!" Ashley makes a noise to indicate that Momi just threw shade.

"He thinks he can get any girl he wants," Momi continues

"Well, he did get you, girl." Ashley brings up the facts.

"Shut up!" Momi starts to get annoyed with her cousin. "Ugh, you wanna know the T? He's overcompensating."

"It's like they say, 'Big Head, Small Head.'" Ashley points to her crotch on the latter 'Head.'

"That's for sure," Momi concurs.

"I like Chico, though." Ashley redirects Momi's focus.

"Oh, I LOVE Chico! He's always so chill, always helpful..."

"Always high," Ashley takes the lead nonchalantly, "and always hooks me up with the best weed!" The two girls chuckle.

Chico is not as tall as Beau or Parker, but not small either. He's an average height Latino male, with a big smile that would make the cheshire cat feel jealous. At a young age, he lost his parents in a tragic car accident, which left him to be raised by his Mexican grandma he calls 'Abuela.' She taught him to see the good in every situation which is why he's always got a positive outlook on life. Liked by everyone, he seems to be the only person at Violet that dodges any drama. However, his amazing advice in every situation often gets brushed off and disregarded because he's a stoner.

"Chico and his boyfriend are such potheads," Momi states.

"And I love it!" Ashley replies. The two girls giggle.

From the other direction, Tisha, another bartender, turns the corner and walks toward everyone with her "right off the runway" look. A tall glass of chocolate milk, she's an African American dream with skin as dark as midnight. A former stripper, she's got the body that make men go crazy, but having dealt with so many abusive men in the past, she's now a full blown lesbian.

Momi notices Tisha right away. "God damn," Momi says under her breath

"What?" Ashley turns to see who or what Momi is looking at. She realizes quickly who Momi is going 'ga-ga' over. "Oh, here she comes," Ashley says, "I'm not even in to chicks, but she's gorgeous."

"You don't even know the things I fantasize doing to her," Momi says with her mouth almost drooling.

"Ok. Calm down horndog. You're like a high school boy right now." Ashley tries to snap her cousin out of it. "Wait, I don't get it. Why don't you just sleep with her and make your fantasies reality? You guys sleep with everyone else."

"I can't," Momi says all depressed. "Parker and I have one rule…"

"Don't tell me he's racist," Ashley tries to guess.

"NO! Not at all. Not that," Momi exclaims. "We can sleep with whoever we want, but we can't sleep with close friends."

"Ahhh" Ashley says being enlightened. "Yeah, I guess she is a close friend, huh? At least I know *I'm* safe," Ashley jokes

"Ew, you're family, you're not even an option!" Momi says grossed out.

Ashley laughs and sarcastically says, " Well, I guess you just gotta sleep with your boyfriend then! What a tough life." Momi rolls her eyes and then goes back to watching Tisha walk toward them.

With one arm holding her purse, Tisha smiles and waves femininely at the group of boys. She B-lines straight to Momi and Ashley.

"Hey girl," Ashley says and then kisses Tisha cheek-to-cheek, pretending as if they weren't just talking about her.

"Look at you, girl, with those red booty shorts on!" Momi flirts.

Tisha turns around and shows off her butt, completely unaware that Momi is checking her out. "You like it?" Tisha asks innocently. "I just bought it today."

"I love it!" Momi responds out loud and finishes her sentence internally …*and I love you*.

"Oh she definitely loves it," Ashley remarks, making fun of Momi. Momi elbows her cousin as to say *Shut up*!

Tisha leans in to kiss Momi hello. "Good Morning, boo."

"Hi babes." Momi receives the kiss and then goes for a hug too. Ashley and Momi make eye contact while the hug happens and Ashley shakes her head in a disapproving, but entertained way. Momi closes her eyes and enjoys the embrace for as long as she can.

Just as the hug is coming to an end, a loud crash startles the girls. Both groups, the girls and the guys, turn to discover Yuki with his ass on the pavement and a trash can overturned. His skateboard is rolling away from him and trash is everywhere.

"Ho her gawd," Momi says mimicking the ever-popular 'Oh My God," another one of Violet's adopted slang. Momi gets irritated with Yuki, thinking he just ruined the perfect moment.

"Are you ok?" Parker yells over to Yuki.

"I'm good, I'm good. That trash can just came out of nowhere," Yuki yells back, still on the ground.

Yuki is a klutz. He's a small, Japanese transgender boy in his early twenties, who's always falling and hurting himself in some way. How he came to be the barback of Violet, no one really knows. Balancing stacks of cups and lugging multiple buckets of ice becomes a daring circus act when Yuki is working behind the bar. Being a transgender male in mid-transition, his hormones can sometimes be all out of whack. Most of the time a goof, he can sometimes go from tears of happiness to tears of sadness in a small amount of time. Regardless of his vices, Yuki is harmless and always means to do well.

"Do you need help?" Beau asks, knowing full well that he has no intention to go over and help Yuki.

"Ugh, I can't with him," Ashley says unimpressed with yet another clumsy Yuki occurrence. Momi just shakes her head.

"Be nice," Tisha tells the other two girls gently with a smile. She turns around and walks toward Yuki to help.

From the boys group, Chico starts heading over to Yuki as well. Chico, being just a pace behind Tisha, does a little skip to catch up to her. "Good Morning!" He says in his usual jolly tone.

"Oh!" Tisha gasps, just the tiniest bit startled. Realizing it's Chico, she smiles and responds, "Good Morning, baby." She kisses Chico on the cheek and they walk together toward Yuki.

Chico offers his hand to Yuki while Tisha just stands back and smiles. Yuki pops up off the ground disregarding Chico's gesture and pretending as if he hadn't just fallen flat on his ass. In his mind, he's humiliated, but wanting to prove that he's one of the boys, he dusts himself off and says, "Sup guys!"

"You ok, boo?" Tisha asks still with a smile on her face.

"Oh who? Me? Yeah I'm good. So good. Totally fine!" Yuki counters, acting as if he isn't going to wake up with a big bruise on his ass tomorrow morning. Yuki runs to grab his skateboard, which is still slowly rolling away like a leaf on a lazy river.

Chico and Tisha look at each other and smile as to non-verbally communicate *Gotta love Yuki*. They wait for him to return with his skateboard then head back to the group.

"Yuki!! WOO!!" Beau cheers mockingly like a frat boy as if Yuki just won gold at the Olympics. The entire group of boys join in, clapping and shouting as to tease Yuki in a loving way.

Yuki blushes in embarrassment, but decides to make his way to the center of the boys and relish in the moment anyway. He bows a grand bow as if he had just finished receiving a standing ovation for his Broadway debut.

"I guess we should go and join them, huh?" Ashley says to Momi from the other side of the car.

"I guess." Momi responds acting more 'over-it,' than she actually is.

As Yuki is taking his final bow, the girls barge into the group. "Alright, alright. Circle Jerk is over boys," Ashley proclaims sarcastically.

"…unless, I'm invited," Momi finishes. The whole group laughs. The girls split up and stand next to their boyfriends.

"Wait. Why are we all still outside?" Yuki interrupts the laughter.

Ashley looks at Yuki and says, "Guess."

"The reason we're always outside, Yuki," Momi responds as if Yuki should already know the answer. Yuki looks at everyone blankly, completely clueless. No one said he was the brightest crayon in the box.

In unison, the group says, "Kaleo!"

9. Blow Job

- 1/2 oz Kahlua
- 1/2 oz Baileys
- 1/4 oz Amaretto
    *Served as a shot, then topped with whipped cream

Kaleo shakes his head with frustration. He's stuck in traffic. Driving his black Toyota Tacoma, his right arm steers as his left arm sits in the window sill, holding his still pounding head. Moving at a snail's pace, he knows he's going to be more than a little late. He grabs his phone and starts to text his best friend, Parker.

"I'm gonna be late," Kaleo texts.

"We know lol," Parker texts back swiftly. This isn't the first time this has happened.

Kaleo and Parker have been friends since high school. Having joined the canoe paddling team as strangers, they quickly became friends when they were placed in the same boat. Over the course of their Junior year, they became so close that seeing them together was as common as seeing rice on a plate lunch. They pushed each other to be the best they could be by making one golden rule: "You gotta finish what you start." Whether it'd be a long distance run for practice, taking a course they weren't comfortable with or even finishing a big meal, they had to see things through 'til the end.

They told each other everything, created a secret handshake and even shared answers on tests, but there was one thing Kaleo never shared. Closeting his true self in high school, Kaleo kept the fact that he was gay a secret from everyone, including Parker. That is, until one day in the boys locker room…

* * *

Canoe paddling practice just finished and while most of the boys leave straight from the Ala Wai canal, Parker and Kaleo head back to school to shower before going home. Having just got his driver's license a couple months prior, Parker would drive Kaleo home everyday after practice. With no rush to go home and do the boring task of homework, the boys take their time and find themselves to be the last ones remaining.

In the locker room, Kaleo and Parker unlock their lockers and slowly undress. Kaleo watches Parker from the corners of his eyes, admiring him and taking in every muscle of Parker's freshly pumped body. Usually, Kaleo could check out Parker without getting *hard*, but today was different.

Just the night before, Kaleo had a wet dream where he was giving Parker a blow job in the boys' locker room showers and now here they were… in the boys' locker room about to head into the showers. Trying to suppress the vivid images in his mind and trying to stop his dick from rising, he stops undressing and sits down on the bench.

"You ok?" Parker asks Kaleo, completely oblivious to the thoughts racing through Kaleo's head.

"Yeah, yeah. I'm good. You go ahead. I'll be right there," Kaleo says calmly on the outside, while slightly panicking on the inside.

"Ok," Parker responds. He casually pulls down his boxer briefs exposing his perfectly pink penis and heads into the showers.

That's all it took. Kaleo's semi-chub turned into a full-on boner with a single glance. He thought to himself, *Shit, this is bad! I can't go into the shower with a raging hard-on, but if I don't shower, he's gonna know something is up. What do I do?!* He tried to calm himself down and started thinking of things

32

that don't turn him on. He started with baseball.

Ok, baseball is not my favorite sport, it's boring, it's hot… oh, but the guys on our baseball team are super hot and they have nice asses… oh shit, NO! Ok, SOFTBALL! Yeah, softball. There's only girls in softball and I don't like girls, so that works.

While still mostly hard, his little friend below slowly began to descend. *Yeah and UGLY girls too. Yup. Ugly girls playing softball. Gross OLD ugly girls playing softball, yeah like grandmas. Ugly grandmas with their old dried up vaginas playing softball with other old ugly grandmas.* That seemed to have done the trick. While not completely flaccid, he went back into the semi-chub stage which hung enough to where Kaleo thought it could just pass as a thick dick.

As Kaleo exhales a sigh of relief, Parker calls from the showers "You coming in?"

Kaleo, having finally calmed his rebellious rod, yells back, "Yeah, I'm coming in now." Kaleo removes his underwear, heads toward the showers and takes a deep breath before turning the corner. *I got this.*

He walks a couple more steps and sees Parker standing under the shower in all of his naked glory just like he was in his dream last night. And, as the old saying goes… "The penis has a mind of it's own." Kaleo's semi-erect dick, once again, turns into a full-blown raging boner. *FUCK!* Kaleo freaks out internally, but before he can cover his junk, Parker looks over and sees Kaleo standing there, looking at him with a stiffy.

"Dude…" Parker is surprised and confused. He's slightly defensive, but remembers that it's Kaleo, his best friend, so he doesn't want to take it too seriously.

Kaleo stands there stunned with his hands covering his dick. His worst fear had just come true. Without saying a word, he runs back to his locker and quickly starts putting on his clothes.

Parker, trying not to think too much of it and actually

finding it kind of funny, turns off the shower, grabs his towel off the bathroom rail and wipes himself down. He wraps the towel around his waist and then heads back to his locker. He turns the corner and notices Kaleo sitting on the bench, fully clothed with his backpack next to him, struggling to put on his shoes. "Dude, it's ok. It happens."

Kaleo looks up at Parker, shakes his head and then looks back down at the floor. "Sorry."

"For what?" Parker responds. "Man, seriously it's cool. I get it. They come out of nowhere sometimes. Like today, I had a hard-on in physics. PHYSICS! What's sexy about physics, right?! And we had a test! So, why was I hard in a completely quiet room, looking at a piece of paper with multiple choice on it? I don't know, but they come when they come. That's why they call it a head, right? Cause it has a mind of it's—"

"I'm gay," Kaleo cuts him off, still staring at the floor.

"What?" Parker, still in his towel, is shocked and finds himself frozen. He had no idea. Kaleo looks up at him and looks Parker straight in the eyes without saying anything. "Sorry, I heard you. I just thought I, uh, *mis*heard you." Parker struggles to find something to say.

Kaleo grabs his backpack and walks out of the locker room, passing Parker on the way. Parker changes into some clean clothes, still trying to process what just happened. He puts his shoes on, locks his locker and heads out the door to look for Kaleo.

By this time, the sun has gone down and it's only getting darker. The campus lights have come on and the last of the other student athletes are finally getting picked up by their parents. Parker walks toward his car looking for Kaleo on the way, but doesn't see him. In the student parking lot, his Toyota Corolla is the last car left. From afar, Parker sees Kaleo sitting on the curb next to his car staring blankly at the ground. He walks up to him and sits ride beside him.

"Well, there's some news for ya," Parker tries to joke to lighten the mood. Kaleo doesn't budge. He remains silent and continues to look at the ground. Parker stops, exhales deeply and looks at the ground too. They sit in silence for a minute until Parker decides to get real.

"Gay, huh?" He starts. "I've never met a gay person before or at least I never knew that they were gay when I met them. Actually, your dad is gay, right? I met him a couple times. Maybe it runs in the family?" Realizing it's probably a silly thing to say, he continues "Look man, I'm not good at this, ok? I don't really know what to say. You kinda gotta help me out." He pauses and waits for a response from Kaleo, but Kaleo is still silent. "So... are you, like, gay for me?"

"No! I mean, yeah I was kinda... shit, I don't know." Kaleo breaks his silence. "Can we just drop it?" He gets up and tries to open the passenger door, but it's locked.

Parker unlocks the car and Kaleo gets in and closes the door quickly. Parker walks around to the driver's side and gets in. They sit in the car looking out at the dark sky, avoiding looking at each other.

"You were kinda what?" Parker asks curiously.

"What?" Kaleo looks at Parker confused.

"Yeah, you said 'I was kinda...' dot dot dot. You gotta finish what you started. That's the rules, remember?" Parker presses.

"Nothing. I mean... I was just... I don't know." Kaleo pauses and sighs a very deep sigh. "I was kinda checking you out."

"I knew it! You like what you saw, huh?" Parker jokes and tries to use this info to lighten the mood. "Were you checking out... this face?" Parker puts his thumb and index finger in the shape of a check mark under his chin, puckers his lips and tilts his head up at Kaleo.

Kaleo chuckles under his breath. "Shut up, will you?"

"Were you checking out... these guns?" Parker flexes his arms in a muscle man pose and kisses his bicep to be funny. Kaleo rolls his eyes, but with a smirk on his face. "Were you checking out... these abs?" Parker lifts up his shirt and displays his washboard abs. He grabs Kaleo's hand and makes him rub his six-pack. Kaleo retracts his hand quickly, but Parker grabs his hand again and places it back on his stomach muscles.

With his left hand on Parker's rock-hard abs, Kaleo looks at Parker shocked. Having always fantasized about feeling his best friend's body and thinking that this is all part of a joke anyway, he doesn't pull away. *Is this really happening?* He thinks to himself and goes with it.

With a smile on his face, Parker is now having fun with the whole situation. He realizes that he is literally, and figuratively, in the driver's seat. Finally, he asks "Were you... checking out.. this?" He guides Kaleo's hand down into his pants revealing that he's been concealing an erection the entire time.

Kaleo, now with his hand around his best friend's cock, is shaking with every emotion: nervousness, fear, confusion, but mostly excitement. He looks Parker in the eyes as to say *What now?*

Parker, with a sly smile, looks at Kaleo and then down at his crotch and nods. "Guess you gotta finish what you started."

* * *

10. B-52

- 1/3 oz Kahlua
- 1/3 oz Baileys
- 1/3 oz Gran Marnier
    *Layered in this order and served as a shot

Back at Violet, the bar and door staff are still locked outside. Having had this happen before, and with no one really wanting to work anyway, the group of friends welcome the delay. Parker, having just texted Kaleo, chuckles to himself and then rejoins chatting with the group. "Kaleo says he's gonna be late," Parker announces to the group, flashing his phone to imply that he just received a text.

"Ladies and Gentlemen... Captain Obvious," Beau states sarcastically, trying to insult Parker, but Parker just laughs. He puts his phone back in his pocket.

"Why is he always late?" Tisha asks genuinely.

"He's lucky he can't get fired," Yuki proclaims.

"He's lucky I don't beat him up for making us wait!" Malu says aggressively.

"Oh, here he goes..." Momi says as she rolls her eyes at Malu's comment.

"All talk," Sam pokes fun at his own friend.

"Nah, nah. I wouldn't hurt him, you guys. I'm a lover, not a fighter." Malu puts his arm around Ashley to imply that he's a loving boyfriend.

"Hoooo Her Gaaawwdd!" Momi cries out loud and rolls her eyes even harder this time.

Ashley smokes a cigarette while she waits. With Malu all of a sudden cozied up next to her, she looks straight ahead with no emotion on her face. "You see what I have to deal with?"

Seeing someone coming from the corner of his eye, Chico turns his head and expects to see Kaleo. Instead, it's a three-part army with an angry female leader. "Uh-oh. Incoming," Chico alerts the group.

Robin walks toward the group hastily, with Chyna and Lopaka a few paces behind. "Why are you all outside?" Robin says loudly and sternly from afar. The group braces for impact.

Finally reaching the group of her employees, Robin asks again "What's going on? What's the hold up?" Everyone avoids eye contact, not wanting to be the one to get Kaleo into trouble.

"We don't have a key," Malu speaks up for the group.

Robin scans the group and realizes that Kaleo is absent. "AGAIN?!" Robin yells. "Oh, that boy! I swear." By this time, Chyna and Lopaka have reached the group, but decide to hang back a few steps while Robin goes on one of her 'ty-rants.' She looks back over to Malu and says in a quiet, but assertive tone "Call your brother and tell him to get his ass to work NOW!"

Robin parts her staff like the Red Sea, walks up to the entrance of Violet and unlocks the front door. She holds the door open and ushers everyone in, giving each of them assignments as they pass her. "Yuki, sweep the floors. Tisha, restock the bar. Beau, you're on ice. Sam, take those boxes to my office…" Robin is taking no prisoners.

As the last of the crew enter the club, Chyna walks up to Robin. "Ok sis, I'm gonna hele (*hele* is a Hawaiian word implying the action "to go" or "to come"). I'm gonna go make me some coin tonight." Chyna kisses her friend on the cheek and heads to her usual spot for *business*.

"Be safe, bitch!" Robin lectures her friend as if she is one of her employees.

While Robin and Chyna say their goodbyes, Malu greets Lopaka, not with a bro-hug, but with a real hug this time. "Guess he's late again, huh?" Lopaka asks already knowing the answer.

"That's your brother for you," Malu says matter-of-factly.

"He's your brother, too!" Lopaka comes back with quickly. "Must be the middle child syndrome."

Malu laughs, "Must be."

Lopaka, Kaleo and Malu are brothers and were born in that order. With a year between Lopaka and Kaleo and two years between Kaleo and Malu, the three brothers have always been close. That is, until recently.

In the past couple of months, Kaleo has distanced himself from his brothers. Having done this a few times before, Lopaka and Malu are expecting Kaleo to come out of his funk and revert back to his normal self like in the past. However, this time seems to be lasting longer than usual.

"HURRY UP, YOU TWO!" Robin yells at the two brothers. "Malu, you're on trash duty and Lopaka, help Yuki sweep."

"But I don't even start gogo-ing 'til 11pm." Lopaka tries to get out of doing any extra work.

"What are you gonna do? Go home and be depressed? Sit by your phone like a little puppy waiting for Ryan to call you? No! You get in here and you help out!" Robin orders.

The two brothers look at each other and smirk before heading in the club, passing Robin at the entrance. "Come on! You guys are already late!" Robin scolds.

11. Key Lime Pie

- 1 oz Whipped Cream Vodka
- 1/2 oz Rumchata
- 1/2 oz Key Lime Juice
    *Rim shot glass with lime juice and crushed up graham crackers, shake and serve as a shot

Inside the club, the majority of pre-shift tasks have already been done. Knowing that the club doesn't really get busy until about 10 or 11pm, the bartenders and door staff try to find things to keep themselves busy. With enough space in Violet for a stage, a large dance floor, and two separate bars (the front bar and the back bar), the staff find themselves spread out and often don't see each other 'til the end of the night. Parker, Beau and Chico man the front bar, while Momi and Tisha wo-man the back bar, making it a battle of the sexes for tonight's set up.

"We got everything we need?" Momi asks Tisha while checking out her body.

"We're all set up and ready to go, boo," Tisha responds with a smile.

"Good. Let's show these boys the power of a push-up bra," Momi jests. The two girls adjust their boobs and fix their hair. They know that sex sells. With every night being friendly competition, the bartenders tend to split up into teams and see which of the two bars can have the highest sales.

At the front bar, Parker and Chico are still cutting lemons and limes for service. Beau, however, is already on his phone, checking his social media.

"Dude!" Parker says to get Beau's attention.

Disappointed with his Instagram post from earlier that's only received 8 'likes,' Beau looks up at Parker. "What?"

"You gonna help out or what?" Parker asks, thinking that it's something he shouldn't have to ask.

"There's nothing left to do," Beau defends himself.

Parker and Chico look at each other as to non-verbally say *Seriously?* Both with knives in their hands, they look at Beau like two murders ready for their next victim. "Wipe down the bar," Parker asserts.

"Alright, alright," Beau throws his hands in the air and then walks away mumbling profanities under his breath.

As Beau is wiping down the bar top near the entrance, Kaleo opens the door and walks in. "Whoaaa, somebody finally decided to show up. Thank you for blessing us with your royal presence, your majesty," Beau says sarcastically and bows on one knee.

"Shut up, Beau. And why are you working the front bar?" Kaleo questions.

"Queen Robin assigned our positions," Beau continues his sarcasm.

Parker and Chico come around the bar and greet Kaleo. "Good morning babe." Chico kisses Kaleo on the cheek and hugs him.

Parker and Kaleo look at each other and then do their 'secret handshake' that they've done since high school. "Suh dude," Parker mocks the ever-popular 'Sup Dude.'

"Suh dude," Kaleo jokes back.

"You smell like shit," Parker tells his best friend.

"I feel like shit," Kaleo responds.

"Well, you're about to feel a lot shittier..." Parker warns. "Robin wants to see you in her office."

"Shit," Kaleo mutters.

On his way to Robin's office, Kaleo stops by the back bar and kisses Momi and Tisha hello. "Looking good, girls," he compliments.

"Thank you!" The girls say in unison. "You're with us in the back tonight." Tisha scrunches her face insinuating that she feels bad for Kaleo.

"Yeah, I heard," Kaleo responds slightly disgusted. "Nah, but it will be fun," he quickly tries to cover, hoping the girls didn't take offense. Usually, Kaleo works the main register at the front bar. Being the lead bartender and the fastest at making drinks, it only makes sense that he is placed at the busiest part of the club, but tonight is a different story.

"Now we'll definitely have the higher sales!" Momi says all excited.

He leaves the girls and sighs deeply to rid his nerves. He knows he's about to get his ass handed to him.

Once he reaches Robin's office, he knocks on the already open door. Robin, in the middle of replying to some emails, looks up from her computer.

"You wanted to see me?" Kaleo opens the conversation.

Robin looks at her watch. "You're an hour and fifteen minutes late," she says stoically.

"Yeah, sorry. I woke up late and then there was traffic because of the construction on the freeway. Then, as I was texting the crew to let them know I was gonna be late, I got pulled over by a cop for being on my phone. Of course, since I was rushing out the door, I forgot my wallet at home. Which means, I didn't have my driver's license, so I got a ticket for that too. Not to mention I wasn't wearing a seat belt. I meant to call you, but I—"

Robin throws up her hand as to say *Enough*. "This is the third time this month, Kaleo." She pauses. "It's the 18th. Do you know what that means? That means, that you've been late three times in less than three weeks."

"I know, I'm sorry," Kaleo apologizes.

"Give me your key," Robin commands.

"What?" Kaleo is caught off guard.

Robin extends her hand without repeating herself.

Shocked, Kaleo realizes she's being serious and obediently reaches for his keys. He takes the club's key off of his key ring and hands it to Robin.

"Tell Ashley I want to talk to her," Robin says before going back to her emails. Her silence insinuates that he's allowed to leave.

Kaleo, understanding that the conversation is done, walks out of the office. He runs straight to the bathroom and closes the door behind him. Feeling mad at himself and frustrated with the situation, he paces back and forth before stopping in front of the mirror. With both hands on the sink, he looks at his own reflection with disgust. He yells one big "FUCK!" loud enough for everyone to hear.

After calming himself down, he leaves the bathroom and B-lines for outside. The girls at the back bar watch him quietly as he passes. As he passes the front bar, Parker asks "You alright?" to show concern, but without coming off as invasive. He looks over in Parker's direction and just shakes his head in disbelief, while continuing his pace toward the door.

As he exits the club, he sees Lopaka, Malu and Sam joking with each other on the left and Ashley and Yuki sharing in a smoke break on the right. He turns to the right and walks up to Ashley. "Can I have a cigarette?" He asks.

"I thought you quit smoking?" Yuki questions.

"Can I *please* have a cigarette?" Kaleo reiterates, ignoring the last remark from Yuki.

Ashley hands him a smoke and lights it for him. It's the first time he's taken a hit off a cigarette in months. He starts to remember the amazing feeling of ease that smoking gives him and he wonders why he ever decided to quit in the first place. As he starts to relax into each puff, Ashley gently asks, "What's the matter, babe?"

Kaleo shakes his head and just wants to enjoy his cigarette while it lasts. Ashley doesn't push any further and just stands next to him, letting him know that she's ready to listen whenever he's ready to share.

Yuki, having finished his cigarette and never doing well with silence, decides it's his time to go. "Ok, well… I'll see you both inside," he awkwardly delivers and slips away. On his way into the club, Yuki looks at the group of boys to the left and just shrugs his shoulders as to say *I don't know what's going on over there*. The three boys take that as their signal to head over.

As Kaleo finishes his cigarette, Lopaka, Malu and Sam approach the smoking duo. "Whoa, whoa, whoa. Alright, what's going on around here? Who do I need to 86?" Malu comes in strong hoping that joking will break the tension and get Kaleo to loosen up. Ashley gives Malu the eyes that say *Cut it out!*

"You wanna talk about it?" Lopaka takes his turn. Kaleo shakes his head 'no' as he throws his cigarette on the ground and stomps it out. "Well, too bad." Lopaka doesn't give his younger brother a choice. "What's up?"

"Are you fired?" Malu asks.

Kaleo scoffs, "No, but I might as well be. She demoted me to the back bar."

It's probably just for tonight, Leo." Ashley shortcuts Kaleo's name.

"Oh and she wanted to talk to you," Kaleo says to Ashley.

"Me? Why me? What did I do?" Ashley's mind starts to race. "Did you get me into trouble too?"

Kaleo chuckles. "If I'm going down, I'm taking every single one of you bitches with me!"

Ashley, realizing that Robin is probably waiting, puts her cigarette out and starts to head inside. Sam, realizing that he should probably leave the three brothers to talk in private, turns around and walks with Ashley into the club.

"So you're in the back bar for awhile, that's not so bad," Lopaka offers positively.

"And she took away my key," Kaleo informs his brothers. "She basically took away my lead server position."

"Damn," Malu says slightly stunned. "Well, you can always work the door with us. We could use another bouncer. Actually, we *need* another bouncer. I've been telling her. This place is too big for just Sam and I. Too many dummies and not enough dummy-removers."

"Well, at this rate, I'll probably be demoted to doorman by the end of the night," Kaleo says negatively.

"Whoa, whoa, whoa. You mean PRO-moted!" Malu laughs, while the other two just look at him. "Ahh come on! You guys are boring. What? Are your panties in a knot?" Malu continues to laugh at his own jokes.

"Whatever brother. Take it for what it's worth… you still have a job," Lopaka tries to get Kaleo to look on the bright side. "At least you don't have a stupid boyfriend that doesn't text you when he says he will." Lopaka is still irritated with is own situation.

"Oh, you're boyfriends now?" Kaleo asks, happy to take the focus off of himself.

"Shut up!" Lopaka is offended.

"No, I'm genuinely asking," Kaleo presses further.

"We've BEEN boyfriends. You guys know that." Lopaka is trying to understand why his brother is asking him this.

"That's not what he told me," Kaleo counters.

"That's not what he told me either," Malu says under his breath.

"What are you guys talking about? What exactly did he say to the both of you?" Lopaka is starting to get pissed.

"He told me that you guys are just having fun, messing

around. Nothing serious," Kaleo informs his brother.

Malu looks at Lopaka and nods, "Same."

"Just messing around for SIX MONTHS?!" Lopaka is heated.

"Sounds like a conversation you need to be having with him, not us," Kaleo tries to offer.

"Yeah, I would if I could get him on the FUCKING phone!" Lopaka has hit his limit with irritation for the day.

"Alright, alright, chill out," Malu says trying to calm his oldest brother. "Look, as I see it, it's pretty simple. You're either in a relationship or you're not. You shouldn't have to wonder whether or not you're in one."

"Yeah, and if you are in a relationship, you're either in an open relationship like Parker and Momi or a monogamous one like Malu and Ashley." Kaleo pauses and then continues, "I think you already have your answer."

"Well, I must say, you've both made me feel really good about my life!" Malu laughs at his own joke again.

"Shut up," Kaleo and Lopaka say in unison.

The three brothers chit-chat a bit more, then head back into Violet to gear up for the night ahead.

12. Three Wise Men

- 1/2 oz Johnnie Walker
- 1/2 oz Jack Daniels
- 1/2 oz Jim Beam

A few hours later, three cute little gay boys with coordinated outfits approach the entrance of Violet. Sam, the size of the three boys combined, stands at the door like an oversized troll blocking his bridge. "IDs," Sam says intimidatingly and thinks, *They almost look like triplets*. The three little gays each hand Sam their driver's license.

"It's his birthday today!" The one in red says pointing to the one in blue.

"Twenty-one! Woop Woop!" The one in yellow cheers.

The birthday boy in blue smiles nervously and doesn't say a word. It's his first time not only to a gay club, but to a club in general. He looks up at Sam, who's looking back at him to make sure the photo on his ID matches his face. Displaying no emotion, Sam hands the birthday boy his ID back. The birthday boy thanks Sam and fumbles to put his card away quickly.

Sam opens the entrance door and cracks a big smile; going from scary villain to lovable teddy bear in 0.2 seconds. "Happy Birthday!"

Just inside the entrance door, Ashley sits at a counter with a register full of cash. As the nightclub's cashier, she's the true troll of the bridge; taking people's money and granting access to the "other side." She sits by herself watching a funny video on her phone; a nice break from always having Malu and her kids around. With the drag show starting in ten minutes, the crowds of guests have already started to make their way in. However, Ashley knows it's just the beginning of the rush.

Trying to savor her solitary moment, Ashley quickly puts her phone down when the front door to the club opens. *Alone time is over*. She looks up to find three little gays entering her area. "Ten dollars each guys," she says as they get closer. She notices their matching outfits and thinks to herself, *The Three Little Pigs*.

Not even a blink later, the door swings open as if it were huffed and puffed and almost blown down. It's the *she-wolves*. The wind from outside blows inward almost in slow-motion, messing up Ashley's hair and rustling some papers. The three little gay boys turn their heads realizing that it's the main reason they came to Violet in the first place… *the Fish y Chicks*.

The little gay in red gasps, while the little gay in yellow covers his mouth in shock. The birthday boy in blue says, "Oh my God!" With stars in his eyes, he touches both hands to his chest, clutching his imaginary pearl necklace.

"Boo!" Alexus, the leader of the Fish y Chicks, says like the Boogeyman.

The Fish y Chicks (pronounced 'Fish E. Chicks,' a play on 'Fish and Chips,' with a Spanish 'y' for the 'and') are Hawaii's premier drag queen performers. Known across the Hawaiian islands as the fishiest queens (*fishy* is gay slang for most likely to pass as a female when dressed up), these girls have racked up quite the following on social media. Just like fish and chips, the Fish y Chicks leave you salivating for more with their fun and flirty performances. Formerly a four-person group, the recent loss of a 'sister' queen has left the remaining three girls a little off their game. However, their "Keep Fierce and Death Drop on" motto has kept the Fish y Chicks from losing any sort of following.

"You're late!" Ashley scolds. "Robin is pissed!"

"Oh my God, is she really?" Alexus asks.

Ashley laughs, "Nah, I don't know. I've been sitting here the whole night. She was mad earlier, but not about you guys."

"You bitch!" Alexus says relieved, but still knowing that Robin might actually be pissed.

"Hurry up! You guys have ten minutes 'til you're on." Ashley checks the time on her phone, "Oh, nine minutes now."

The three drag queens scurry in their high heels pass Ashley's station blowing kisses to her as they pass. They wave hi to the starstruck, matching little gay boys and lug their rolling suitcases, full of costumes, to the dressing room.

"That'll be thirty dollars total, boys," Ashley says trying to snap the three little gays back into reality. As she waits for them to pay, she looks the boys up and down and thinks to herself *The Fish y Chicks: Next Generation.*" She laughs inwardly.

"Oh my God, I'm so sorry!" The little gay in red apologizes after realizing that they've all just been standing there in a trance. He hands Ashley exactly thirty dollars cash to cover all of them.

With Violet's infamous butterfly stamp, Ashley stamps the inside of their left wrists as each of the three little gays pass one-by-one. "Have fun!" She says with a smile.

Finally making it to the other side of the troll's bridge, the three little gay boys jump up and down with excitement. "WE MADE IT!" Arm in arm, they enter the main part of Violet ready to celebrate the night.

13. Fish Bowl Punch

- 1 cup Light Rum
- 1 cup Vodka
- 3/4 cup Blue Curaçao
- 1 1/2 cups Sweet and Sour
- 4 cups Pineapple Juice
- 4 cups Lemon-lime Soda
- Swedish Fish candies
- Optional: Citrus fruit slices

Business has started to pick up and with the drag show about to start, the bartenders know it's about to get even busier. At the front bar, Parker, Beau and Chico are each dealing with three very different customers.

"What's good here?" A female customer asks Parker.

"What do you mean?" Parker responds.

"Like, what do you recommend?" The same girl continues, trying to be cute and flirt with Parker.

"Well, what do you like?" Picking up on the fact that she's trying to flirt, but not finding her attractive, Parker ignores her sly signals. He tries to decipher what exactly she wants to drink.

"I like sweet drinks, but, like, not too sweet. Fruity-ish. Make it strong though, so I can taste it, but I don't want it to taste like alcohol. I wanna get drunk! WOO! But not like too drunk 'cause I still wanna look cute, you know what I mean?" The girl describes her drink of choice in a very valley girl type of way.

No, I don't know what you mean, Parker thinks to himself, but answers with, "Uh, ok." Still not exactly sure as to what she wants, Parker pours a 'Sex on the Beach' cocktail with an extra shot of vodka and slides the cup across the bar.

She pulls her hair back with both hands and leans over to sip the drink without holding it. As her lips reach the straw, she looks up at Parker with her eyes, pretending as if she's sucking something else. She recoils back up to a standing position and says "Ew. I don't like it."

Bitch... he thinks to himself.

To Parker's left, Beau is engaged with a female customer of his own. Unlike Parker, Beau finds his customer super hot. Tall and blonde, with a big butt, she's just his type. He's already begun his usual sleazy spiel .

"So, where you from?" Beau inquires while pouring her a Vodka Cranberry.

"I'm from L.A.," she answers.

"No way, me too!" He responds quickly.

"Oh really? Cool! Small world. Well, I'm originally from Michigan, though," she reveals truthfully.

"No, no. Still counts. I'm technically from the OC, so we're even," Beau says trying to flirt. "What brings a beautiful girl like you to Hawaii?"

"Oh, me and a couple of my girlfriends are just here on vacation for a week. We've never been, so we figured, why not?" She explains.

"Well, lucky me." Beau hands her her drink and tries to make eye contact. "Where are you guys stay—"

"Hey what do I owe you?" She interrupts and opens up her purse looking for her wallet.

"No, no. It's on me." Beau gives her a free drink in hopes that it will seal the deal.

"Oh my gosh, thank you so much!" She closes her purse and grabs the drink off the bar. "You're the cutest gay guy I've ever met," she admits.

"No, no. I'm not ga—," Beau tries to correct her.

"Thank you!" She shouts over the music, cutting him off

and already halfway back to her group of friends. She waves to Beau one last time before turning around and enjoying the rest of her free drink.

"BITCH!" Beau says out loud.

On the other side of the bar, Chico is serving a group of four older gay guys. "Hola Papis!"

"What do you guys want, what do you guys want?" The leader of the group asks his friends. The rest of the guys are dumb-founded as if it were an S.A.T. question. Chico smiles and waits patiently.

With his friends taking too long to decide, the leader of the group makes a rash decision. He looks back to Chico and says "Screw it. Give me four Patron." His friends over hear his order and make sour faces disagreeing with his choice. "Hey, you guys couldn't decide, so I decided for you!"

"Shots or on the rocks?" Chico clarifies.

"Uhh, shots please," the leader responds.

"Four shots it is, boss!" Chico says, still with a smile on his face. He lines up four shot glasses and is about to start pouring when the leader interrupts him.

"And pour yourself one too," the leader offers. "A cutie like you deserves a shot having to deal with old queens like us."

Chico nods his head 'yes' and says, "Gracias!" He adds another shot glass to the line and starts pouring. He hands out the shot glasses when finished, one for each guy and one for himself.

The leader hands Chico his credit card. "Leave it open, bub. We'll be back," he says, implying that he wants to start a tab. He winks at Chico.

Chico slides the card on his touch screen POS and opens a tab for the group. He grabs his shot off the bar and holds it up toward the group of men. "Salud!"

"YASSSS BITCHES!" The group of older guys yell before

downing their Patron shots.

In the dressing room, The Fish y Chicks are scrambling around doing any last minute touch-ups before their performance begins. With their earphones in and marking their dance moves, the queens try to practice the songs that they're about to lip-sync. While mostly ready, the queens stick a couple extra bobby pins in their wigs, add extra powder to their nose and spray their crotches with perfume just in case.

Amidst the chaos, the door to the dressing room opens. The three queens look up from their mirrors and stop what they're doing.

"It's showtime, girls," Robin says from the door without much emotion on her face. This is the first time they are seeing her tonight. The girls greet Robin and kiss her hello, still unsure if she knows how late they were.

"Alright girls, let's go," Alexus commands. The three girls leave the dressing room and head up onto the stage behind the main curtain. Still out of sight of the audience, the three girls stretch and warm up before their music starts.

"Ready?" Robin asks from the side of the stage.

Alexus looks over at Robin and nods. The girls strike their first pose and get ready to put on a show.

At the back bar, Kaleo hands Tisha and Momi shots that he just made. Checking to see if Robin is around, the three friends cheers below the bar and quickly take their shots. Throwing the shot glasses in the sink to get rid of the evidence, they swiftly turn back around and continue serving the next people in line.

Kaleo's next customers are three straight boys. He can tell by their nervous eye-contact and short exchange of words. "Uh, can I get a Heineken," one of the guys mumbles.

"Yeah, me too," a second guy tags on. Kaleo knew this

would probably be the case, since most straight guys need to prove their *straight-ness*, while in a gay club. No fruity cocktails, only manly beers.

The third guy decides to take a different approach. He's asian with chiseled cheekbones. Taller and handsomer than his other two friends, he seems as if he is the leader of the pack. Trying to make his two friends laugh, he looks to Kaleo and says "Give me the *gayest* drink that you have!" He turns around, high-fives his friends and laughs.

Kaleo, having dealt with assholes like this before, grabs the most expensive whisky off the shelf and pours it into a shot glass. He slams the drink down on the bar and says, "Gay enough for you?"

The third guy turns around and notices the shot of whisky. He realizes that Kaleo didn't think it was a funny joke.

"Twenty bucks, faggot," Kaleo demands.

To Kaleo's left, Tisha is serving a straight guy of her own. Being a former stripper, she knows the best way to get a straight guy to leave a big tip is to make him think he has a chance to hook up with her. With no intention of ever sleeping with a man again, Tisha knows exactly how to play the game.

"Can I buy a lovely lady a drink?" The straight guy asks.

"You can buy a lovely lady whatever you want, but you can buy *me* a shot?" Tisha counters in a sassy way. She knows straight guys like a challenge.

"Two shots it is." The straight guy smirks. "What time do you guys usually get out of here?"

"Who wants to know?" Tisha smiles and flirts.

"A guy I know just might wanna meet up with you after this," the straight guy asks her out in a roundabout way.

"Oh really? Do I know this guy?" Tisha continues to lead him on.

"You're about to." The straight guy looks Tisha up and

down.

"Cheers!" Tisha hands him his shot and they take a shot together. The straight guy hands her his credit card, she swipes it and hands it back to him with a credit card slip for him to sign. After taking longer than it usually takes a person to sign, the straight guy hands Tisha back the slip. He walks away while still making eye contact for the first few steps, but then disappears into the crowd.

Tisha grabs the credit card slip off the bar and just as she expected, he's written his phone number at the top. She scans the slip a little further down and realizes he didn't leave her a tip; she wasn't expecting that. She looks on the bar to see if maybe he left some cash, but there's nothing. She goes over to Kaleo and shows him the slip.

"How the hell you gonna flirt with me, tryna get in my pants, leave me your phone number and not tip? Da Fuck? Cheap ass muthafuckahs! I am so over men," Tisha says irritated. Kaleo laughs.

Momi finishes up her last customer in line and then looks over to see Tisha, who looks bothered. She walks up to Tisha, hoping she can be a shoulder to cry on, "What's the matter, girl?"

"Nothing. Just some jerk who didn't tip," Tisha explains.

"Who is he? Which one? Nobody fucks with my girlfriend!" Momi says like a wind-up toy.

Tisha laughs, "Oh, you would be a good girlfriend."

"You're damn right!" Momi cracks and then fantasizes about what it really would be like to be Tisha's girlfriend. At that very moment, Momi looks across the bar and inhales as if she's just seen a ghost. She stares at something in the middle of the room.

"You ok, boo?" Tisha asks, trying to figure out what Momi is starting at.

"I'll be right back." Momi tells Tisha and leaves the bar.

Just then, Robin takes the stage with a microphone in hand. "Come one, come all! Come my little gay children. Hele mai kakou. Make your way to the stage. Follow the sound of my voice…" Robin jokes, knowing that her voice is coming from every speaker in the club. The music starts to fade and Robin's mic starts to get louder as more and more people start to gather around the stage. "YASSS!!! Come closer, come closer, oh aren't you cute?" Robin says to a little white boy in the front row.

"How many of you are ready for our show?" A lackluster response leaves Robin underwhelmed. "Oh come on, I've heard better responses from a senior day care. HOW MANY OF YOU ARE READY FOR OUR SHOW?" She repeats louder. The audience responds with more enthusiasm. "There we go. That's more like it!

"Welcome to Violet! I'm your MC, host and owner of your favorite club, Robin DeCraydle. Thank you, yes, yes, I will fuck you later." Robin points to the same cute white boy in the front row as the audience cracks up.

"Now tell me, how many of you have been to Violet before?" More than half the audience screams. "Very nice. How many of you have seen our drag show before?" About half the audience screams. "Ok, not bad, not bad. Do we have any Violet Virgins tonight?"

Two of the three little gays from earlier scream from the side of the stage while the little gay birthday boy in blue tries everything he can to hide his face.

Robin notices the three little gays from the stage. "Don't hide little gay boy. We don't bite… hard," she cracks. "Well, we'll get you up here in a second baby, don't you worry, but the time has come… for our show. Are you ready?" The audience screams. "I said, are you ready?" The audience screams even louder. "This is… the Fish y Chicks!"

The song "Faded" by Zhu begins to play over the entire club as Momi approaches a female who is visibly excited for the start of the drag show. She taps her on the shoulder and the girl turns around. It's Simone from the ice cream shop. "Hey! I thought that was you."

"Oh hey!" Simone says slightly hesitant.

"Did you see Parker at the front bar?" Momi wonders.

"No, actually, there were a lot of people over there when I first came in. I heard one of the drag queens say 'Come to the stage' over the microphone, so I just came here instead," Simone explains.

"I didn't think you were gonna come. You didn't text me. Did you have to pay? I could've got you in for free," Momi questions.

"Oh no, I mean yeah, I was going to text you, but when I was outside, one of the bouncers just let me in for free," Simone describes the situation

"Big guy, kinda looks like a Samoan Shrek?" Momi tries to decipher.

"Yup, that's the one!" Simone giggles.

"Sam." Momi is not surprised. "You're hot, that's why he let you in. He does that a lot," Momi explains.

"Oh," Simone responds. She thought she was getting special treatment.

"Oh, no, that's not to take anything away from you." Momi catches herself. "You ARE hot. I mean, look at you. Like really, look at you. How can you blame Sam? I'm just jealous because I wanted to be the one to let you in," Momi spells it out for Simone. She gets really close to Simone and whispers in her ear "I hope you'll let *me* in."

Simone nervously laughs off Momi's last statement and tries not to think too much of it. She looks back to the stage just as the curtain is parting. The audience goes wild as the Fish y Chicks begin their routine. The two girls stand next to each other as they watch the queens performance.

"Ok, see the one on the right? That's Karmen Sense." Momi gently touches Simone's arm and begins to describe each of the Fish y Chicks. "She's all body, no brains; a true blonde. The irony of her name, right? She's the only trans girl in the group and she's had a lot of work done to her body in the past year. Oh, here we go, you'll see all of her new 'assets' in 3, 2, 1…"

Karmen tears away her outer costume to reveal she's only wearing nipple pasties and a G-string underneath. The audience goes crazy. "She's done enough blow and blown enough guys to win her a medal. She's the newest to the group, but she's not that new. Although, she be actin' *brand new* some days; saying some racist ass shit." Momi pauses. "Haole."

"How-Lee?" Simone doesn't know the word.

"White… basically. It has a deeper meaning in Hawaiian, but you can look it up later," Momi educates Simone. "Ok, that one there, on the left, is Arita Bitch."

"I like her name," Simone chuckles.

"Yeah, apparently it's a play on the phrase, 'I'll read a bitch' and boy does she live up to it. She's Portuguese, so she doesn't shut the hell up," Momi continues.

"Is that really a thing?" Simone asks.

"It is in Hawaii," Momi responds. "See that big mouth of hers? It matches her big hips and it gets her into A LOT of trouble. I can't tell you how many times Robin almost kicked her out of the show. She's local, but her fair skin often makes people assume that she's from the mainland... until she opens her mouth. Full-on pidgin."

"Pigeon?" Simone imagines birds flying out of Arita's

mouth like a magician.

"Yeah, pidgin. You've never heard of it?" Momi remembers that Simone said she just moved to O`ahu. "Man, you really are new to the island, huh? Pidgin is our local version of English; broken English basically."

"Oohhh." Simone still wishes birds would fly out of Arita's mouth.

"And last, but not least, the leader of the pack, the diva with the hot bod, who tucks her hot 'rod'… Alexus Convertible." Alexus, at the front and center of the stage, jumps into a split. The crowd roars and showers Alexus with dollar bills.

Simone laughs. "You're kidding! A Lexus Convertible? Like the car?"

"Yup, that's her, but she drives a Toyota Camry." The two girls share a laugh. "She's the *Fish* in the Fish y Chicks. She's the Filipino Beyoncé, while Arita and Karmen are Kelly and Michelle. I'll let you choose who's who." She winks at Simone. "She's got a million followers on Instagram and it's rumored that she's going to be on the next season of that TV show 'America's Next Top Drag Queen,' but no one really knows for sure."

Simone watches the queens perform their opening number, bopping along to the beat. Feeling like this is the perfect opportunity, Momi grabs Simone from behind. With her hands around Simone's waist, they groove together to the music. Simone, having never had a female embrace her like this, lets it happen. The two girls dance and get lost in the music, losing focus of the show that's happening right in front of them.

Momi takes complete advantage of the situation by caressing Simone's feminine curves. She presses her hips right up against Simone's butt and smells the sweet scent of her hair. Everything is going according to plan until Momi leans in and kisses the back of Simone's neck.

Feeling like she just woke up out of a trance, Simone comes back to her senses and freaks out internally. Instantly feeling uncomfortable, she creates an excuse to leave, "Uh, I just remembered, I gotta go."

"What? But you just got here?" Momi says confused.

"Uh, yeah, I know, but, um, Casper's at home… by himself… and I… I forgot to take him out to pee before I left, so yeah, I just…I gotta go check on him," Simone says backing away. She awkwardly waves bye to Momi and heads toward the exit.

"Shit," Momi mumbles to herself.

On her way out, Simone passes right in front of Parker's part of the bar. "Hey!" Parker tries to yell over the music, but it's too loud. Simone continues straight out the door, obviously bothered by something. Parker, not having any clue as to what just happened, chases after her. "Watch the bar," he says to Chico on the way out.

Parker swings open the front doors in a hurry, almost hitting Malu. "Whoa! What the fuck, Parker?" Malu barks.

"Sorry dude. Hey, did you see a chick about yay high?" Parker gestures to the middle of his chest, "Cute, dark brown hair, big tits?"

"That's literally every chick that walks in here, bro. Give or take the big tits part," Malu comments.

"Blue dress, walking out in hurry?" Parker tries again with more information.

"Oh yeah, you mean her?" Malu points to Simone, who is getting into an Uber. She shuts the door and confirms her destination with the driver.

"WAIT! Parker yells trying to stop her, but before he can even start running toward the car, the Uber takes off. "Shit."

Just then, Momi exits the club looking for Simone herself. She stands next to Parker and asks, "Did you see—" Parker cuts her off by just pointing at the car taking off. "Oh."

"What happened?" Parker asks his girlfriend.

"Nothing. I didn't do anything out of the usual," Momi starts. "I just… kinda gave her the express track."

"BABE!" Parker exclaims.

"What? Don't get mad at me just because you didn't get to sleep with another chick. I was doing *you* a favor. It's not my fault she was a virgin or whatever." Momi counters aggressively. She walks back into the club. Parker just shakes his head as everyone smoking outside looks at him.

Malu walks up to Parker and asks, "You ok?"

Parker nods, "Yeah, I'm good."

"Chicks, brah," Malu relates.

"Chicks, man. For real," Parker sighs. "Sometimes I wonder if it would be easier to just be gay."

Back inside, the Fish y Chicks continue to perform their number. Waiting for the show to finish so his go-go shift can start, Lopaka decides to watch the queens to pass the time. From the back of the audience, he observes the way the girls move, how they look and how they interact with the audience. He thinks to himself, *I can totally do that*, his thirst to try performing in drag starts to grow, *and I would do a lot more too!*

Finally getting over the hurt he felt earlier, Lopaka looks at his phone and shrugs. As expected, no new messages. Trying to stick to his new motto of "No expectations, no disappointments," Lopaka keeps calm and carries on. That is, until he looks over to the back bar.

Just in front of where Kaleo is serving drinks, Lopaka sees Ryan flirting with another guy. Lopaka, deciding not to jump to conclusions, stays where he is and just watches from afar. He talks to himself internally, *Ok, calm down, Paka. He hasn't done anything wrong yet. I mean, he didn't call me when he said he was going to, but PHYSICALLY he hasn't done anything with this guy yet. Who knows? Maybe they're just friends? Maybe he's a cousin?* Lopaka watches Ryan as he starts to make-out with the other guy. *MAYBE HE'S A TWO-FACED DOUBLE-CROSSING SLUT FACE WHO'S ABOUT TO GET HIS DICK RIPPED OFF!!!*

Lopaka storms all the way over to Ryan and pushes him from behind. "Who the hell is this?" Lopaka gestures toward the other guy.

"Jeez, what the fuck, Paka," Ryan quavers.

"Answer the question, Ryan. Who the hell is he?" Lopaka repeats.

"I'm gonna go." The other guy turns and disappears into the crowd.

"He's just a friend," Ryan attests.

"Oh, a friend who's tongue you just had down your throat?" Lopaka questions sarcastically.

"Calm down, you're causing a scene." Ryan looks around and notices that people are starting to pay more attention to the two of them than the Fish y Chicks on stage.

"Good, let them see! Let them see how much of an ASSHOLE you really are!" Lopaka is outraged. "I waited for you. I waited an hour and a half for your ass to text me, call me, send me a fucking letter... ANYTHING! But did you? No."

"What are you talking about?" Ryan asks.

"Dinner ASSHOLE! We were suppose to go to dinner tonight, remember? Or were you too busy rimming that guys asshole like the asshole that you are. And to bring him to Violet of all places." Lopaka scoffs. "You're a real piece of work, you know that?"

"Hey, I didn't think I'd have to spell this out for you, but here it is: We're not in a relationship! That was you assuming that we were in one," Ryan snaps back.

"You know what, Ryan…" Lopaka looks Ryan straight in the eyes, "Fuck. You. I'm done." He walks away and heads for the entrance.

At that very moment, Momi returns back to the bar. Kaleo, having watched the whole fight happen, but having been too busy serving customers to intervene, finishes up with his last customer and tells Momi and Tisha, "I'll be right back."

"Tag team," Momi says and high fives Kaleo as to say *your turn*.

Kaleo points at Ryan, who's now standing alone. "Not cool, Ryan," he scolds and then chases after his brother.

Outside of Violet, Malu and Parker are still chatting. As the two boys are about to walk back in, they see Lopaka running out in tears.

"Whoa, whoa what's going on now?" Malu asks his brother, but Lopaka just runs right past them and hops into a cab quicker than they can comprehend. And just like that, Lopaka is gone.

"Damn. We got some fast taxis in Honolulu tonight," Parker says half jokingly.

"What the hell was that all about?" Malu is completely lost.

A second later, Kaleo comes running out the front doors and yells to the other two boys. "Where'd he go?"

"He just left in a cab." Parker gestures to the street.

"Can somebody please tell me what the hell is going on tonight?" Malu asks.

"Ryan made out with another guy," Kaleo informs his brother.

"HE WHAT?!" Malu shouts.

"Yeah, he made out with this random guy, right in front of my bar and Lopaka caught him, so they got into this huge fight and I guess they're over now." Kaleo fills in the blanks for his brother and best friend.

Malu starts to head into the club with a determined look. "Watch the door," he says to the boys as he walks away.

"Where are you going?" Kaleo asks, but Malu doesn't answer. "Malu. MALU! Don't do anything stupid, Malu!"

"I'm not," Malu yells, and then mutters to himself, "I'm gonna do something smart." He disappears into the club.

"What are you doing out here?" Kaleo asks Parker. "Taking up smoking?"

Parker laughs. "No. Although, I probably should right now."

"Why? What happened?" Kaleo inquires.

"Nothing big. Momi and I just got into a fight over a girl."

"Which girl?" Kaleo is interested.

"Just some girl we met earlier. Doesn't matter, she's gone now, so…" Parker exhales.

"See, you might as well just be gay," Kaleo teases.

"I'm thinking about it at this point." Parker jokes back. The two boys look at each other, then look away and chuckle. They both know, first hand, that Parker has had gay experiences in the past. They stand in silence for a minute until they hear the front doors swing open dramatically as Sam walks out.

"SAM!" Kaleo shouts and starts heading over to the entrance. Parker follows.

"It wasn't me," Sam jokes and throws his hands up to prove his innocence.

"Where were you?!" Kaleo asks.

"I had to piss," Sam explains.

"We just got jumped by a group of Samoans!" Kaleo tries to fool Sam.

"What?! When?" Sam worries.

"Just now! And, they took Kaleo's wallet." Parker joins in on the fun.

"Yeah and they called us all a bunch of queers and took off in a taxi!" Kaleo elaborates.

"Yeah and they said 'Sam is the biggest queer of them all!'"
Parker exaggerates the story.

"Yeah and they said 'Tell Sam we'll see him at home,'"
Kaleo overdramatizes.

"Aaaahhhh you fuckahs! You guys so lie!" Sam finally
realizes they're playing a prank on him. "How can any of that
be? My family don't even know what a 'queer' is. Plus, how can
a group of Samoans fit in *one* taxi? They cannot even afford a
taxi!" The three boys crack up.

"Alright, we better get back in," Kaleo says to Parker. The
two boys shake hands with Sam and head back to their
respective bars.

Inside the club, the Fish y Chicks are still performing for a
fully-engaged audience. They've already collected a bunch of
tips in the short amount of time that they've been onstage. Ryan,
trying to forget about the drama that just happened, searches
through the sea of people to find his 'friend' that he was just
making out with. Finally spotting him across the room, he
waves to him and starts heading over. He makes it halfway
before running into Malu.

"Sup Ryan," Malu says to get Ryan's attention

"Oh hey Ma—" Ryan starts, but before he can finish his
sentence, Malu punches him right in the nose. Ryan falls back,
but doesn't fall down. The crowd of people gasp and jump back
as if there was a snake in the middle of the room (even though
there are no snakes in Hawaii). Woozy and in pain, Ryan grabs
his nose, which is now bleeding.

Just as Ryan gets his nose bashed in, the Fish y Chicks finish
their number. They hit their last pose and wait for the audience
to go nuts… but it's silent. The three girls are confused and
slightly offended. They look down and realize there's a
commotion going on in front of the stage. Not knowing what to

do, and not even exactly sure as to what's going on, the Fish y Chicks leave the stage unnoticed.

"Oh my God!" A random girl says.

"What the fuck man!" A random guy shouts at Malu.

"Call the security!" Another girl says.

"He *is* the security." Robin walks toward the center of the crowd. She shoots a sharp glance at Malu as to say, *I'll deal with you later*.

Trying to break the awkward silence in Violet, Robin smiles a fake smile and speaks jovially into the microphone. "Alright guys, girls and everyone in between, the Fish y Chicks will be back to take your bucks after they fix their tucks. So, until then, grab a drink from your favorite bartender and let's get this dance party started! HIT IT, DJ!" She motions to the DJ to turn the music volume up quickly.

She puts down the mic and puts down the front. Robin's stern face says it all. She looks at Malu and then at Ryan, "Boys, my office. NOW!" The two boys look at each other with resentment like two elementary school enemies that just got busted by the principal.

Malu and Ryan enter Robin's office and shut the door. Robin is sitting on her desk facing the door with her arms crossed at her chest. She's been waiting for them. She throws Ryan an ice pack and asks, "What the fuck was that?!"

"Yeah, tell her, Ryan?" Malu taunts.

"You tell me! I don't even know. I didn't do shit to you! I literally was just walking across the room and then you fuckin' punched me out of nowhere," Ryan says holding the ice pack to his nose.

"You know why! No act dumb," Malu says with a serious tone.

"I don't care what happened. It is NEVER ok to hit another employee." Robin speaks directly to Malu. Ryan looks at Malu with a smug look on his face.

"Shut up, Ryan. 'Fore I knock you out!" Malu is still heated.

Robin points her finger at Malu, "Cut it out! You heard me?"

She switches her focus over to Ryan. He's starting to feel like Robin is on his side. "And you... I know what you've been doing to Lopaka. Being careless and playing with his emotions." She points her finger at Ryan this time, "Cut it out! Both of you better cut this shit out, you heard me? You guys know that our guest count has been low recently. We can't be having any bad word-of-mouth. The last thing we need is for everybody to be afraid that our own security is gonna punch them out if they come to Violet," Robin reprimands. "Ryan, you're not gogo-ing tonight."

"What! No, I'm good," Ryan counters.

"No, you're not. You're gonna go to the hospital and get your nose checked out," Robin orders. She looks over to Malu, "And you're taking him."

"What?!" Malu is shocked

"What?!" Ryan has the same reaction.

"Yes. Now, shut up and get out of my office," Robin demands. The two boys eye each other out while leaving Robin's office and head off to the Emergency Room.

Once the boys leave, Robin starts coughing profusely. Her health has been wavering recently. Alone in her office, she gasps for air in between coughs. She can barely catch her breath. She knows that she has to keep her stress levels down in order to stay healthy.

Robin's coughs start to get heavier and deeper. Trying her best to steady herself, she clings to her desk for stability. Luckily, after a couple minutes of constant coughing, Robin finally calms herself down. She takes a few deep breaths in and exhales slowly. She repeats this until she can breathe normally. She's been so busy that she forgot to take her medication; a common occurrence with Robin trying to run the club herself.

After she's gathered herself, Robin dusts off her dress and grabs the microphone off her desk. Pretending as if nothing happened, she steps out of her office with a smile on. She turns on her mic and says, "Who's ready for the rest of the show?"

14. Cosmopolitan

- 1 1/2 oz Vodka
- 1 oz Cointreau
- 1/2 oz Fresh Lime Juice
- Splash Cranberry Juice

It's 2:15am and the club has been closed for fifteen minutes. Outside of Violet, there's still a few groups of people waiting for rides and chatting. The smoke-filled air and alcohol-filled guests slopping around look like a scene out of a zombie movie; a typical Friday night.

Back inside, the Fish y Chicks pack their belongings and tidy their dressing room. They take off their false eyelashes and stuff their dollars bills into their suitcases; they made a lot of tips performing tonight. As they take off their heels, Robin walks in.

"Here you go girls," Robin says and hands them each a white envelope containing their payment for tonight's performance. "Good job tonight. Despite the little hiccup we had in the middle, we did pretty well."

"Yeah, what happened?" Alexus asks. "We were performing and everybody was living for it and then the next thing I know, there's a boy with a bloody nose."

"Gay boys and their drama, you know how it goes," Robin states pragmatically trying not to reveal more than she needs. "Anyway, I've been thinking. We need to amp up the show, we need to bring in more people and since Jamba Nay left us—"

"God bless dat girl," Arita interrupts.

Robin shoots Arita a sharp look for interrupting. She repeats, "Since Jamba Nay Transy is gone, we need someone else to fill the role of the fourth girl. Plus, it'll give you guys more time to change between numbers."

"Honestly, I no tink we need a fourt' girl anymore," Arita says in full Pidgin English. "We good wit just da tree of us. Da audience loves us and we cannot have anyone ruin our *fishy* reputation. Plus, no more dat many pretty drag queens and we —"

"Shut up, Arita," Alexus says under her breath.

"This is not a *dragocracy*," Robin starts, "This club is a business, and it's *my* business. When you have your own club, you can make your own rules, but for now, what I say goes."

"What happened to Jamba Nay again?" Karmen asks out of the blue, interrupting an intense moment with her lack of social cues. Robin, Alexus and Arita look over at Karmen, who's looking back at them blankly. "Is there something on my face?"

"You really are a blonde," Arita makes fun of her drag sister.

Karmen checks herself out in the mirror, making sure there's nothing on her face, but then gets distracted by her own reflection. She puckers her lips at herself in the mirror starts pretending she's doing a photoshoot.

"She went to heaven, Karmen, remember?" Alexus explains for what feels like the millionth time, "You were here for her last show."

"Oh yeah. I forgot." Karmen says, not really remembering. She puts her hands into a prayer position and says "R.I.P. Miss Transy."

Robin shakes her head with disbelief of how dumb Karmen really is. "Anyway, I'm throwing a competition next Friday. It's going to be a drag competition and the winner will be our fourth Fish y Chick."

The three girls gasp in unison. "What!" Alexus says in shock.

"You can't do dat to us!" Arita pleads.

"Cool!" Karmen says with a smile. Alexus and Arita both

shoot Karmen a dirty look. Karmen looks in the mirror again thinking that she really does have something on her face this time.

"Well, it's too late now because I just posted it to the club's Instagram." The girls gasp again, even bigger this time. "The competition will take the place of your show next week, however, you still need to be here. Right after the winner is announced, you will perform a number with her to present the *new* Fish y Chicks to the world. Oh yeah, and the winner will be chosen by the audience."

The girls lose it. "Ho her God!" Arita says dramatically and holds her head as if she's going to faint.

"So, by this time next week, the three of you will have a new sister," Robin informs, "And I expect you all to welcome her with open arms, no matter who she may be." Robin points a stern finger at Arita and she nods in agreement. "Alright, good night. I'll see you tomorrow."

Just as she's about to exit the dressing room, Robin turns back around and tells the girls, "And don't be late. I deducted twenty bucks from each of your pay tonight for starting the show late. Good night." She leaves the room and closes the door behind her.

The three girls open their envelopes and realize she wasn't kidding. "Shit, she did," Arita confirms. "I was hoping she never see us come running in."

"That bitch sees everything," Alexus comments, then instantly fears that Robin overheard her. She looks to the door, which remains closed, and sighs in relief.

"Yay! We're gonna get a new sister!" Karmen cheers. The other two girls look at her with contempt in their eyes.

"Oh Nay, Karmen. Not Yay," Arita corrects her 'Fish y' sister. "We don't want another a girl."

"Oh, no other girls. Got it." Karmen takes note and quickly

changes her stance on the matter to fit in.

"Alright girls, here's the deal," Alexus starts to devise a plan, "We can't stop the competition from happening, but we can affect who will win."

"How we gonna do dat?" Arita asks.

"Leave that to me," Alexus replies.

In the main part of the club, the Violet staff are closing up. At the front bar, Kaleo counts the money in the bartenders' registers, while Ashley counts the money she made at the door. Sam and Chico sweep the floors, Yuki washes the rest of the dirty cups and the other bartenders close down their respective bars.

The club is silent. As with most nights, the staff quietly wrap up their tasks. They welcome the quietness after having had pop music blaring over the speakers for the entire night.

The Fish y Chicks leave their dressing rooms lugging their suitcases behind them. They wave goodbye to Tisha and Momi at the back bar and head toward the exit. As they pass the front bar, they each kiss Kaleo goodbye.

"Bye guys!" Alexus shouts out loud, so she doesn't have to kiss everyone else individually.

As they finish kissing Kaleo, Sam stands in their way, blocking their path. "You weren't gonna leave without telling me goodbye, were you?" Sam questions playfully.

"Of course not!" Alexus says. Sam, trying to take what little affection that he gets, gives each of the girls a big bear hug.

"Whoa, what about me?!" Beau shouts sarcastically. Alexus and Arita look at Beau and stick the middle finger simultaneously as they head out the door. "Oh come on!"

Karmen, trailing the other two, looks at Beau and blows him a kiss out of pity. She quick-steps and tries to catch up to her friends. As she runs, her ass bounces in her tiny booty shorts, leaving nothing to the imagination. Beau stares and checks out her ass, then quickly remembers that she's a trans girl and cuts his gaze. Having such a narrow mind, Beau fears that someone might call him gay. He looks around to make sure that no one saw what he was doing and goes back to cleaning the bar.

At the back bar, Tisha and Momi finish cleaning and shut everything off. They head over to the front, where everyone else is. "Hey boys. How'd you do?" Tisha asks with a smile. Momi, following just behind her, doesn't ask and doesn't have a smile. She's still upset with Parker.

"Pretty good," Parker answers Tisha. He looks to Momi, who's avoiding eye contact. He realizes that she's still mad.

"There were a lot of bitches tonight," Beau adds to the conversation.

"Good. You deserve to get ALL the bitches." Momi takes her frustration out on Beau.

"Well I did get you, so I guess you're right," Beau claps back, bringing up the fact that they slept together.

"Ugh. Shut up, Beau!" Momi shouts.

"Dude," Parker exclaims as to say *I'm standing right here. Her boyfriend, remember?*

"What? This ain't news to you," Beau responds to Parker's reaction. Parker just shakes his head.

"How long you been working here, Beau?" Kaleo asks without looking up.

"About a year," Beau replies.

"Then act like it," Kaleo shuts him down.

"Ohhh. Burn!" Sam says and laughs from across the room. Beau acts like he doesn't care.

"How long have you been in Hawaii?" Tisha questions Beau.

"Uhhh I don't know, about eight years. I came for college, but I stayed for the ladies," Beau flaunts. Momi rolls her eyes.

"What did you study?" Tisha asks kindly.

"Psychology," Beau answers. Everyone bursts out with laughter. "What?"

"People would go psycho, if they ever went to you as a psychologist," Ashley joins in the conversation.

"Oh, so you have your B.A.?" Tisha inquires while everyone is still laughing.

"No," Beau answers under his breath.

"Oh, you're B.S.?" Tisha explores further.

"No," Beau is short with his answer.

"Yeah, tell her why you don't have your degree, Dr. Phil," Momi jumps in sarcastically.

"Why?" Tisha asks curiously.

"Cause I got kicked out," Beau responds.

"For masturbating in one of his classes!" Momi interrupts and finishes the sentence. Everybody cracks up again.

"What?!" Parker exclaims while laughing. This is the first time he's hearing this.

"This ain't news to you, Parker!" Beau fights back.

"Yes. Yes, it is, pervert!" Parker responds.

"Whatever you guys, it's not that big of a deal," Beau defends himself.

"That's what she said," Kaleo cuts in, implying that Beau's dick is 'not that big of a deal.'

"That's what I *know*," Momi confirms Kaleo's last remark and holds her thumb and index finger in an inch measurement implying how small his penis is. She squints at her fingers with one eye.

"OHHHHH BURN!" Sam says again as he and Chico join the group.

"Shut up, Sam!" Beau is embarrassed. The staff cracks up again, for a third time, at Beau's expense.

From the sink area in the corner, they hear a loud crash

74

followed by a "Sorry!" As per usual, Yuki's butterfingers dropped a stack of cups. "I got it, I got it," he reassures the group.

"Yuki!" The entire group says in unison.

"You ok?" Kaleo yells in his direction while still counting money.

"I'm good, I'm good. I got it," Yuki continues to reassure and collects the dirty cups off the floor.

"Didn't you come for college too, Tisha?" Beau asks and tries to get the focus off of himself.

"No, I came in high school actually, in the middle of my junior year," Tisha informs. "My dad was in the military, he got stationed at Pearl Harbor, so he moved my mother, my brother and I out here and we've been here ever since."

"You guys must've been happy when you found out you were moving to Hawaii," Sam assumes.

"Yeah, we were, but biiitch... that plane ride though... that was no joke," Tisha enlightens the group. "I'm black, I don't know if you've noticed," the group chuckles, "and I'm not gonna speak for all black people, but my ass cannot swim! So when we were flying over the Pacific ocean and all you could see was blue... ooo, I closed my window shade and prayed to the good Lord above."

Yuki walks over with a stack full of clean cups and adds them to the others. He's been listening to the conversation from his corner. "I remember that flight," Yuki gets involved in the conversation, "except I was coming from the other direction."

"Oh yeah?" Tisha turns to Yuki in interest.

"Yeah, my dad was in the military too. Air Force. Here's a fun fact about me: I was actually born in Illinois. Random, right? Of all places. So, I'm a legal U.S. Citizen, but I spent most of my childhood in Japan."

"That's pretty cool. I wish I could've grown up in Japan."

Parker shows his interest.

"Yeah, it was pretty cool actually," Yuki confirms.

"I'm hapa (*hapa* is a hawaiian word meaning 'half' or 'part'). My dad is white and my mom is Japanese, and my mom really wanted to go back home to Japan after I was born. So, when I was about three, we moved to Japan, just outside of Tokyo, and that's where I grew up."

"So when did you come to Hawaii?" Tisha asks.

"Well, my dad got transferred here when I was twelve, so we packed up everything and relocated. When we first got here, I was in complete culture shock."

"Me too!" Tisha concurs.

"Really?" Ashley asks Yuki. "But there's so much asian influence here."

"Yeah, that's exactly why! There were so many Japanese people here, but most of them didn't speak or understand the Japanese language. I couldn't wrap my head around it at twelve years old. I mean, I get it now, but it was weird for me back then."

"Ahhh, yeah. I never thought about it that way," Ashley admits.

"Right?" Yuki confesses. "I mean, now that I'm a little older, I love it. I love the mix of cultures here in Hawaii. You know, I lived in Japan for a long time and I've been back to Illinois to visit my dad's side of the family, but in both places… I've never felt as accepted as I do here.

"Why's that?" Ashley asks curiously.

"Well, I wasn't asian enough in Japan and I was too Asian in Illinois, so when I came to Hawaii and everyone looked like me, I cried. I finally fit in somewhere. Anyone can fit in here and that's why I love it. Not to mention the whole trans thing. People just seem to get it out here in Hawaii."

"Yeah, we do. It's more about who you are in Hawaii and if

you have the Aloha Spirit," Kaleo offers his opinion.

"Awww, that's so sweet." Tisha goes to hug Yuki, but Yuki runs away.

"I may be only half asian, but I still fully hate hugs," Yuki yells as he runs away. The groups laughs.

"I was stationed here too," Chico joins in the conversation. He redirects his focus to Beau, "Can I have a beer, brother?"

Beau takes out two Bud Lights. "Anybody else for a shifty?" Beau asks the group. Sam gestures to hand him a bottle and Momi displays the beer that she's already sipping on.

Beau hands Chico a bottle, "Thanks brother. Yeah, I was stationed here at eighteen years old, fresh out of high school. I didn't know a single soul and I never even been on an airplane before."

"Seriously?" Beau is shocked.

"Yup. I grew up in East L.A., you know, like the ghetto. We never had no money. We were lucky if we had enough money to buy tortillas, you know what I mean?" Chico jokes. "Nah, but my abuela took good care of us, me and my cousin, José."

"What happened to your parents, if you don't mind me asking?" Ashley asks.

"Nah, it's cool. Um, my mom and dad were in a car accident when I was little, I barely remember it. And then, my cousin José's mom, my Tia Rosa, she got caught up in drugs and abandoned him, so our abuela took us both in. She was the best woman I ever knew, man, with the kindest heart.

"You know, where we grew up, you didn't get out. You either ended up in a gang, sold drugs or if you were lucky, you went to prison. My abuela, she knew we lived in a bad area, so she signed me up for the military and sent me away."

"Aren't you still in the military?" Tisha asks.

"Nope. Honorable discharge," Chico chuckles.

"What's that?" Ashley asks.

"Well, it's better than a dishonorable discharge, I'll tell you that." Chico makes the group giggle slightly, "Nah, but basically, my abuela, she was sick. She had cancer for years, you know. Her health went up and down and up and down… and I got mad at her when she sent me away because who was gonna take care of her, you know? But my cousin, José, he reassured me. He was a year younger, so he stayed back and took care of her. I remember him telling me, 'Go Chico. You have to go. Go out and make some money for our family.' So, I did… and that was the last day I ever saw my cousin." Chico pauses and starts to tear up.

Everybody looks over at Chico. They've never seen him emotional. "On the day of his high school graduation, he was in the wrong place at the wrong time… and he got shot. He didn't even get to graduate. He was so smart, you know, smarter than I ever was. He was my brother. I still feel bad… I shouldn't have left him." The entire staff is silent and let Chico tell his story.

"Anyway, my abuela couldn't take care of herself, so the military gave me an honorable discharge. They let me go home and take care of her, but she passed the next year." Chico pauses to gather himself. "I didn't have a big family, you know, but my family had a big heart. There wasn't anything left for me in East L.A., so I sold my abuela's house and I moved back to Hawaii. I always knew that I would end up back here. There's just a warm feeling in Hawaii that you don't feel anywhere else and I couldn't wait to get back to it."

"It's true. I feel that way too," Tisha agrees, while wiping a tear out of her eye.

Chico brightens his tone, "But, life is good now, you know? I got a nice place, I have friends like you guys and I have a hot boyfriend."

"Yeah you do!" Ashley encourages.

"Ugh, he is. I wish I found him first," Kaleo confesses and

they all laugh.

"You know what's funny, he's the first person I met when I came back to the islands. And you know what's even funnier, I came all the way back to Hawaii, where everybody is mixed-raced, and I found myself a white boy. My abuela would be so *proud*," Chico jokes sarcastically.

"Sometimes, I imagine bringing Riley home to my abuela for the first time. She'd smile and be nice and then take me to the other room and say 'Un gringo, mijo?' I'd just laugh and tell her 'He loves me, Abuela' and she'd get it. But, I know she's with me, they all are... my parents and José too. I see it in the way Riley looks at me and cares of me. It's the same way my abuela used to look at me."

"Damn, man. One for the homies." Beau ruins the mood. He pours a little bit of his beer on the floor.

"Shut up, Beau! God!" Momi says, having had enough of Beau's dumb comments.

"Dude, you're the kind of white guy that's ruining it for all us other white guys," Parker tries to get Beau to understand.

"What? I'm showing my support." Beau pours his beer on the floor again. Parker just shakes his head.

"Don't mind him," Momi speaks to Chico, "he thinks he's Eminem." Chico doesn't take offense and just laughs.

"Wait. Don't you speak Mexican, too?" Beau directs his question at Momi.

"Seriously, shut up, Beau," Momi spouts and then turns back to Chico, "I'm Puerto Rican. Half Puerto Rican."

"Duh! I was just joking. I know Mexicans and Puerto Ricans don't speak the same language." Beau tries to back track and seem smart, but actually making himself look dumber. The whole staff looks at him with disbelief, but they don't correct him.

"Ah, Hablas español?" Chico asks.

"Un poco. Like MUY poco." Momi quickly stops Chico from thinking that she is fluent in Spanish. "My grandma was from Puerto Rico, but my mom was born here, so I would only hear Spanish when my grandma was around, but she passed away when I was little."

Yuki comes back around with more clean cups. "Does that mean, you're Puerto Rican too, Ash?" Yuki looks at Ashley waiting for a response. "You guys are cousins, right?"

"Yeah, we're cousins, but not on that side of the family. Our dads are brothers. So, we're both Hawaiian from our dads, but her mom is Puerto Rican and my mom is Filipino," Ashley clarifies.

"Oh, gotcha," Yuki responds, learning something new about his co-workers. "Aren't you guys Hawaiian and Filipino too?" Yuki turns his focus over to Kaleo, but being too deep into counting money, he doesn't respond.

"Yo, Kaleo," Parker gets Kaleo's attention.

"What?" Kaleo realizes everyone is looking at him. "Oh sorry, I didn't realize you were talking to me."

"Nah, it's all good. I was just wondering what your ethnicities were," Yuki repeats.

"Oh, uh, we're Hawaiian, Filipino, Chinese, English and Spanish." Kaleo lists them off as he's done his entire life.

"Damn!" Yuki responds.

"Yeah, but that's pretty much the norm in Hawaii. Everyone's mixed," Kaleo responds.

"You and your brothers are so lucky. I wish I had that many ethnicities. I'm just black. Proud of it, but just black." Tisha gets the group to laugh.

"Which, by the way, where is my younger brother?" Kaleo looks around the club. "Ash, where's Malu?"

Ashley sighs, "He's at the hospital."

"What?" Parker questions.

"How come no one told me earlier?" Kaleo asks slightly irritated, thinking his brother got hurt somehow.

"No, no, he's fine. Ryan, however, is a different story," Ashley states.

"Wait, wait, wait. Start from the top please," Kaleo insists.

Just then, Robin appears from around the corner and begins to explain, "Your brother took it upon himself to avenge Lopaka and punched Ryan right in his face. I think he broke his nose." She continues with no emotion on her face, "I sent him to take Ryan to the E.R. He caused the problem and now he has to take responsibility."

"Shit, I told him not to do anything stupid," Kaleo explains.

"You would've known if you were behind the bar," Robin states matter of factly. She really does see everything. "Where were you?"

"I went chasing after Lopaka, but he hopped in a cab and took off before I could get to him," Kaleo defends himself.

Robin doesn't respond. "Alright gang, I'll see you all tomorrow." She notices the beer that Beau is drinking. "Finish your beers inside. If any of you take any alcohol out of this building, you didn't get it from Violet. Got it?"

"Got it," the group says in unison.

"Ashley, make sure to lock up," Robin speaks to Ashley directly. She opens the entrance doors and heads home.

"What does she mean 'Ashley, make sure to lock up?'" Kaleo inquires once Robin is gone.

"Nothing," Ashley responds.

"No, not 'Nothing,' Ash. What did Robin mean by 'make sure to lock up?'" Kaleo persists. Ashley just looks at her phone. He's put two and two together. "She gave you the keys to the club, didn't she?!"

"Well, what was I supposed to do? Not take them?" Ashley justifies herself.

"Yes, that's exactly what you're supposed to do. Those are *my* keys!" Kaleo argues.

"Ok guys, calm down," Parker says trying to ease the tension.

"Sorry, Kaleo, but you fucked up. Honestly, I don't even want these keys, I don't want the responsibility, but I can't just give them back to you. Robin will know." She pauses to gather herself, "Just give it a week or two," Ashley asserts. She then takes the lead, "Alright guys, everything's finished, right? Yuki are you done?"

"Yup, I'm done," Yuki replies.

"Ok guys, let's go home. It's been a long night." Ashley tries to usher everyone out, so she can go home. "Momi, can I catch a ride with you and Parker? Malu took our car and he's still at the hospital. Guess where he's sleeping tonight. Hint: Not in my bed, I'll tell you that."

"Actually, I'm going with Tisha," Momi responds. She looks over to Tisha, "Can Ash jump in with us?"

"Yeah, of course," Tisha responds.

"Whoa, whoa. Were you gonna discuss this with me?" Parker is offended.

"Well, you obviously have other plans in mind for tonight that don't involve me, so I'm gonna hang out with Tisha," Momi says sassily.

"And where are you guys gonna go this late at night?" Parker asks.

"I got the hook-up at the strip club that I used to dance at. They stay open later just for the employees to hang out and drink. Don't worry, Parker, I got her," Tisha persuades.

Parker looks at his girlfriend. Momi looks back at him and finally says, "I'll text you tomorrow." She kisses him on the cheek before heading out the door.

"Alright guys, I'm turning off the lights," Ashley yells from the front door. She turns off the lights and the rest of the staff scurry outside like cockroaches.

Outside the club, the boys hang out and chat in a semi-circle as Ashley locks the entrance. Tisha and Momi are already halfway to Tisha's car.

"Hello! Wait for me!" Ashley yells to the other girls. "Bye guys," she says to the boys as she tries to catch up.

The boys slowly depart one-by-one until Kaleo and Parker are the last two left. "You and Momi gonna be alright?" Kaleo asks.

"Yeah, we'll be fine," Parker assures. "What about you? You ok?"

"Yeah, I'm pretty sure Lopaka just went home and Malu will probably end up sleeping on the couch, but he'll be fi—"

"No, I don't care about them. Are *you* ok?" Parker interrupts. "I can tell you've been off your game recently."

"Yeah, I'm good. I'm just…" Kaleo pauses, "I'm good."

"Well, whatever's going on, you know we can talk about it, right?" Parker assures his friend.

"I know. I'm good, though," Kaleo reassures his friend and smiles.

"Cool." Parker leaves it at that. "Surf tomorrow?"

"Yeah, maybe. What time you thinking?" Kaleo asks.

"Whenever I wake up," Parker chuckles.

"Shoots, text me when you wake up then," Kaleo responds.

"Rajah! Need a ride to your car?"

"Nah, I'm right around the block."

"You sure?" Parker double checks.

"Yeah, yeah. I'm good," Kaleo confirms.

"Alright, I'll hit you up tomorrow then," Parker concludes. The two boys do their secret handshake and start heading in opposite directions.

Kaleo looks back at his friend walking away and yells,

"Hey!" to get Parker's attention. "Thanks." Kaleo thanks his friend for reassuring him that they can always talk things out. Parker flashes his eyebrows and smiles. He turns back around and heads toward his car.

Kaleo watches his friend turn the corner and disappear into the night. He thinks about how long they've known each other and everything they've been through together. He thinks to himself, *My next boyfriend better be as good as Parker*, and imagines what it would be like to be in relationship with him. *Man, we would be such a good couple.*

Kaleo heads toward his car and passes the after-hours bar on the way. *They're still open.* He fights with himself internally, *Get in your car, Kaleo, and go home.* He looks in the window and sees his friend Josh working the bar. *Well, maybe just one...* Kaleo opens the door and heads inside for 'just one.'

15. AMF (Adios Mother Fucker)

- 1 oz. (30ml) Vodka
- 1 oz. (30ml) Rum
- 1 oz. (30ml) Gin
- 1 oz. (30ml) Tequila
- 2 oz. (60ml) Sweet & Sour Mix
- 1 oz. (30ml) Lemon Lime Soda
- 1 oz. (30ml) Blue Curaçao

Almost a week has gone by and Lopaka has barely left his apartment. Still dealing with the heartache of losing Ryan, who he thought was his boyfriend, Lopaka has secluded himself from everyone at Violet. His phone starts to ring; one of many times this week. It's his brother Kaleo. He looks at his phone and declines the call. He's been ignoring everyone all week.

With his phone already in his hand, he decides to check his social media. He scrolls through Instagram and passes a post from the Violet page. There's a picture of the Fish y Chicks with a black silhouette of a female's body next to the three girls. The caption states "Will you be the next *Fish y Chick*? Don't miss our drag competition tonight at 11pm." A variation of this picture has been posted everyday since last week Friday.

Lopaka looks over at a dress he bought the other day, laying on the bed next to a pair of heels. He's been strutting around his apartment in them with all week. *Am I really gonna do this?* He thinks to himself and then looks back to his phone.

He scrolls down a little further and the very next post he sees is from Alexus. She's also been posting all week. However, her posts have been of Arita's fresh-out-of-the-closet, younger brother, Matt.

Matt is a twink. He's fair-skinned, way tinier than Arita and looks really pretty in make-up. All week, Alexus has posted photos of Matt and his transformation into his new drag persona, "Matt Make-up;" a name, ironically, thought up by Karmen Sense.

With being presented to the world, not only on Alexus' Instagram, but on Arita's and Karmen's as well, Matt's following has almost tripled over the past week. Creating this hype and getting people excited to see Matt Make-up perform at the drag competition was Alexus' plan from the start. If there was going to be a new addition to the Fish y Chicks, she knew it had to be someone that wouldn't pose a threat.

Lopaka looks at the beautifully photo-shopped picture of Matt in full drag. *Shit, she's really pretty*, he thinks to himself, *I don't stand a chance.* He looks back over at his dress and changes his mind. *Fuck it!* He declares with conviction. *I may not be the prettiest, but I'm a damn good performer.* With Ryan out of his life and having always wanted to try drag, he figures, *I have nothing to lose.*

16. Mai Tai

- 1 1/2 oz Gold/Amber Rum
- 1 oz Dark Rum
- 1/2 oz Triple Sec
- 1 oz Pineapple Juice
- 1 oz Orange Juice
- 1/4 oz Lime Juice
- 1 dash Grenadine

It's another Friday night at Violet and about an hour before the drag competition begins. The music is bumping and the crowds of guests are starting to trickle in.

Having shown up on-time today, Kaleo thought that he would be reassigned back at the front bar like usual. However, Robin delegated the same positions as last week, leaving Kaleo at the back bar. Not knowing if he will ever go back to the front, Kaleo tries not to think about it and focuses on pouring drinks.

At the front bar, a girl and her gay guy friend walk up to Beau's side of the bar. "Hi handsome!" The girl says to start conversation.

"Hey!" Beau responds looking her up and down. She's a tall brunette with big tits. Beau is instantly interested. "What can I get you?"

"Well, you can get me your phone number first of all and then…" She looks over and asks her guy friend, "What do you want?"

She's pretty straight forward for a chick, Beau thinks to himself. *I like it!*

"Uh, can I get a Mai Tai, please?" The gay guy asks meekly.

"Yup and for you?" Beau flashes his eyebrows and smiles at the girl.

"Just a Heineken for me," she answers.

Beau is slightly surprised at her drink of choice, but then thinks to himself, *Well, she can hang with the boys. I like that too.* He pours the Mai Tai, cracks the beer and hands both drinks to her. "That'll be twelve dollars."

She gives him a twenty dollar bill and says, "Keep it."

Damn! And she's a good tipper! Beau thinks it's too good to be true. "Thank you!" He says and expects her to walk away.

"You never gave me my first order," she states.

Beau tries to rack his memory, *Shit, what was it?*

"Your phone number..." She flirtatiously reminds him.

Man, this is my lucky day, Beau thinks. "Yeah, sure. Give me your phone." She hands Beau her phone and he quickly enters in his phone number and saves it.

Just then, Yuki comes by to pick up some dirty cups off the bar top and sees the phone number exchange between Beau and the brunette.

"Hit me up," Beau says before she waves and walks off with her friend.

"Wow, Beau, I'm proud of you," Yuki confesses.

"Proud? What do you mean?" Beau is confused by Yuki's last statement.

"You know that's a T girl, right?" Yuki asks Beau.

"What's a T girl? Beau counters.

"T girl, you know, Transgender. She's trans," Yuki informs

"Shut up, Yuki!" Beau says in disbelief. "No she's not!"

"Beau, I'm a trans guy. I think I would know," Yuki persuades. "She's pretty passable though."

"Fuck, Yuki, are you being serious?!" Beau asks desperately.

"Dude, look at her," Yuki testifies. "Look at her hands. Those are some big hands."

"SHIT!" Beau panics. "I just gave my number to a dude!"

"She's not a dude, jackass, she's a chick!" Yuki condemns.

Beau looks at Yuki with half fear, half anger in his eyes, "I'm not gay."

"And neither is she," Yuki responds. "You know, you say some pretty ignorant things sometimes, but I'll give you a pass because you're my friend," Yuki reprimands. "You're a guy, she's a girl. What's the problem? Have you ever even been with a trans girl before?"

"No," Beau replies.

"Then, don't knock us 'til you've tried us," Yuki speaks on behalf of all trans men and women. "You 'straight' guys are so small-minded sometimes." He grabs a couple more cups off the bar and takes them back to his dish station to wash.

Beau can tell that he's offended Yuki. He looks back at the girl that he just gave his number to and begins to imagine what it would be like to sleep with her, but then quickly starts serving another customer to divert his thoughts.

At the back bar, a group of six, three girls and three guys, walk up to Momi. One of the girls takes the lead, "Hi! Can I get six shots please."

"Sure, what do you want?" Momi asks politely.

"I'll have one lemon drop shot, two STPs, one Vegas bomb, a blueberry vodka straight and a chilled tequila shot with salt and lime." She recites her order like she's reading a grocery list.

Momi looks at her, trying to hide her irritation, and thinks, *Really, bitch?* Knowing it's not illegal to order a bunch of different drinks, she turns around and looks at Kaleo and whispers, "Ho her Gawd."

Kaleo, having overheard the order, rolls his eyes and asks "Do you want me to make any of them for you?"

"Nah, I got it. It's just irritating," Momi replies.

Kaleo nods, then looks back to see if there are any new customers for him to serve. Straight ahead and walking directly toward him is the same Asian guy that ordered from him last week. *Shit, here we go again*, he thinks to himself.

"Hey," the guy says hesitantly. Kaleo just looks at him blankly. "Hey, I'm not sure if you remember me—"

"Oh, I remember you," Kaleo interjects.

"Yeah… I was here last Friday with two of my buddies and uh…" He pauses, "Look, I came to apologize."

Kaleo is stunned. He was not expecting that. Kaleo looks at him in a way that says *I'm listening*…

"Yeah, um, I didn't mean to offend you last week when I said 'Give me your gayest drink!' He mocks himself. "That was dumb and I—"

"What? Wanted to look cool in front of your friends by making fun of us gays," Kaleo snarls.

"Yeah, about that…" The guy continues, "Uh, those are my friends from high school and uh… I haven't seen them in awhile, so…"

"Come on, I have other customers waiting," Kaleo interrupts, trying to hurry the story along, even though there are no other customers waiting.

"They don't know that I'm gay," the asian guy admits.

"Oh." Kaleo is shocked. He wasn't expecting that either. "Uh, well…" Kaleo is at a loss for words.

"Yeah. Pretty dumb, huh?" The guy confesses. "I'm Jimmy, by the way." He sticks his hand out and Kaleo receives it. "Hey, look, I'm pretty embarrassed about the way that I acted and I was thinking maybe I could take you out sometime and make it up to you."

Only then does Kaleo notice how handsome he is. Being too clouded earlier by how mad he was, Kaleo now starts to observe this tall asian man. *He's got great hair, really good skin and he's got a nice set of teeth too*, Kaleo takes note. He checks out his toned body that is shown off perfectly in his fitted clothes. For a second, Kaleo considers taking him up on his offer, but quickly replies, "I don't date guys that are still in the closet."

"Touché," Jimmy responds with a smile. "Well, can I at least buy you a drink?"

"Which one? 'The gayest drink we have?'" Kaleo says sarcastically.

Jimmy laughs. "Ok, ok, I deserve that." He looks at Kaleo and smiles, "Sure, two shots of whiskey for this 'faggot,'" Jimmy mocks Kaleo this time, for aggressively calling him a faggot last time. Kaleo chuckles and pours a shot for Jimmy and a shot for himself. They cheers and take their shot together.

"Sorry again," Jimmy apologizes, "and if you ever change your mind, the offer stands." He puts a hundred dollar bill down on the bar along with his business card. He smiles, waves goodbye and walks away.

Kaleo picks his business card off the bar which has his phone number on it. It states, 'Real Estate Agent.' He, then, looks down and sees the hundred dollar bill. *DAMN! AND HE HAS MONEY TOO!* Kaleo thinks to himself. Jimmy has managed to shock Kaleo three times in a matter of minutes. *Maybe I really should take him up on his offer.*

Just outside of Violet, Lopaka pulls up in an Uber in full drag. As this is his first time ever being dressed as a woman publicly, he feels nervous and wonders what everyone will think. He gathers his courage and steps out of the car. The Uber driver helps him get his suitcase full of accessories out of the trunk. Lopaka thanks the driver and starts heading toward the entrance of Violet.

With the competition entry just being a mere sign-up sheet at the front desk, Lopaka knew that he didn't have to reveal his intentions ahead of time. However, having not seen or spoken to anyone from Violet since last Friday, he knows that his look will come as a surprise.

He walks up to the front door, rolling his suitcase behind him. He looks at his younger brother, Malu, who is guarding the door and waits for a reaction.

"ID," Malu requests.

"Malu, it's me," Lopaka says trying to get his brother to comprehend the situation.

Malu looks at the drag queen in front of him and starts thinking really hard. He racks his brain trying to remember if he's met this specific queen. Being the doorman, he sees a myriad of drag queens nightly. *Am I supposed to know this queen? She obviously knows my name. Maybe she's a friend of Robin.* He looks her up and down one more time, then finally admits defeat, "Uh, sorry… who are you?"

"Your older brother, dumbass!" Lopaka spells it out.

"OH SHIT! LOPAKA!" Malu is completely taken aback, but then immediately hugs his brother. "What the fuck! Where have you been? We were all worried."

"Yeah, I just needed some time to myself," Lopaka responds.

"Yeah, we figured. Ho, so I guess this is the new you, huh?" Malu questions.

"And so what if it is? And how come you can't recognize your own family?" Lopaka scolds and slaps him on the arm.

"Hey, to be fair, I wasn't expecting to see you here tonight… and especially not like this." Malu defends himself. "So, you're a drag queen now, huh?" Malu makes fun.

"Shut up, Malu!" Lopaka is on the defense this time, "Don't judge me!"

"Are you kidding me? I don't care. Look at me, I'm a straight dad working at a gay club. Plus, I have two older brothers, who are both gay. One of you was bound to end up in drag," Malu wisecracks. "Come, let's go show Ashley!" Malu opens the entrance door and let's Lopaka in first. "Look who I found…" Malu says to Ashley in a sing-song way.

"OH MY GOD, LOPAKA!" Ashley screams with excitement and runs around her little desk to hug him.

"What?! How did you guess that so fast?" Malu is dumbfounded.

"Duh, doofus! You can tell it's him," Ashley scoffs at her boyfriend. She redirects her attention back to Lopaka, "How have you been? You been ok?"

"Yeah, I'm good. I just needed some time," Lopaka reassures.

"Yeah, we all figured," Ashley assures.

"What if I was dead? You guys didn't even come and check on me!" Lopaka accuses.

"DRA-MATIC!" Ashley cries out dramatically herself. "Don't act! We knew you were alive by how many times the phone rang. Every time any of us would call you, it would ring like two and a half times. A HALF! Phones don't half-ring unless somebody is on the other side declining it."

The three of them crack up. "Ok, ok fiiiiine. You caught me," Lopaka admits.

"You here for the drag competition?" Ashley asks.

"Oh yeah! The drag competition!" Malu suddenly remembers.

Ashley rolls her eyes, m*y boyfriend, the genius*, she thinks sarcastically to herself, then looks over at Lopaka, "Do you see what I have to deal with on a daily basis?"

"No, no! I remember we have the competition tonight, but I thought maybe he was here in drag just because," Malu justifies.

"No. I'm definitely here for the competition," Lopaka clarifies.

"Good for you, babes. You're gonna kill it! I know you are," Ashley encourages. She hands him the sign-up sheet, there's already three other girls signed up. The first on the list, of course, is Matt Make-up. Lopaka writes his name down and hands the clipboard back to her. Ashley looks at it and laughs, "Is that your drag name?"

"Yup," Lopaka chuckles.

In the dressing room, all of the contestants for tonight's drag competition are getting ready. The Fish y Chicks steal two of the best spots in the room, nearest the doors, and help Matt Make-up get ready. Karmen teases his wig to get maximum volume, while Arita touches up his *matte* make-up. Alexus, being the leader of the brigade and the charade, is on her phone posting a new photo to Instagram. *Tonight. Violet. 11pm. Matt Make-up Domination*, her caption reads. The hype around Matt is already at an almost unsurpassable high.

"I'm good. I'm very good. I should be a politician," Alexus says out loud, still looking at her phone. "Look at how many 'likes' you already have Matt." Alexus flashes her phone to the other girls.

"No, I'm the politician. You're my promoter," Matt jokes.

"Oooop!" Karmen makes a noise indicating that shade has just been thrown.

Arita slaps Matt's head. "Cut it out!" She looks to their leader, Alexus, hoping that she isn't offended.

"Careful now. Don't bite the hand that feeds you, daughter," Alexus says calmly. She knows all it would take is one bad post about Matt and all of her followers would turn on him.

The dressing room door opens and all of the contestants including the Fish y Chicks look over. Lopaka enters the room with his suitcase in tow and closes the door behind him. The girls just stare at him. He's the buffest queen in the room.

"Oh my God. Lopaka?" Karmen decodes. She's not so dumb after all.

"Guilty," Lopaka jests awkwardly.

"Whoa, I neva know you was in dis competition," Arita says with her pidgin accent. Alexus is silent and just stares at him trying to hide the disgust on her face, but not doing a good job at it. She wasn't expecting this curveball, but by what she sees in the room, she knows Matt still has no competition.

"Guilty again," Lopaka answers. "Um, is there an open spot someplace for me to get ready?" He asks the crowded room of queens.

"You can sit over here," a browned-skinned drag queen with red hair says from the corner. She points to an empty chair and mirror that's right next to her.

Lopaka nods and scoots his way through the Fish y Chicks, hitting a few of them with his broad shoulders on the way. He passes an older looking queen, who he assumes is another contestant. She waves hi and then goes back to applying her make-up. As Lopaka settles into his little work station, he looks to the queen who offered him the seat, "Hey thanks!"

"Of course, girl," the red-head reassures. "Nothing like not having a place to set your things. I'm Arrriba, by the way." She rolls the R's in her name, letting Lopaka know that she's hispanic. "Arrriba McEntire."

"That's HI-LA-RIOUS!" Lopaka says and laughs out loud. "Like a latina Reba McEntire?"

"Yup, exactly that!" She confirms. "I do all Reba McEntire songs, but in spanish."

"Oh, you win already. I love that," Lopaka admits.

"And you are…" Arrriba asks.

"Oh, I'm Lopa—" He pauses, then corrects himself, "I mean, I'm Jenna."

"Nice to meet you, Jenna," Arrriba says warmly. "First time?" She asks.

"Yeah and kinda nervous," Lopaka confesses.

"Don't worry. The first time's the best time. I think so anyway," Arrriba comforts. "Plus, you have beginner's luck on your side."

"I hope so," Lopaka remarks. He pulls out his make-up and starts adding his final touches to his look.

The door opens again, but this time it's Robin. "Hey girls," Robin starts. She glances around the room quickly, but with a million things on her mind, she doesn't notice Lopaka in the corner. Thank you for signing up tonight. This show would not be happening without you." The girls applaud for themselves and each other.

"Ok, so here's the deal. You'll each perform your song of choice and you'll go in the order that you signed up." Robin looks down at her clipboard, "So, Matt Make-up, that means you're up first." Matt nods. "Make sure to give your CD or thumb drive or whatever you have, to the DJ, if you haven't already.

"After you all perform, we'll bring everyone back up onstage and the audience will cheer for the best performer. The queen with the loudest round of applause will win and become one of our very own Fish y Chicks!" The girls applaud again. "This is a great opportunity, so please treat it as such. Do your best and give the best damn performances of your life, ok?" The girls applaud one last time. "Ok girls, good luck! You've got ten minutes and then we're gonna start the show." Robin turns around and exits the room.

The queens continue to get ready for the show. The Fish y Chicks start pulling and pushing at Matt, while he sits and makes faces of pain. Arrriba puts in her earphones to practice her lyrics. Lopaka looks around the room, then back at himself in the mirror. He inhales deeply and then exhales all of his doubts. *I got this*, he thinks to himself and finishes applying his make-up.

At the entrance, Malu and Ashley are arguing in between each customer passing through. Malu checks a girl's ID, Ashley takes her money and then stamps the inside of her wrist. Once the girl enters the club, the couple begin their fight again.

"I told you this a month ago!" Ashley reiterates.

"No, you didn't!" Malu responds.

"Yes, I did. I made sure I did because I was trying to avoid this situation we're having right now," Ashley says irritated.

"Well, I don't remember, so you can't blame me," Malu defends himself.

"What do you mean 'I can't blame y—'" Ashley cuts herself off. A group of four gay guys walk in the door. "Hi guys!" Ashley says with a fake smile. The gay guys enter the club and Ashley starts again. "They're your kids too, you know. I shouldn't be the only one knowing their schedules."

"I DO know their schedules! I pick them up from school every fuckin' day! Don't give me that." Malu is heated.

"Well why don't you remember about tomorrow then, huh? Tell me, Malu, why don't you remember?" Ashley says in a low, sassy tone.

"I just forgot maybe. I don't know. Shit," Malu replies.

"No! I'll tell you why—" Ashley cuts herself off again as a lesbian couple comes through the entrance. "Hi guys!" Ashley says, once again, with a fake smile on, trying to hide her anger. She doesn't realize, but she stamps the inside of their wrists a little too hard. The lesbian couple shake out their wrists in pain as they enter the club.

She waits 'til they're far enough away and repeats herself. "I'll tell you why you conveniently don't remember… because tomorrow is your stupid UFC fight on TV."

"It's not stupid, it's for the championship belt," Malu explains.

"So record it! We have a DVR!" Ashley yells.

"I can't! The boys are coming over tomorrow. We have the whole thing set up already. I can't cancel on them now. It's too late!" Malu protests.

"So you're choosing your friends over your own kids?" Ashley uses those words to stab deep.

"I would do ANYTHING for my kids and YOU KNOW THAT!" Malu is pissed that Ashley would even say that.

"Your daughter has been practicing for this hula performance for two months. What am I suppose to say when she doesn't see daddy in the audience? Huh? Tell me." Ashley tries to prove her point.

"Ash, I can't be missing at my own house party. That's messed up," Malu tries to reason.

"You're unbelievable you know that," Ashley says with disgust in her voice.

Just then a handsome guy walks through the door and says to Ashley, "Hey pretty lady!"

Malu, having bottled up most of his aggression, immediately head-butts this guy and knocks him to the floor.

"OH MY GOD!!!" Ashley screams.

"Who is that guy? HUH? Tell me right now!" Malu gets defensive.

"HE'S GAY, DUMBASS!" Ashley scolds as she runs to check on the guy. "Fuck, he's knocked out." She grabs her phone and calls 911. As the phone is ringing, she talks to Malu, "You can't keep knocking people out, Malu. You're not Max Holloway!"

The operator answers and Ashley redirects her focus. "Hi, I need an ambulance to Violet Nightclub... yeah, there's a guy that got knocked unconscious... uh, yes, again..." Ashley gives her boyfriend the look of death.

17. Love Potion

- 1 1/2 oz Raspberry Vodka
- 1 oz Cranberry Juice
- 1/2 oz Fresh Lime Juice
- Splash Grenadine

Robin looks at her phone, it's 11pm. *Show time!* She makes eye contact with the DJ and nods her head to signal him, *We're gonna start, turn down the music.* From the side of the stage, she turns on her microphone and begins speaking as the music is fading.

"Gather round, gather round! Come to the stage and see the incredible six foot four woman, with hands the size of baseball gloves and an adam's apple the size of... well... an apple." Robin improvs and makes fun of herself to draw a crowd. She speaks like an old-timey reporter, "Yes, for one night only, this glamazonian circus freak is here at our very own Violet, your favorite nightclub. Come lay eyes on this gender-fucking, mind-bending, totally gorgeous, excuse for a human being."

The guests laugh and start to gather around the stage. "This is a once in a lifetime opportunity, but beware, she does bite. She also splits and kicks, but she's too old for that." Robin continues the joke, "Yes, yes. You probably, maybe, most-likely, hopefully never seen anything like this before." She steps onto the stage with her back facing the audience, hiding her face. "Oh here she is ladies and gentlemen, the one, the only... Robin DeCraydle." She turns around with the ugliest face she can possibly make and screams into the mic as if she's trying to scare a child on Halloween. A couple of girls in the front row actually jump back, but the rest of the audience just cracks up at Robin's hilarious monologue.

She changes her expression to a smile, "Aloha no kakou my beautiful Violet children and yes, I am a monster." The audience laughs. "Go ahead take a picture, it'll last longer. I'll wait." She puts down the mic and poses. She makes eye-contact with random people in the audience and lips the words "Thank you" multiple times.

"Who knows why we're here tonight?" The audience cheers. "I see *some* of you do. Who is here just to get fucked up?" The audience cheers even louder. "Well, you're in the right place. Say hello to our stunning bartenders." The bartenders wave from behind the bar. "Take care of them and they'll take care of you.

"Tonight is a very special night. A night of all nights, if you will, where one queen's dream will come true! And, who that lucky queen will be… is up to you." She extends her arm and gestures to the audience with an open palm. *Ooos* and *ahhs* rumble over the crowd with just learning this information. "A twist! Yes, we all love a good twist. Tonight, we are looking for a fourth Fish y Chick. You know our Fish y Chicks, right?" The audience applauds. "Let's bring them out.

"First, she's got the body with no book smarts, but it's ok, it's *Karmen Sense*!" Karmen steps onto the stage in her shiny silk robe and catwalks forward. At the front of the stage, she takes off her robe and reveals her sexy lingerie piece underneath. The audience screams.

"Next up, she doesn't read books, but, trust me, she will read a bitch, it's *Arita Bitch*!" Arita comes to the stage in a rhinestone leotard that hugs her thick figure. She walks to the front of the stage and grabs the mic right out of Robin's hand.

"I'm Arita Bitch and I will read a bitch!" She shouts into the microphone.

Robin snatches the mic back and gives Arita the death glare. She quickly puts on a fake smile and looks back to the audience.

100

"And last, but definitely not least… she will take you where you wanna go, she's got a high mileage, but who's counting? It's the luxurious… *Alexus Convertible!*"

Alexus comes to the stage in a floor-length gown made of peacock feathers and a huge, matching feathered headpiece. "Oh God, here she comes," Robin says sarcastically, but steps to the side of the stage to let her have her moment. She takes her time walking to the front of the stage, posing at different points like she's in a pageant. The audience goes wild.

"And those are your Fish y Chicks, ladies and gentlemen. Give them a round of applause. Thank you, ladies." The girls leave the stage the same way they came up. "Alright, who's ready to start this competition?" The audience is revved up and ready to go. "We have four contestants tonight, so make sure to show all of them some love, but remember… at the end of the night, there can only be one. So, choose wisely. Are you ready to start the show?" The audience hollers. "I said, ARE YOU READY TO START THE SHOW?!" Robin shouts and the audience shouts back even louder. "This is your first queen of the night. Don't call her glossy, it's contestant number one… MATT MAKEUP!"

Matt takes the stage behind the closed curtain. "Crazy in Love" by Beyonce begins to play over the speakers and the audience starts to get excited for what's about to come. This is the moment that more than half the audience came for. After all the promoting on Instagram, all Matt has to do is deliver a solid performance and the fourth spot is hers.

The intro music vamps as Matt waits behind the curtain. She sways back and forth, trying to shake off the nerves and get into the groove. On the first lyric of the first verse, Matt bursts through the curtain and starts attacking the song. The audience goes nuts.

Alexus, Arita and Karmen run to the front of the stage to

watch Matt's performance. "She looks stunning! Good job girls." Arita pays herself and her friends a compliment. "GET IT, MATT!" She yells over the already yelling crowd.

The first verse and chorus go by as Matt works the stage like an amateur runway model. The second verse and chorus pass and the audience is starting to lose confidence. Although lip-syncing all of the words correctly, Matt keeps doing the same moves and just walks around the stage like a bad Naomi Campbell impersonator. The Fish y Chicks forgot that Matt can't dance.

As the song comes to an end, Matt starts twerking to try and regain the audience. The only problem is that Matt has no ass, making her look like a chopstick breaking itself over and over again. The song ends and Matt smiles confidently, completely unaware that the audience was unimpressed.

"Well, she looked great," Arita says to the other two Fish y Chicks.

"It's ok. She's still gonna win," Alexus says to reassure herself mostly. "This competition is slim pickings anyway. Have you seen those other girls? Lopaka? Please! They don't stand a chance."

Robin takes the stage again. "Wow! Our very own Wannabe-yoncé. Let's hear it for your contestant number one, Matt Makeup!' The audience claps, but the cheers are less enthusiastic than before. Robin looks at a random person in the audience, "Did you like that? Yeah, you did. Alright, who's ready for more?" Robin holds the mic toward the audience to get them to scream louder. "Let's go ahead and bring out our next contestant. She's got the country sugar and the latina spice, it's contestant number two… ARRRIBA MCENTIRE!"

The music starts and the curtain opens revealing Arrriba at the center. The theme song from Reba McEntire's TV show *Reba* begins and Arrriba walks to the lip of the stage with a microphone in hand. The first verse is about to begin and Arrriba pulls the mic up to her mouth. She starts singing the country song, but in Spanish.

"Is she really singing?" Karmen asks her friends.

"Ew. She sounds like a man," Arita says with disgust.

"She is a man," Alexus reminds her friend. "You're a man," she insults just because she can.

"I know, I just meant—" Arita starts to defend herself.

"Let's go check on your brother," Alexus interrupts. The three girls walk toward the dressing room.

The audience likes the gimmick that Arrriba McEntire brings, but with the majority of the crowd not understanding Spanish, mixed with the lack of country music fans, Arrriba's performance fails to reach its full potential. Looking like a red-headed Selena with no *Dinos*, Arrriba still attacks the song with true Latina style and pride.

She finishes her last lyric and the music fades out. "Gracias!" She says into the mic. The audience gives her a mild, but polite round of applause as Robin takes the stage again.

"Well, I've seen a lot of things, but I've never seen that before. Have you?" Robin looks at another random person in the audience. "Arrriba McEntire everybody! Let's hear it for her! Alright, let's keep this ball rolling, shall we?

"This next queen is a dear friend of mine. We've been friends a loooooong time, so show her some love. She may have nieces and nephews, but don't call her uncle... this is contestant number three... AUNTY PERSPIRANT!" The audience laughs at her name as Aunty takes the stage.

At the front of the stage, a mic stand is placed directly center. Aunty walks straight up to the mic and cues the DJ to start the music. Birds starts to chirp as Aunty's track begins; it's Minnie Riperton's "Lovin' You." Having just watched Arrriba perform, the audience thinks Aunty will sing live as well.

However, once Minnie's voice plays over the speakers, the audience realizes that she's lip-syncing.

Aunty does a decent job with such a slow-paced song. She knows for her age, she won't be doing a dance number to Beyonce without breaking a hip. So, Aunty decided a cute homage to her favorite childhood song was the best way to show her talents. She hits the high note of the song and acts it out dramatically and the audience claps in support.

The song finishes and Aunty takes a grand bow. She walks off stage passing Robin on the way up and kisses her friend on the cheek.

"Well, what a lovely performance. Did you like that? Let's hear it for contestant number three, Aunty Perspirant, you guys. Love you, girl," Robin says as the audience gives a respectful amount of applause.

Back in the dressing room, the Fish y Chicks congratulate Matt. "Good job, girl!" Karmen says.

"You goin' win!" Arita assures her brother.

"It was good, right? It felt good," Matt says confidently. Alexus is silent, while the other two girls continue to compliment her.

Just then, the dressing room door swings open and Lopaka comes running in. "Shit, shit, shit," he mutters to himself as he rummages through his things to find his asian-style folding fan. He knows it's almost his turn to perform.

"Whoa, easy killah," Arita says sarcastically.

"Is that what you're wearing?" Alexus asks with disgust in her voice. The other girls stare in silence.

"Yeah, why? You don't think I look pretty?" Lopaka says sarcastically, all the while knowing that they don't. He's wearing a long silver-haired wig, that's done up in a very Merrie Monarch kind of way, with a bunch of flowers pinned into the left side. He's also drawn wrinkle lines on his face to make himself look elderly and his long muumuu grazes the floor as he searches for his large fan. "AH! FOUND IT!" He grabs his fan and jets out the door.

"Good luck," Alexus says sarcastically, but is too late. Lopaka is already out the door. "He's gonna need it."

Back on stage, Robin starts to introduce the next performer. "Alright, alright. We've got one more performer. Are you guys ready for it?" She checks the audience's energy level. She looks down at her clipboard to check the name of who's next and laughs into the mic, "Oh my God! Well, I don't know what to say about this next queen, but this is our last and final competitor tonight. This is your contestant number four... JENNA TALIA!"

Laughter takes over the entire audience at Lopaka's choice of a drag name. He takes the stage behind the main curtain and waits for his music to start. He closes his eyes and takes a deep breath to calm his nerves. "I got this, I got this, I got this..." He repeats quietly to himself. The music starts and he opens his eyes. *Let's win this fuckin' thing!*

The Fish y Chicks run out of the dressing room to watch Lopaka's performance.

"Oh God, this is gonna be an epic fail," Alexus tells her friends as she pulls out her phone to record his performance, hoping that he'll fall at some point.

"Hanaiali`i Nui La Ea" by Amy Hanaiali`i plays over the entire club. The curtains part and reveal Lopaka, but he has his back facing the audience. Using a large black cloak to hide his muumuu and the asian-style fan he found earlier to cover his face, he turns around and starts walking toward the audience. On the first lyric, he closes the fan to reveal his elderly-looking face and starts lip-syncing in complete Hawaiian.

Robin looks up and instantly notices his face even through the makeup, *Is that Lopaka?!*

The audience's reaction is mixed. Half of the audience is cracking up at Lopaka, while the other half is confused as to why he looks old. There's a lot of talk happening throughout the audience as Lopaka performs, but he continues to give his all.

For the first verse of the song, Lopaka works the stage cracking his large fan dramatically, in time with the music. He puts the fan in his fake boobs and runs to the side of the stage to grab his prop ukulele. He mimics playing the ukulele for the repeat of the first verse and runs all over the stage, pretending he's a rock star. The audience is slowly taking a liking to him. For the third verse, he puts the ukulele on the floor and starts dancing around it like a Mexican hat dance, then ends up doing the Macarena. The audience cracks up.

For the first bridge of the song, Lopaka rips open his large black cloak and reveals his loud, flower-print muumuu. He grabs a big black cauldron from the side of the stage that he set up earlier. He brings it to the center and goes to his knees. He starts pretending like he's a witch creating a potion and begins throwing things into the cauldron. He starts with the ukulele and reacts dramatically. He takes off his cloak and throws it in. He then rips one of his fake flowers from out of his hair, smells it, makes a sour face pretending it stinks, licks it and then throws it in as well. With each item that goes into the cauldron, the audience reacts with him by yelling a loud "OH!" He takes out two little dolls that look like Hansel and Gretel that were hiding in his bra. The audience cheers him on to kill the kids and he throws them into the cauldron as the last ingredients.

The next verse starts and he grabs the cauldron and starts pretending to throw his newly concocted potion onto different parts of the audience. He, then, holds the cauldron over his head and pours all of the items out over his head and body and pretends he's in a wet T-shirt contest.

The second bridge of the song starts and he parts the

audience in half, creating a walkway for himself. Completely "soaked" in his imaginary potion, he makes his way down into the audience and starts working the crowd.

At the top of the last verse, he jumps into a split in the middle of the crowd. The audience goes nuts! He bounces a couple times and then pretends he broke his hip. Playing up the old lady role, he jokingly acts like he can't get up and asks a random audience member to help him up. He makes his way back onto the stage, hunching and playfully writhing in pain the whole way.

Back onstage and with the song about to end, Lopaka turns back to face the audience, acting as if all his old-lady pain vanished in an instant. On the last two beats of the song, he rips open the top of his muumuu and his fake boobs fall to the floor mocking old ladies' saggy boobs. He throws his hands up in the air as the song finishes and the audience goes insane! They are cracking up, cheering and screaming for Lopaka. Someone starts a chant, yelling "JEN-NA! JEN-NA! JEN-NA!..." and the rest of the audience joins in.

Lopaka takes it all in. He's proud of what he just did. He bows as his old lady boobs still drag on the floor. He picks them up, throws his boobs over his shoulders and waves to the audience. He starts heading offstage, but is stopped by Robin.

"WOOOOW!!!" Robin yells into the microphone. "How was that shit?!" The audience is still going mad. She brings Lopaka back to the front of the stage and continues, "Wow! That's all I can say is wow! Now, that's what we call a competition, ladies and gentlemen." The audience continues to cheer. "Let's hear it one more time for your contestant number four, Jenna Talia!" Robin puts down the mic and covers it with her hand. She smiles and speaks to Lopaka privately, "Good job, babe. Very good job." She puts the mic back to her mouth, "Ok, ok, ok, let's bring all the contestants back to the stage."

Matt, Arrriba and Aunty walk up the stairs and join Robin and Lopaka onstage. Robin steps to the side of the stage as the four contestants line up in the order that they performed. "Give it up for you four contestants, ladies and gentlemen." The audience cheers obediently.

"Now, as I said earlier, the winner of tonight's competition will become our fourth member and the newest addition to our dynamic girl group, the Fish y Chicks. She will also perform a number with the current members immediately after being declared the winner. Yes, that's right. Tonight! In just a few minutes, you will see a brand new performance from our brand new Fish y Chicks.

"And, who declares the winner?" Robin pauses and holds her hand out to the audience, "You. By a round of applause, I will go through each contestant and you'll cheer for who you want to win. The person with the loudest applause will be your new Fish y Chick. Got it?" The audience cheers to show they understand.

"Now don't make this hard for me, ok?" Robin playfully lectures. "Don't be cheering loud for everyone and making my job difficult. I know how all you mahus (*mahu* is a hawaiian word that means gay boys and/or transgender people) get when you drink. Alright, are we ready?"

Robin takes a slight pause before proceeding and then steps next to Matt, "Let's hear it for contestant number one, Matt Makeup!" The audience cheers generously. Despite her underwhelming performance, she's obviously still got a lot of fans. "Ok, thank you."

Robin steps next to Arrriba, "Let's hear it for contestant number two, Arrriba McEntire!" The audience is less generous with their cheers. A supportive "Woo!" is yelled to fill the lack of applause. "Ok, thank you."

Robin steps next to Aunty, "Let's hear it for contestant

number three, Aunty Perspirant!" The audience is even less generous. The pathetic applause fades quickly. "Ok, thank you."

Robin steps next to Lopaka and a few scattered 'woos' and 'yeahs' are already being yelled from the audience. "Let's hear it for contestant number four, Jenna Talia!" The audience erupts! The cheers are deafening. The crowds of guests yell and scream and eventually start chanting again, "JEN-NA! JEN-NA! JEN-NA!..."

Without second guessing it and without waiting for the audience's applause to die down, Robin announces, "Ladies and gentlemen, the winner and your newest Fish y Chick is..." she pauses for half a second, "contestant number four, JENNA TALIA!" The audience continues to go mad and chant "JEN-NA!"

Lopaka is stunned. Robin grabs his hand and escorts him to the front of the stage where he waves and bows to thank the audience. He can't believe he just did it!

From the side of the stage, the Fish y Chicks look at each other shocked. "Shit!" Arita says for the three of them. They still had hope that Matt would take it.

"Thank you, girls. You all did an amazing job tonight. Let's hear it for the other contestants!" The audience cheers for the losing queens as they leave the stage. "And now, as promised, the new and improved, FISH Y CHICKS! Hit it DJ!" Robin leaves the stage as Alexus, Arita and Karmen unwillingly join Lopaka on stage.

The Moulin Rouge version of "Lady Marmalade" starts to play and the audience starts to dance. Alexus, Arita and Karmen walk right pass Lopaka and pose front and center. Lopaka yells over the music to the other girls, "What's my part, who am I?" The girls ignore him and continue with their choreography. Feeling like he'll just figure it out and start lip-syncing when the other girls are not, Lopaka doesn't worry.

The first verse begins and Alexus takes the lead. She lip-syncs every word that Mya sings and the audience eats it up. The second verse starts and Arita comes in as Pink. She mouths the correct lyrics, but her pidgin accent makes it look like she's not saying the right words.

Ok, well, I'm either Lil' Kim or Christina Aguilera, Lopaka thinks to himself. *Thankfully I knows this song like the back of my hand.* He stands to the side and grooves in his own little corner, waiting for his turn.

Lil' Kim's section begins and Karmen charges forward. The audience laughs at this white chick pretending to rap. *Oh sweet! They left me Christina, the best part!* Lopaka thinks. Karmen finishes up her portion and Christina Aguilera starts to riff before her section actually starts.

Lopaka begins to make his way slowly to the front of the stage, taking his time to create drama. As he reaches the lip of the stage and right as Christina start's her first lyric, Alexus pushes Lopaka out of the way and takes over the front of the stage. She starts lip-syncing Christina Aguilera's portion of the song while Arita and Karmen create a wall trying to block Lopaka from getting any attention.

Realizing that the three girls aren't going to let him have any part in this song, Lopaka gets pissed. He tries to work his way to the front of the stage, but the three girls keep creatively finding ways to block him while still performing for the audience. He tries a couple more times before finally giving up. *FUCK THIS! I don't need this shit!* He walks off the stage while the song is still playing, leaving the three girls to finish performing without him.

The three Fish y Chicks watch Lopaka leave the stage from the corner for their eyes and smirk; their plan worked. With only about thirty seconds of the song left, Alexus goes down into the audience, grabs Matt Makeup and brings him back onstage. Half of the audience is too drunk to comprehend the situation, while the other half is completely turned off by Alexus' bold move. As the song comes to an end, the Fish y Chicks, now with Matt onstage, take their final pose. A mix of drunken cheers and sober boos fill the club.

Back in the dressing room, Lopaka packs his things. He's upset with the situation that just happened, but not surprised by the Fish y Chicks childish reaction. He knew going into this competition that they weren't going to accept anyone into their group, except Matt. Now that Matt lost, however, they don't really have a choice. He weighs his options and thinks, *Maybe I should stay in the group just to piss them off, but I would be fucking miserable having to spend every weekend with them.*

The Fish y Chicks walk into the dressing room giggling with cynicism. They side-eye Lopaka as they walk in, but don't say a single word to him. They go about chatting to each other as if Lopaka is invisible.

"Ho her God, that was so much fun! Wasn't it, girls?" Alexus says making sure she's loud enough for Lopaka to hear.

"Yeah, it was!" Arita agrees like the good right-hand woman that she is.

"You did so good, Matt!" Karmen compliments.

"I know, right?" Matt overconfidently accepts.

Lopaka, trying not to start a commotion, remains quiet and gathers the rest of his belongings as quickly as humanly possible.

"Yeah, you were the best!" Alexus passive aggressively taunts Lopaka.

"Da best by FAR!" Arita agrees with Alexus again. "And when we brought you up to da stage at da end, the audience went crazy! Good one, Alexus!"

"Well, you know, I had to bring the *real* winner on stage to join us," Alexus continues to verbally poke the bear. "The only reason *he* won was because he works here."

With being less than ten feet away from them, Lopaka can't drown out the voices of Fish y Chicks any longer. Having heard every word that they strategically chose to prod him with, he finally has had enough.

"You know what, Alexus…" All four girls look in Lopaka's direction. "You can have your stupid *Fish Sticks* show, I don't want any part of it." Lopaka looks directly at Matt, "Congratulations Matt, the spot is yours. I hope you like doing a two-step in the background." He changes his focus back to Alexus, "Just remember… I won. All of your "millions" of followers… voted for *me*. Yup. And don't think that you're fooling anyone. We all know you bought every follower you have on Instagram, well, except for your three minions here. Like they say back in your country… Putang Ina Mo! (*Putang Ina Mo* is the Filipino equivalent of 'Fuck You' in the Tagalog language). Lopaka grabs his things and walks out of the dressing room.

"I WAS BORN HERE, BITCH! I'M AN AMERICAN!" Alexus yells and then starts cussing in Tagalog under her breath.

Just outside of the dressing room, Lopaka runs into Robin. "Hey, you ok? I saw what the girls were doing to you in that last number," Robin asks.

Lopaka just throws his hands up and shakes his head. He points at the dressing room and still without any words spoken, he gestures to Robin that he's going to leave.

"Ok." Robin understands his body language. Lopaka starts to walk away, but Robin stops him and says, "I'm proud of you." Lopaka nods his head and smirks a fake smirk, then turns around and walks out.

Robin kicks the door open to the dressing room. "What the hell was that?!"

18. Surfer on Acid

- 1 oz Jägermeister
- 1 oz Malibu Coconut Rum
- 1 oz Pineapple Juice
   *Shake and serve as a shot

A couple of days later in the middle of the ocean, Kaleo and Parker are out surfing at one of their favorite spots. Having surfed together for many years, they know each other's surf style well. However, with Kaleo having recently been in a funk, Parker starts noticing his friend is struggling more than usual.

"You good?" Parker asks.

"Man, I'm outta shape!" Kaleo huffs and puffs. He paddles his surfboard up to Parker and sits in the line-up next to him.

"Yeah, you haven't been out in awhile," Parker mentions.

"Yeah, I've just been busy with a bunch of shit," Kaleo tries to cover, still trying to catch his breath.

"You're looking a little pale, too!" Parker jabs.

"Shut up!" Kaleo splashes water at his best friend. "I'm still darker than you, haole!"

"Barely!" Parker counters. "Oh, here comes a set."

A set of waves start to make their way toward the boys. They both start paddling a little further out to be in the right spot. Parker blazes ahead of Kaleo and catches the first wave of the set. Kaleo duck-dives through the first wave and sees the next one coming. He tries to get into the perfect position to catch the wave, but he's not quick enough. Another surfer, with a stronger stroke, stands up and takes the wave before he does. A couple more waves roll through, finishing the set, and Kaleo misses them all.

"Shit, I missed the whole set," Kaleo says as Parker paddles up next to him.

"Nah, that was just a warm up set," Parker down-plays.

Kaleo looks at his sexy best friend and can't help but check out his body. Now that Parker's wet, Kaleo starts to have flashbacks of the time in high school when he saw Parker standing in the locker room shower completely naked. He catches himself and quickly tries to make conversation to stop his wandering mind. "So, what's up with you and Momi? She still not talking to you?"

"Nah, she is… but she hasn't really been sleeping at my place that much," Parker confesses.

"For real?" Kaleo inquires.

"Yeah, it's weird. Like, we used to sleep together every night, if not at my house, then at hers, but… she's been going out a lot," Parker reveals.

"With who? By herself?" Kaleo asks.

"Nah. She's been hanging out with Tisha a lot," Parker tells his friend. "Almost every night."

"Do you think she became a stripper?" Kaleo half-jokes.

"Fuck, I hope not! I thought about that, though, to be honest. Cause Tisha used to be one," Parker admits.

"Nah, I'm pretty sure we'd all know if Momi did," Kaleo consoles. "Oh, another set's coming in."

The two boys paddle out again hoping to line themselves up with a good wave. This time, Kaleo gets slightly ahead of Parker. Having not caught a wave yet, Kaleo starts to surf more aggressively. The first wave passes them both by, but Kaleo sets his eyes on the second. He sees someone already paddling for the wave, but he starts paddling anyway. The other surfer stands up and starts to surf the wave, but Kaleo doesn't care; he's getting this wave no matter what. He paddles a little harder and drops-in on the other guy, blocking the other surfer and taking his wave. Parker watches the whole thing unfold.

114

After the set passes, Parker and Kaleo meet up again. "Dude, you totally dropped-in on that guy," Parker calls Kaleo out. In surfing, there's an unspoken etiquette. It differs slightly from place to place, but the overall theme is always the same: *Respect*.

"So? He wasn't that good anyway," Kaleo counters. "I didn't want him to waste a perfectly good wave."

Parker shakes his head and thinks, *Whatever*. "So, anyway, what's going on with you?"

"What do you mean?" Kaleo says, caught off-guard.

"You know… you've been… off, recently," Parker answers hesitantly, unsure of how Kaleo will take it.

"No, I haven't. I've been at work all week," Kaleo deflects.

"No, not like off of work, like off-track, off your game. Something's up and you're not telling me," Parker finally confronts his friend.

"I don't know what you're talking about," Kaleo tries to convince his friend.

"C'mon Leo," Parker isn't buying it, "I tell you everything about Momi and my family and all that. What's up?"

Kaleo is silent for a second and then speaks up, "So… there's this guy…"

"OHHH! So, it's guy trouble! Why didn't you tell me earlier?" Parker exclaims. "Guys love me!" He says smugly.

Yeah, don't I know it, Kaleo thinks to himself, *I'm one of them*. Kaleo has been in love with Parker since high school. Over the years, their friendship has grown into a type of brotherhood, but Kaleo has always hoped that one day, Parker would wake up and change their relationship status from 'bromance' to 'romance.'

Having fooled around with Parker when they were younger, Kaleo knows they've been through just about everything with each other. The trust and bond that they share is so sacred to

Kaleo that even compared to his past relationships, Kaleo still holds Parker higher than any boyfriend that he's ever had. Without realizing it until recently, Kaleo has held out for the possibility that he and Parker might end up together.

"Yeah, no, I don't know..." Kaleo starts. "He came in once and was a complete asshole and then he came back this past weekend and apologized. He said that he wasn't 'out' to his friends yet and all that bullshit... and then he asked me out..."

"And you said 'yes,' right?" Parker asks hoping he's correct.

"No." Kaleo disappoints his friend.

"WHAT?! Why? Dude, you need to get out, go on dates. You haven't even hooked-up with anyone in awhile," Parker scolds.

"You don't know that," Kaleo counters.

"Why? Have you?" Parker checks Kaleo.

"No," Kaleo answers quietly.

"See. I know you, Kaleo." Parker grins, "I can read you like a book."

"It doesn't matter anyway, I can't go out with him," Kaleo says under his breath.

"Why? You got something else important going on?" Parker pushes the issue.

"No because..." Kaleo stops himself.

"What? Say it. Come on. Hey, remember, 'You gotta finish what you started.'" Parker brings up the motto of their friendship.

"Because I'm in love with another guy," Kaleo blurts out.

"Who? Oh, don't tell me you're still hung up over your ex, Joey," Parker scoffs

"No..." Kaleo pauses and takes a deep breath.

"Who then?" Parker presses the issue. "Come on! Tell me! It's just me, Leo. You gotta tell me now."

Kaleo exhales heavily and thinks *Fuck it. It's now or never.*

He looks Parker right in his eyes and says, "You!"

"What?" Parker is stunned.

"You, Parker. I'm in love with you. I've *been* in love with you." Kaleo looks to Parker for a reaction, but his face is blank. "I don't think I was aware of it until recently and I didn't want to say anything because I don't know... I don't want things to get weird between us if you don't feel the same way..."

"I, uh...I..." Parker takes a breath and gathers himself. "I love you too..."

"Really?" Kaleo says excitedly. *Maybe he's been feeling the same way this whole time, but we both didn't want to say anything!*

"...just not in that way," Parker finishes his sentence. "You're like a brother to me. You know that. And yeah, I know we fooled around way back when, but I'm with Momi now and... even though things are a bit complicated at the moment... I'm in love with her."

Kaleo's short-lived hope that Parker's feelings were mutual died in a matter of seconds. With his heart shattered and feeling completely embarrassed, Kaleo responds quickly, "Yeah, I know you do. Sorry, it was stupid of me to say anything. I love Momi and I love the two of you together, I hope you know that. I wasn't trying to...whatever... just forget I said anything, ok?"

Just then, another set of waves come rolling in. "Oh look a set's coming in," Kaleo says and starts paddling away from Parker.

"Hey, wait! Kaleo!" Parker yells.

Kaleo paddles up to a wave, this time lining himself up perfectly. He turns around and catches it. As he's on the wave surfing he sees Parker paddling to get out his way. He yells, "I'm going in! I'll catch you later!" and rides the waves all the way to shore.

"No, wait!" Parker tries to stop his friend from leaving, but

Kaleo is already long gone.

Parker tries to catch the next wave, but someone is already on it. He tries for the wave after that, but the wave is too weak. Before he knows it, the set is over. He looks back to the shore and sees Kaleo getting out of the water. Without a wave to catch, Parker is stuck out in the ocean until the next set rolls in.

Once back at his truck, Kaleo wipes himself down with a towel. Although still decently toned, he notices that he's starting to put on a little bit of chub from drinking every night. He grabs at his developing love-handles, *Man, I need to work out*. He replays what just happened out in the water and can't believe he just confessed his love for Parker. *What was I thinking?*

With his surfboard already thrown into the bed of his truck, he wraps the towel around his waist and opens the door to the driver's seat. With the towel covering his surf shorts and still without a T-shirt on, Kaleo looks like he just got out of the shower to anyone passing. Before he even sits, he hears something vibrating from the middle compartment of his truck, where he hides his phone. He opens the compartment and grabs his phone. It's Lopaka.

"Hey, you alright?" Kaleo answers his phone.

"Yeah, yeah. I'm fine," Lopaka assures from the other side. "What are you doing right now?"

"Uh, I just finished surfing. I'm still at the beach, but about to go home. Why?" Kaleo inquires.

"I need a favor," Lopaka appeals.

"Sure. What do you need?" Kaleo wants to help his brother, especially after what has happened to him over the past couple of weekends.

"Can you take me to the airport?" Lopaka asks.

"Yeah, when?" Kaleo questions.

"Right now," Lopaka answers.

"RIGHT NOW?!" Kaleo shouts. "Wait, hold up. Where are you even going?" Kaleo's thoughts quickly shift from Parker to Lopaka.

"I'm moving." Lopaka is short.

"MOVING?!" Kaleo is completely confused. "Whoa, whoa, whoa. Since when are you moving? And to where?"

"I'm going to L.A.," Lopaka informs.

"L.A?!" Kaleo is starting to get slightly angry. "God, Lopaka, were you gonna tell any of us?"

"I'm telling you now," Lopaka defends himself.

"Yeah, right before you're leaving," Kaleo comes back with angrily.

"I just need a change of life, ok? There's nothing for me here already," Lopaka explains.

"Nothing for you? What about us? What about your family? Does Robin even know that you're leaving?" Kaleo asks a myriad of questions to get the whole picture.

"No," Lopaka remarks shamefully, then quickly changes his tone to a stern one, "Look, can you take me or not? I gotta catch a flight. Should I just call an Uber?"

"No, no, I can. I'll be right there." Kaleo puts aside his anger for now, wanting to at least see his brother once before he leaves.

"Thank you," Lopaka responds.

"Yup," Kaleo replies dismissively.

The two brothers hang up and Kaleo shakes his head. *Fucking Lopaka! He always does spontaneous shit like this and doesn't think about the consequences.* Kaleo gets in his truck, starts the engine and heads over to Lopaka's apartment.

19. Hot Toddy

- 1 oz Bourbon
- 1 Tbsp Honey
- 2 tsp Lemon Juice
- 1/4 cup Boiling-hot Water

Robin and Chyna sit in the exam room of a doctor's office waiting for the doctor to arrive. Robin was just here last week to get her blood work done. Her health has been fluctuating and she's developed a bad cough.

"Thanks for coming with me, girl," Robin thanks her friend.

"Of course, girl. I don't have anything to do today," Chyna reassures. "Plus, nobody should go through this alone." Chyna touches her friend's arm. She knows it must be hard to be living with HIV. With all of her own late night escapades, Chyna knows she tempts fate. She knows she's lucky for remaining HIV negative. "How are you feeling, sis?"

"I'm ok," Robin assures. "I'm just a little weak. It's weird though, I get bursts of energy, but then come back to this feeling of exhaustion."

"You have been working a lot," Chyna reminds her.

"Yeah, but not more than usual," Robin counters.

They share a quick moment of silence before Chyna speaks up, "What's going on, Robin?"

"I don't know. We'll find out, I guess," Robin answers.

"No, not that," Chyna investigates. "I mean, I know your health isn't a hundred percent, but what's going on? I can tell there's something on your mind."

"Nothing," Robin deflects, "Really, I'm good, it's just my health and—"

"Cut the crap," Chyna says, seeing through the bullshit.

120

"Come on. We tell each other everything, right? So, spill."

Robin sighs. She grabs her purse and reaches for an envelope. She pulls it out and hands it to Chyna.

"What is this?" Chyna asks. She opens the envelope and unfolds the paper. At the top, it states *Final Notice* in bold print. "Final notice? For what?" She reads further and her jaw drops. "ROBIN! Why didn't you say anything?"

The letter states that they have forty-five days to evacuate Violet. Since the rent hasn't been paid for two months and they are now into their third month of deliquency, the building owners have finally decided to take action.

"I didn't want anyone to worry," Robin defends herself.

"No wonder your health is dropping. This is huge! You should've told me earlier," Chyna scolds like a concerned parent. "Does any of the staff know?"

"No, and please don't tell them," Robin requests.

"Robin! You have to tell them," Chyna reprimands.

"Tell them what?" She continues in a mocking tone, 'Oh hey guys, here's the list of duties for tonight. Oh, by the way, you're all about to be jobless.'"

"Well, it'd be better than them finding out the day of the eviction," Chyna argues her point. "Robin, they can help. We can all help. It's not over yet. We still have a little over a month. If we come up with enough money, I think we could convince the building owners to keep Violet open."

"Mary, they're Chinese. The Wongs. They're not gonna budge," Robin expresses.

"You don't know that. Plus, they may be Chinese, but I'm Chyna. I AM the Motherland, bitch!" Chyna jokes to lighten the mood.

"You're not even, Chinese. You're Korean, you slut," Robin reminds her friend.

"Bitch, I'm anything I want to be! Plus, it's called a 'street corner professional,' thank you very much, and I *make* things happen. My name isn't 'Chyna Make' for nothing. I be *chyna make* that coin, *chyna make* that change… and you know first hand, that if there's anything I know how to do, it's how to make that money, honey! But right now, I'm *chyna make* you believe in yourself again because this pity show is ovah! You know what else is *ovahz*? Me." Chyna points to herself and Robin rolls her eyes. (*Ovahz* is gay slang in Hawaii interchangeable with 'stunning' or 'overly beautiful.')

Chyna gets serious again, "You know what's not over… this club. It ain't over, 'til it's over. And even then, we're too stubborn to take no for an answer. We've always been like that. So, what's different about this situation?"

"I'm tired, sis. I really am," Robin admits.

Chyna slows her pace, "I know you are, babe, but we gotta fight. As long as we're alive, we need to fight. We fought for our rights, we fought for equality and now we're fighting for this club. Don't you give up before it's over," Chyna asserts. "We need to start thinking of ways to make money. Maybe a fundraiser?"

"Who's gonna give money to a gay club?" Robin says with zero hope.

"The *gay* community. DUH! I'm sure they would love to get involved!" Chyna points out matter-of-factly. "Violet is not just a place for people to get drunk and party, it's a safe-space. Violet is where you can be anybody you want to be: male, female, gay, straight, trans or anything in between, and no one will judge you… except for those shoes you're wearing." She looks down at Robin's sneakers covered in a butterfly print.

"Stop! It's a daytime look," Robin justifies.

"Well, it's a *look*. That's for sure." Chyna makes fun of her friend and then continues, "Look, remember when everyone shunned us for wanting to transition? Remember how hard that

122

was? We were lucky that we had each other. Violet is that place that we needed back then. It's a place where you can run away from your super conservative family and find others who think the way you do. Think about everyone that you saved from committing suicide because they felt they weren't alone. Violet is important and you know that! That's why you started this club in the first place!"

A knock at the door cuts into the girls conversation. Robin's doctor walks in and makes eye contact with her. "Robin, nice to see you again," he says kindly with a smile. He looks over and notices Chyna, "Oh, hello. I'm Doctor Patel." He extends his hand toward Chyna.

Chyna meets his hand with hers and begins to flirt, "Wow, Robin never mentioned that her doctor was tall, dark and handsome. I hope it's ok that I'm here."

"Would you behave yourself!" Robin scolds and then redirects her focus to Dr. Patel, "Sorry, she doesn't get out much."

He laughs, "Oh, it's quite alright." He looks back to Chyna, "Thank you, I'm flattered and if Robin is ok with you being here, then it is ok by me." He redirects his focus, "Robin, how are you?"

"I'm ok, doctor. I've had this cough that I can't get rid of and I've been feeling really weak," Robin informs.

"Ok. Now, Robin… I have a little bit of bad news, nothing drastic though. Your white blood cell count is low. That is, perhaps, why you've developed this cough that you are complaining of. Have you been taking your medication?"

"Um… yes, well, kind of," Robin responds. "I've missed a couple of days here and there."

"Robin!" Chyna speaks up. Robin shoots a sharp look at her friend and Chyna falls back.

"I need you to start taking your ARVs regularly," Dr. Patel

advises. "Do you have something that you can log whether or not you've taken it? It will help you stay on track."

"Yes, I have one on my phone," Robin assures.

"Good." Dr. Patel looks at Robin's patient chart. "Now, you've also developed some high blood pressure. Is there anything in your life that's giving you a hard time?"

Robin looks over the doctor's shoulder and sees Chyna peering at her with her arms folded in front of her. "Well, work's been a bit stressful recently, but I can handle it."

"Ok. If it starts getting too much for you, I want you to back off and maybe ask someone else for help," Dr. Patel suggests. "Is there someone that can help you with your tasks at work?

Chyna butts into the conversation, "Yes, doctor. I can help her."

"Very good. In your condition, Robin, I need you to keep your stress levels down, ok?"

"Got it," Robin assures.

"I'm going to prescribe you a high blood pressure medication for you to take at the same time as your ARVs, so you won't have to remember different times for different pills. If your cough persists, come back and see me. We want to make sure that we stay on top of that."

"Thank you, doctor," Robin says with a smile.

Dr. Patel shakes Robin's hand and then shakes Chyna's, "It was a pleasure to meet you."

"Likewise, doctor," Chyna flirts.

"Take care, ladies." He opens the door and walks out.

"He was CUTE!" Chyna blurts out as soon as the door closes.

"You think everyone is cute," Robin says disapprovingly.

"And he's a doctor. I bet you he has money! Do you think he was into me?" Chyna gets carried away. "Maybe we could get married and Dr. Patel and I can just buy the whole building that

Violet is in. Then, you'll just have to pay *me* the rent!"

Robin rolls her eyes. "Oh my God. Let's go."

20. Black & Tan

- 6 oz Pale Ale Beer
- 6 oz Guinness Stout Beer

   *Pour Pale Ale Beer into pint glass, then float Guinness Stout Beer on top by slowly pouring it over the back of a spoon.

Back at the beach, Parker paddles back to shore; he's had his fill for the day. After Kaleo left him suddenly, he wasn't exactly sure how to feel; it was a lot to take in. He decided to stay out and surf a couple more waves to clear his head. With his focus and concentration all over the place, Parker's surfing mirrored just the same. Falling off of his board and getting tossed by the waves, he looked like a beginner again. Figuring that he had embarrassed himself enough for one day, he decided it was time to go home.

Once he reaches the shore, he looks around and sees a variety of people on the sand. To his left, he sees a bunch of friends playing volleyball. *Man, I haven't played volleyball in a long time. We should get the Violet crew together and set up a tournament.* Right in front of him, there's a family of five: a mom, a dad, two young boys and a girl. The mom reads her book as the dad buries his three kids in the sand. *Cute! I wonder if Momi and I will ever have kids. I wouldn't mind being a dad.*

To his right and at a distance, he looks over and sees two girls walking away from him: a local Hawaiian girl and a black girl engaged in conversation. *Those girls look like Momi and Tisha. It couldn't be, though. Momi said she was helping her mom with something today.*

Walking up the beach with his surfboard under his arm, he squints and tries to decipher if it really is Momi and Tisha. *THAT IS THEM! Did she lie to me? Well, I don't want to jump to conclusions. Maybe she finished helping her mom early and now she's just hanging out with Tisha. That's not a crime.* He yells to get their attention, "MOMI!"

Being far enough away and without hearing or noticing Parker at all, Momi and Tisha start to make-out. Their kiss is a passionate one and one that lasts longer than a kiss between two *friends* should. The two girls hold each other for a little bit and then continue on their walk, now hand-in-hand.

WHAT THE FUCK?! Parker stops in his tracks. He can't believe his eyes. *Wait, maybe that's not them. Maybe it's some other chicks.* "MOMI!" He yells out even louder this time. The family of five look at him like he's a crazy, homeless person.

Momi looks back. She heard her name, but she can't find who or where it's coming from. Tisha heard it too, but she can't find the source either.

Nope, that's definitely them! Parker throws his surfboard down on the sand and starts running toward the girls. When he's halfway to them, he yells again, "MOMI!" This time he knows he's within range for them to hear.

Momi looks back again, but this time sees Parker charging toward them. "OH MY GOD!"

Hearing Momi's reaction, Tisha turns around. "Holy Shit!" She says out loud, when she finally sees Parker coming at them like an angry bull.

Parker catches up to the girls, he's visibly upset. Now with a mix of ocean water and sweat dripping down his face, he confronts the girls. "Oh, hi!" He says sneeringly.

"Dude, you can't come charging at a black person like that," Tisha warns.

"What are you doing here, Parker?" Momi asks, trying to play casual.

"Oh, I don't know. Not making out with another chick, that's for sure," Parker answers sarcastically.

127

"What are you talking about?" Momi plays dumb.

"I saw you guys making-out, Momi. Don't act like it didn't happen," Parker challenges.

Tisha looks over at Momi, "Wait, I thought you said he was cool with this."

"I'll explain later," Momi says calmly to Tisha.

"Like hell you will, you'll explain it now. For all of us. Cause God knows I don't know what the fuck is going on," Parker fumes.

A few people look in their direction. "Can we not do this here?" Momi tries to avoid any public confrontation.

"No, we're doing this right here, right now!" Parker demands. "I don't give a fuck who hears!"

"Yeah, actually, I'd like to hear what you have to say too," Tisha sides with Parker.

Momi looks at Parker and says nonchalantly, "We're in an open relationship, remember?"

"Open to sleeping with other people, not being in other relationships!" Parker rages.

"That's all we're doing. It's not that big of a deal." Momi tries to downplay the whole situation.

"I'm sure," Parker says sardonically. "Walking on the beach romantically, holding hands and making-out. No big deal, huh?"

"It's no different than what you were planning to do with that ice cream chick!"

"What are you talking about? It's COMPLETELY different! That is a WHOLE different situation that *you* were in on. Plus, nothing ever happened, so don't try and use that against me." Parker changes his focus and looks over at Tisha, "Seriously, Tisha?"

Tisha throws her hands up, "I don't really know what's going on either."

"Don't bring her into this!" Momi defends Tisha.

"Well, *excuse me* for breaking up your little romantic date here," Parker states sarcastically. "And, even if you are just sleeping together, I thought we weren't supposed to sleep with close friends." Momi is at a check-mate. She looks down and remains silent. Parker pauses to calm himself down. He starts back up with a quieter tone, "What the fuck is going on, Momi?"

Momi doesn't say anything for a bit, Tisha turns her back and steps off to the side and Parker stands there waiting for an answer. Momi finally looks up at Parker with tears in her eyes, "I don't know, babe." Parker's heart starts to melt slightly, but he's still too amped. He doesn't break and stands there waiting to hear more.

"I just… I love you so much…" Momi says, trying to catch her breath while crying. She calms herself down and continues, "I don't know how it got this far and I never had any intention of hurting you…"

"What are you saying?" Parker wants Momi to clarify.

Still in full tears, Momi pauses. She takes a deep breath in and finally looks up at Parker, "I'm gay." Tisha turns back around and looks at Momi; this is news to her as well.

"What?" Parker is shocked, but also confused.

Momi nods and looks him straight in the eyes, "I love you, Parker, and I always will, but I'm a lesbian. I didn't realize it until recently."

Parker grabs Momi and hugs her. As confused as he is, he knows that no one should have to feel guilty for coming out.

Still embraced by Parker, she speaks into his chest, "I think that's why I always loved our open relationship and I only wanted threesomes with girls." Momi then looks up at him, "You're an amazing person, Parker, and you've been the best boyfriend a girl could ever hope for and you deserve to be with someone who can give you that in return. I can't."

Parker starts to tear up, but holds himself back from crying. He nods his head, but doesn't say anything.

"I'm so sorry and I hope you can forgive me." They kiss one last time and hug each other tightly. They pull apart and Momi gestures to Tisha, *Let's go*. The two girls head back to Tisha's car in silence, this time with distance between the two of them.

Parker just stands in a daze, watching the two girls walk away. *What the hell just happened?* Parker thinks to himself. *First Kaleo, now Momi.* He starts to feel like he just got emotionally slapped in the face. Realizing that his surfboard is still on the sand, he heads in that direction. Still trying to figure out if this is reality, he jumps back in the ocean at the shoreline hoping it will help cleanse his overcrowded mind. *Man, what a fucking day.*

21. Lava Flow

- 1 oz Light Rum
- 1 oz Malibu Coconut Rum
- 2 oz Strawberries
- 1 Small Banana
- 2 oz Pineapple Juice
- 2 oz Coconut Cream
- 1 cup Crushed Ice
  *Blend together

Two weeks go by and what once was a simple idea thought up by Chyna, has now become a fully developed reality. Thanks to Violet's Instagram page, the gay community buzzes with talk of the *Violet Fundraiser*. One post reads, *$45 gets you dinner and a drag show. Come be entertained by the legendary Fish y Chicks and possibly even win a prize. *All tips collected on this night, from the performers and the bartenders, will be donated to our cause.* Tonight is that night.

The bartenders set up their two bars like usual. Kaleo, having proved himself over the past few weeks, is assigned back to his usual register at the front bar. He, Parker and Chico arrange their wells and configure their bottles to prepare for the fun night ahead.

"I see you got your old position back," Parker starts conversation with Kaleo. "Congrats."

"Thanks, but she still hasn't given me back the keys to the club," Kaleo worries.

"Baby steps," Parker reassures, "you'll get them back in time."

The conversation ends. The two boys share a slightly, but not overbearingly awkward silence. Since their last surf session together, Parker and Kaleo have been pretending as if Kaleo never confessed his feelings for Parker. Trying to go back to their usual playful friendship, the two boys have lost their natural chemistry. Now on two different wavelengths, Parker wonders if they'll ever get back to normal.

Parker looks over at Kaleo who's looking down at the bar towel that he's folding. He thinks, *This weirdness between the two of us has gone on long enough*. He sticks out his tongue and crosses his eyes, pulling his face in a weird way. He stands there and waits for Kaleo to look over.

From his peripheral vision, Kaleo notices that Parker has stopped moving. He looks over to see if he's ok and starts to laugh. "You're stupid," Kaleo chortles, then makes a funny face back at his friend.

Parker walks up to Kaleo and gives him a big bear hug. Kaleo hugs him back. Feeling like it was exactly what they both needed, they embrace for a little longer than usual. They pull a part to look at each other, but keep their arms around each other's waists. Parker looks down at Kaleo and in a mocking, but light-hearted way says, "I love you, Kaleo."

"Pfffft," Kaleo sneers and tries to push his friend away.

Parker holds tighter so Kaleo can't get out of his grasp. He waits until Kaleo stops resisting and finally looks back up at him. "I do, though. And for what it's worth, you know that if I was ever to be with a guy, it would be you." Kaleo smirks and nods in response. "So, are we good?"

"Yeah, we're good," Kaleo affirms.

As the two boys are still holding each other, Beau comes walking up to their bar and shouts, "GAAAAAY!"

The two boys break their embrace and Kaleo fires back, "Shut up, Beau! You're the biggest homo there ever was."

"Ooop!" Chico yelps, signifying that a gauntlet has been thrown.

"Jeez, you guys are over here making-out, Momi and Tisha are back there all over each other… actually, I don't mind that one, now that I think about it…" Beau drifts off, imagining the two girls in a scene out of a Lesbian porno.

"What do you want, Beau?" Kaleo asks in hopes of getting rid of him quickly.

Beau snaps back to reality, "I just read the Insta-post…we're not making any tips tonight?"

"No, we're donating our tips to the club," Kaleo confirms.

"So, we're basically working for free?" Beau asks

"You'll get your hourly," Kaleo clarifies.

"Uh, nobody becomes a bartender to make minimum wage," Beau scoffs.

"It's one night. Think of it as an investment, you give back to the place that allows you to make those tips. We use that money to make this place better, and then, eventually, we make even better tips," Kaleo explains.

"Patience, young grasshopper," Parker chimes in.

"Patience? Pfft, I'm a millennial. I need instant gratification!" Beau asserts. "Plus, I need to make rent." Everybody ignores him. "What is this fundraiser even for?"

"It's so we can start bringing in bigger names and better talent," Kaleo answers.

"Ooop!" Chico yelps again.

"Shaaaade!" Beau says fervently.

"No, it's not shade, it's the truth," Kaleo defends. "Robin wants to be able to fly in mainland DJs and famous drag queens to provide the best entertainment for our community."

Chyna walks in on the ending of the boys conversation. She hears Kaleo's reason for what he thinks the fundraiser is for and immediately realizes that Robin didn't tell them anything. *There's a whole other situation going on here. These kids might even lose their jobs and they have no idea. I'm gonna kill her!*

"Hey boys! Everything going alright so far?" Chyna questions without mentioning anything to them.

"Well, look who it is… the sexy ladyboy from the meat-packing district," Beau says, thinking he's funny.

"Careful, boy. You might end up meat packed by this ladyboy… and like it!" Chyna comes back with wittily. The other boys crack up laughing at Beau's expense. "Hey, where's Robin?"

"I think she's in her office," Kaleo informs.

In her office, Robin is having another cough attack. She clings to her desk and gasps for air in between coughs. She waits for it to pass, but this one is lasting longer than usual. Just when she thinks she can't take another breath, the coughs stop. She sits on her office chair and takes deep breaths to calm her heart rate.

Robin hasn't been taking her HIV medication. Being so busy with planning this fundraiser and still trying to run the club as normal, she's lost track of all days. That is, all days, except for today. Today, Robin has been a strict drill sergeant barking orders at everyone. Making sure that everything is set up correctly, she's become a dick-tator; ten inches further than a normal dictator.

Just as Robin finally catches her breath, there's a knock at the door. "Hold on," Robin yells. She collects herself, fixes her hair and takes a deep breath to make sure no one can tell what just happened. "Come in!"

Chyna walks in and closes the door behind her. "I overheard the staff talking..." She walks up and kisses Robin hello, "You didn't tell them?"

"What for? We're gonna raise enough money to pay off the Wongs, we'll get to keep the club and this will all be a distant memory… that only you and I will share," Robin asserts.

"Wasn't that your plan all along?"

"Well, yeah, but—" Chyna starts, but gets cut off.

"Then, that's it. They'll all get to keep their jobs, we get to continue serving the LGBT community… no use having everyone run around worrying about something that might never happen, right?" Robin states very matter-of-factly.

"Well, I see someone has had a change of heart since the last time we spoke," Chyna says surprised.

"People change, darling." Robin smiles and then begins to have another cough attack. She's paler and thinner than she was just a few days ago.

"Oh my God, are you ok?" Chyna starts to get worried, "Here, drink some water." She hands her a water bottle that's sitting on Robin's desk.

Robin starts to catch her breath. She grabs the water bottle and takes a sip. "Thank you."

"Girl, now don't take this the wrong way, but you don't look too good," Chyna admits.

"I'm fine. I just caught a little cold," Robin downplays.

Chyna feels Robin's forehead for a quick second before Robin pulls away. "Whoa, you're burning up! That's not just a *little* cold. You have a fever, Robin! We should go to the doctor."

"I said I'm fine!" Robin says sternly.

"Sis, don't be stubborn!" Chyna tries to convince her friend.

"What do you want me to do?" Robin fumes, "Everything is riding on tonight. I can't just leave. Who's gonna run everything? Huh? If tonight doesn't go over well, we're losing this club. Do you even get that?"

"Of course, I do. It's just your health is—" Chyna tries to reason.

"I gotta set the tables," Robin interrupts, then walks out.

Outside the club, Malu and Ashley are having yet another fight. They've been at each other's throats constantly since Malu missed their daughter's hula performance. Sam, being outside as well, stands to the side and looks at his phone. He eavesdrops on their conversation and tries not to draw attention to himself.

"Everyday it's something else. I can't win with you." Malu throws his hands up in the air and starts to give up.

"Well, maybe if you weren't drunk every night and actually spent time with your kids," Ashley fires.

"Why you always gotta bring up the kids?! I do spend time with them. They're not complaining," Malu defends himself, "And who are you to talk? You burn every chance you get. You burned right before we left the house." Malu brings up the fact that Ashley smokes weed constantly.

"Yeah, cause you stress me out!" Ashley exclaims.

"And what, you don't think you stress me out? Why do you think I drink? Cause YOU, that's why!" Malu points out.

"Don't blame me! You make your own choices," Ashley deflects.

"Brah, you give me so much shit! Like today! You yelled at me for sleeping in... it was 10am! It wasn't even that late," Malu rants. "I work two jobs *and* I pick the kids up from school. You don't think I'm tired?"

"It's Sunday. We were supposed to go to church, dumbass," Ashley reminds him sassily.

"Go! You guys shoulda went. Nobody was stopping you."

"See, that's the problem right there, Malu... we're a family! We're supposed to do things together."

A Toyota Camry pulls up to the entrance of Violet. Malu and Ashley pause their argument and watch the car settle. The engine stops and the trunk pops open before anyone even gets out. All four car doors open almost simultaneously and the Fish

136

y Chicks, including Matt Makeup, step out the car in half drag. Alexus gets out of the driver's seat and stands just outside her door. She extends her arm and holds out her car keys as if she's about to drop them. Arita comes running around the car and grabs the keys quickly.

"Park the car," Alexus commands, "and somewhere close. I don't care if you have to pay."

"Got it," Arita replies obediently and hops into the driver's seat.

At the trunk of the car, Matt and Karmen take out the queens' suitcases full of their costumes. Alexus comes around the back and pulls out her tiny Louis Vuitton purse. "Matt, grab my bags," Alexus orders, "And you got Arita's, right Karmen?" Matt and Karmen nod in submission like two puppies to an owner. "Good. Let's go." The three Chicks head toward the entrance and Arita drives off with the Toyota's trunk still open.

On the way in, the Chicks pass Malu and Ashley. "Good Mornting!" Alexus announces, bursting through the awkward silence between the couple with no hesitation. The three chicks kiss the couple hello like an old assembly line, one right after the next.

Noticing Karmen and Matt struggle with two suitcases each, Malu sees this as an opportunity to get away from Ashley. "Here, I got it," he says as he takes one suitcase away from both Karmen and Matt.

"Ai, such a gentleman," Karmen comments.

"Oh my God, Thank you!" Matt thanks Malu and shakes out his weak arms.

"Yeah, no worries. I'll walk you guys in." Malu heads into the club, leading the pack.

Alexus, feeling like her tactic of proving power over Karmen and Matt was spoiled by Malu, stands to the side and gives him a fake smile as he passes her. As Karmen and Matt follow Malu in, Alexus' fake smile turns into a hard stink-eye. The other two girls cower and duck their heads in shame. Alexus stops them with her hand and cuts in line, walking in front of them while entering the club to assert dominance once again.

Once inside the club, the three Fish y Chicks pass the front bar. Beau, standing on the customer side of the bar, lowers his voice and says, "Sup" as the girls walk past him. Feeling the need to prove his heterosexuality, he stands with his head slightly tilted upward and his hands clasped in front of his crotch.

Alexus doesn't say anything. Instead, she looks at him with one eyebrow raised and continues to walk right past him. Matt follows right behind Alexus like a servant. He smiles at Beau, but quickly passes through. Karmen, bringing up the rear, passes Beau and flirtatiously says, "Hi handsome!" She touches his chest and winks at him, then follows the rest of the girls like an ant trail.

Beau, not exactly sure of what to do or how to feel, stands there tense and stiff as a board. He looks to see if the queens are far enough, so that he can talk shit, but ends up checking out Karmen's ass instead. Knowing that she's trans, but loving a good pair of cheeks more than anything else, Beau causes an internal battle in his own mind.

Malu comes back to the front bar after dropping off the girls bags in the dressing room and sees Beau's gaze. "Jeez, can you stare any harder?" Malu makes fun.

"Shut up, Malu! I wasn't looking at her!" Beau says defensively.

"What were you looking at then?" Malu asks.

"At the, um... the lights," Beau stutters.

"Oh, the lights, yeah? Ok," Malu chuckles unconvinced.

"Beau, shouldn't you be helping Momi and Tisha set up the

back bar," Kaleo jumps in. Beau turns and walks away, making a sour face and mocking Kaleo all the way back to his bar.

"Speaking of which, how are you and Momi?" Malu asks Parker.

"Uhh…" Parker starts, "We're ok, I guess. I don't know… I mean, we're fine, but it's not like we talk that much anymore."

"Are Momi and Tisha together now?" Malu inquires.

"I don't know and truthfully, I kind of don't want to know. It seems like it, though," Parker admits. "I mean, if she's happy, then that's all that matters, right?"

"Yeah, but what about you?" Kaleo jumps into the conversation.

"Yeah, that's what I'm still trying to figure out," Parker confesses.

"Well, it's better than me and Ash," Malu confesses. "I'd rather be in your position and have her not speak to me sometimes."

"Ho her gawwd, every time with you guys." Kaleo rolls his eyes. "You guys are always on the rocks."

"Brah, it's not me! It's her. All she does is yell at me and scold me like I'm one of the kids," Malu discloses.

"What happened this time?" Kaleo obligingly asks his younger brother.

"Nah, nothing big. We just didn't go church this morning 'cause I slept in, but I was tired!" Malu argues his side of the story. "Shit, we worked super late last night and I've been working a lot. We just got into it again outside. That's why I'm over here."

"Malu, go say sorry!" Kaleo commands.

"For what? I didn't do anything," Malu says defensively.

"So, it's all her fault then?" Kaleo tries to prove a point.

"No…" Malu acknowledges the fact that he's not completely innocent, "Ugh, you sound just like Dad." Malu pauses and then changes the subject, "And what about my brother? Has Lopaka called you?"

"No. He texted me when he first landed in LA to say he got there, but he hasn't texted me since," Kaleo explains.

"That fuckah!" Malu exclaims, "Well, at least you got that. He didn't even tell me he was leaving."

"He didn't tell anyone! He literally called me and asked me to take him to the airport, like, right before his flight. He's lucky I answered," Kaleo describes the situation. "I think he's trying to run away from everything: Ryan, the Fish y Chicks, us…"

"Yeah, well he succeeded," Malu says still offended. "He better not turn out like Mom."

Parker looks at Kaleo and sees this as an opportunity to ask, "You know, I've been your friend for over ten years and I've always wanted to know what happened to your mom."

"Oh, it's a boring story," Kaleo downplays. "She got caught up in drugs and abandoned us, so our dad raised us. I barely have any memories of her."

"Yeah and now Lopaka is doing the same thing," Malu jabs.

"No, he's not Malu! Don't say that," Kaleo scolds his brother. "You're just mad because he asked me to take him to the airport and not you."

"HELL YEAH I AM!" Malu exclaims, "He could've, at least, called both of us."

"He'll call when he calls, ok? Just give him some time," Kaleo defends Lopaka. "Now go talk to Ash before I fire you," he jokes to lighten his brother's mood.

"Yeah, you wish!" Malu snipes and walks away.

22. Buttery Nipple

- 1 oz Butterscotch Schnapps
- 1 oz Baileys
   *Layered in this order and served as a shot

7pm rolls around and about a hundred and fifty people show up for the fundraiser. There's a buffet line full of delicious local food and on the stage, Robin's old friend, Derek, plays Hawaiian music. His voice and guitar serve as background music to balance all the chatter. The guests make themselves plates of food and take their seats; they know the drag show is about to start.

On the side of the stage, Chyna and Robin look at everyone sitting and talking. With not as many people showing up as they hoped, Robin starts to worry that they're not going to make their goal.

"What's with the gay community in Hawaii?" Robin grumbles. "Don't they have any pride?"

"Don't worry, sis. They'll come," Chyna reassures her friend.

"Yeah, well they better or else we're shit outta luck," Robin responds. "You got this?"

"Yeah, I'm good," Chyna replies.

Robin, knowing that she hasn't been feeling well, asked Chyna a couple of days ago to host tonight's show. With a microphone in her hand, Chyna closes her eyes and gathers herself before she takes the stage; it's been awhile since she's MC-ed. Derek plays his last strum of his guitar and thanks the audience for listening to him play. He starts to make his way off stage and Robin signals to Chyna that it's time.

"Now, girl. Go!" Robin nudges Chyna to head on stage.

Chyna starts heading up the stairs to the stage, but then looks back at Robin for last minute encouragement. "You got this. They're gonna love you!" Robin motivates her friend.

Chyna smiles and blows Robin a kiss. Robin blows one back. She takes a deep breath, turns her mic on and walks out onstage.

"Well, look what the cat dragged in!" Chyna starts. The audience looks up and starts applauding. "Let's give it up for Derek everyone! Gracing us with some beautiful Hawaiian music tonight. Yes, hello all you beautiful people out there. Wow! You all look so gorgeous!" She pauses and sees one of her old clients in the audience, "Ben…" She says in a very unimpressed tone. The audience cracks up. "Yes, hi everyone! If you're still in the back, come have a seat. The show is about to start." She looks at a random person and asks, "How's the food? Good, yeah?"

"Yes! Hi everyone, I am your MC tonight. Thank you, thank you. You're too kind. My name is Chyna Make because I'm chyna make that money, honey!" The audience laughs. "They used to call me Chyna *Take* when I was younger, cause if you pissed me off, I would *take* your man, but I've changed. I don't do that anymore… I'll take your man even if you don't piss me off." The audience laughs again.

"Yes! Tonight, we are here to support Violet. Who loves Violet?" The audience applauds. "With you supporting us, we can support you and bring you bigger and better things that Hawaii has never seen before. You guys want that?" The audience cheers and Chyna smiles on the outside, but on the inside, she knows that all of this is a lie. They need the money to save the club from going under.

"This all wouldn't be possible if it wasn't for the owner of this club, the beautiful, the wonderful, my best friend, Miss Robin DeCraydle. Yes! Give it up for Robin! Shine the spotlight on her." The light goes over to side stage where Robin is standing. The audience looks over and hollers, they all know the infamous Robin. Robin waves and takes in the moment, but quickly fans the light away, gesturing to go back to Chyna. "Ohh, gorgeous and modest! What a package... and what a *package*, am I right, fellas?" Chyna jokes.

"Alright, who's ready to start the show?" Chyna asks, "I said... who's ready to start the show?!" The audience screams. "Well, here they come. These are the hottest queens in Hawaii. Is it a duck? Is it a goose? No... this is the Fish y Chicks! The music begins and the curtains draw back presenting all four girls. The audience goes mad as Karmen takes the lead.

As the show begins and everything starts going as planned, Robin starts to have more faith in the fundraiser. She knows that this is her last and only chance at keeping her club alive. If she doesn't make enough money to pay off the overdue rent and convince the Wongs to let her stay, Robin knows this will all be over.

She watches the Fish y Chicks from afar with her hands folded across her chest. She begins to cough and decides to remove herself from the public eye. Trying not to seem sick in front of her guests, she quickly makes her way to her office and shuts the door.

Once inside, she coughs heavily and clings to her desk with a death grip. Trying to stabilize herself, she tries to take deep breaths... but it doesn't work. Barely being able to breathe at all, Robin starts to panic. Her thoughts go back and forth between hopeful and desperate: *It will pass, it will pass, these cough attacks always do. Oh God, I can't breathe, I can't breathe. I'm gonna die!*

She looks around for her phone, she knows she needs to call for help. Now breathing shallow breaths, her vision starts to blur and she starts feeling like everything is moving in slow motion.

With her last ounce of energy, she lunges for the door knowing that as long as someone sees her, she stands a chance. She tries to scream, but having no breath to do so, she gasps and then blacks out. Her body hits the floor like a bag of bricks and she lays there with no one noticing her absence.

The music continues to blare and the Fish y Chicks continue to entertain. The guests holler as each Chick takes their turn performing and the bartenders pour drinks almost in rhythm with the music. Feeling back in his groove, Kaleo starts slinging drinks as quickly as he did before. *I'm back baby!*

Looking around, he knows that the club has been way more packed in the past, but he's hopeful that more people are on their way. He looks to his right and watches Parker help a customer. *Man, that's my gorgeous friend. Maybe in another life we were together, but not this one. That's ok, he's my best friend though and I will take that.*

He looks back to his left and notices a hot asian guy waiting to order. Kaleo notices his slick hair and his dapper suit and starts to check him out. This asian 'Rico Suave' smiles as Kaleo walks up to him. *I know that smile*, Kaleo thinks to himself and then immediately realizes it's Jimmy, back for another round.

"You again?" Kaleo pretends to be irritated, but smiles back at Jimmy.

"I'm back!" Jimmy flirts.

"What do you want, Jimmy?" Kaleo asks.

"Oh, so you remember my name I see?" Jimmy declares, knowing that he would.

Kaleo rolls his eyes. "How could I forget someone as annoying as you?"

Jimmy grabs his heart pretending as if he just got stabbed, "Ouch."

Kaleo looks at him with no remorse, "Do you want a drink

or not?"

"Yeah, my *usual* please," Jimmy jokes, referring to his original order of 'the gayest drink you have.'

Kaleo rolls his eyes again, knowing exactly what Jimmy means. "So, two shots of whiskey then?"

Jimmy nods, "Please."

Kaleo pours the two shots. He hands one to Jimmy and keeps one for himself.

"Oh, did you want one?" Jimmy asks waiting for Kaleo to hand him the second shot as well.

"Uh…" Kaleo feels dumb for assuming that one of the shots is for him.

Jimmy cracks up, "I'm just playing! It's for you." Kaleo reaches over the bar and slaps his arm playfully. "Hey, you're not the only one that gets to have fun," Jimmy laughs.

They cheers and shoot the whiskey. Jimmy makes a face suggesting that the shot was strong.

"What? Can't handle?" Kaleo teases.

"Oh, I can handle. Wanna go again?" Jimmy readies himself for another round.

"No. I want you to go away," Kaleo jabs.

"Hey, did you see my business card I left last time?" Jimmy asks.

"Maybe…" Kaleo responds with a tone that says, *What's your point?*

"Oh, well, I never got a call, so I thought you might not have seen it." Jimmy waits for a response.

"Was I supposed to call?" Kaleo counters sassily.

"So, you admit it. You did see it!" Jimmy imparts.

Kaleo scoffs, knowing that he just got caught, "I might've."

"I thought we agreed that I would take you out?" Jimmy tries a swift one.

"*Agreed?* Boy, please. I told you that I don't date guys, who are in the closet," Kaleo responds matter-of-factly.

"Yeah, about that..." Jimmy starts, "Because of you, I came out to my friends."

"What?" Kaleo questions if he heard correctly.

"Yup, so I just wanted to come in and say thank you," Jimmy gets serious, "You triggered something in me that night that made me look at the way I was living. I realized I had to change... so I did."

"Wow." Kaleo is impressed. "I'm happy for you."

"So... about that date?" Jimmy tries again.

Kaleo rolls his eyes and chuckles, "Ho her God."

Just then, an older asian couple comes walking up to Kaleo. Ashley leaves her station at the door and waves her arms trying to get Kaleo's attention. When she finally makes eye contact, she points at the older asian couple that's just in front of her and makes a face saying *trouble's coming your way*.

"Mom! Dad!" Jimmy is shocked to see his parents at Violet. "What are you guys doing here?"

Mom? Dad? Are these Jimmy's parents? And why is Ashley trying to warn me about them? Kaleo thinks to himself.

In a very heavy Chinese accent, Jimmy's dad replies, "We own dis place."

"We here for show. We get invitation," Jimmy's mom informs.

"Why you at gay bah?" Jimmy's dad asks.

"Uh... I was invited too," Jimmy thinks quick on his feet.

Knowing that Jimmy didn't get an invitation, Kaleo puts two and two together, *So he's out to his friends, but still not out to his parents. Got it.* Kaleo watches the whole conversation take place.

Jimmy looks back over to Kaleo and hesitantly says, "Uh, Mom, Dad, this is, uh, my friend, Kaleo." His fun, confident demeanor seems to have vanished instantly.

Friend? Kaleo thinks to himself, but not wanting to start a family drama, he responds respectfully, "Nice to meet you."

"Kaleo, these are my parents," Jimmy introduces. "They own the club apparently."

Jimmy's dad bows his head slightly, while his mother says a stern "Hello."

"Oh, you're the Wongs!" Kaleo exclaims, finally realizing that Ashley's look meant that they are the building owners. He looks over at Jimmy with big eyes of realization, "Oh, you're a Wong!" *Shit! Maybe I shouldn't have been treating the building owners' son like crap this whole time.*

"Yup," Jimmy nods his head. He shrugs his shoulders as to say, *What can I say?*

"Mr. and Mrs. Wong, please, let me find you a seat." *Jeez, you would think that Robin would've reserved seats for the building owners or at least told us that they were coming.*

"Is Robin here? We want to say hello," Mrs. Wong asks politely, but with her heavy Chinese accent, makes it sound like she's barking a command.

"Yeah, sure, of course. I think she's in her office. I'll take you to her." Kaleo walks around the bar to guide them. He looks at Parker and says, "Parker, watch my side please." Parker nods in confirmation.

Kaleo and Jimmy walk just ahead of Jimmy's parents and speak to each other quietly, so that his parents don't overhear. "So, when were you gonna tell me that you're a Wong?" Kaleo inquires.

"Hey, to be fair, it said 'Jimmy Wong' on my business card," Jimmy challenges.

"Yeah, but there are a million people with the last name 'Wong.' How was I supposed to know that you were one of THE Wongs? Was that your tactic this whole time?" Kaleo questions with conviction.

"What? No, I didn't even know my parents owned Violet. They own a bunch of places in town, I stopped keeping track," Jimmy admits. He recognizes that he finally has the upper-hand, "But, I guess that means… you kind of have to go out with me now, huh? Considering I'm the owners' son and all."

Kaleo scoffs playfully, *He just won't give up!* "I told you, I don't date guys who are in the closet," Kaleo refers to the fact that Jimmy's not 'out' to his parents.

Jimmy laughs and shakes his head, "Touché."

Outside the club, there's a few different groups of guests having a smoke break. Malu mans the door while Sam uses the bathroom. He peeks into the club and looks at Ashley. She looks back at him, but they both quickly look away. After their argument earlier, Ashley has been giving Malu the silent treatment. With such a small crowd and not really having anything to do, Malu looks up at the stars. *I wonder if the girls on Mars are bitches too.*

From around the corner, a gang of five rowdy-looking guys start to make their way past the entrance of Violet. One of them rides a bicycle slowly and trails the rest of the gang, while another has his shirt off to establish dominance. He's the shortest of the group with the tallest ego and with his shirt slung over his shoulder, he walks like an overconfident chihuahua leading a bunch of dumb pit bulls.

They look at Violet's flamboyant exterior and start laughing and cracking jokes at the club's expense. Sensing that they could be trouble, several of the Violet customers put out their cigarettes and head back inside. This makes the gang feel empowered. Preying on people's fears, they start to follow a group of gay guys making their way back into the club.

Once the gang reaches the door, Malu stops them, "Whoa. Where you guys going?"

"Inside," the little gang leader says matter-of-factly. "We're homos." He looks back to his gang and they start laughing and egging him on.

"You got an invitation?" Malu asks the gang. The fundraiser is not an "invite-only" event, but Malu pretends that it is.

"No, we no need one. We invite ourselves!" The gang leader spits back.

Trying to defuse the situation, Malu keeps calm. "Chill out, brah. Don't get nuts."

"Nuts? NUTS?! Boys, he think I getting nuts." The gang leader gets right in Malu's face, "You think this is nuts?! Brah, I SHOW you nuts!" He throws his shirt on the ground and starts bouncing around with his fists up like he's in a boxing match.

"Brah, I not goin' fight you," Malu comments, still keeping calm, "but you guys cannot go inside."

"Oh boys, he telling us what we can and cannot do now! How's dis fuckah!" The gang leader starts to get hyper with hate for Malu. He starts getting up in Malu's face, acting as if he is going to hit him, but then backs away. He does this a couple times.

With his back up against the doors to make sure the doors stay closed, Malu stands firm with his arms crossed at this chest. He stares down the little gang leader as the leader does his whole street fighter routine.

"WHAT?! What kind door man you? You panty, yeah? I bet you one mahu like all the oddah fags in there!" The gang leader barks.

"Brah, you pushin' it," Malu says, starting to get ticked off.

"What? You tink you can stop us? You cannot stop nothin!" The gang leader keeps pushing, "We goin' in there and we goin' take this club," he gets right up in Malu's face, "and I goin' take your chick too!"

Having bottled up all of his anger from arguing with Ashley

earlier and now this situation, Malu can't keep a cool-head any longer. Although Ashley has been irritating him recently, Malu doesn't let anyone talk about her like that. The last comment about 'taking his chick' was the last straw. With the little gang leader right up in his face, Malu head-butts him with all of his might.

Not expecting that Malu would actually do anything, the little gang leader gets, literally, hit by surprise. Feeling woozy, he falls to the ground. The other gang members instantly jump on Malu to defend their leader. Malu swings and makes contact, punching one guy and then throwing another guy off him. Another guy tackles him to the ground and they start wrestling in the middle of the walkway.

A few of the guests outside gasp and watch from afar, not wanting to get into the middle of the brawl. Malu continues to struggle with one of the guys, but finally gets him into a headlock. Trying to cut off his breathing and knock him out, Malu holds him tight.

The fifth gang member gets off his bicycle and heads toward Malu. With the little gang leader dazed and confused on the ground, two of his other friends thrown across the way and his other friend trapped in a headlock, he knows he has to do something drastic. He sneaks up on Malu from behind, takes out a knife and stabs him on the right side of his ribs.

"AAAHHHHH!!!" Malu yells and drops the guy out from his headlock. He grabs his side and falls to his knees. He looks at his ribs that's now pouring blood and then looks back at the guy who stabbed him.

As the guy walks toward him, possibly to stab him again, someone grabs the guy from behind and slams him on the ground. It's Ryan, Lopaka's ex-boyfriend. The knife falls to the ground far enough away from him and Ryan picks it up. He holds it at the gang member's throat and threatens him,

150

"Leave."

At that moment, Sam comes back from his pee break. He opens the door and sees guys thrown on the ground and Ryan threatening one of the gang members with a knife. "WHOA, WHAT THE FUCK IS GOING ON?!" He looks to his feet and sees Malu on the ground bleeding. "Oh shit! Malu! Are you ok?"

The gang members look at the size of Sam then look at Ryan with a knife and begin to back away. They pick up their gang leader, who's still dizzy, and start running away like cockroaches scattering.

Ryan watches as the gang disappears around the corner and then looks back at Malu, who's down on all fours. He sees Sam at his side, down on one knee, trying to decide whether or not he should pick him up. Ryan runs into the club to get Ashley, who has no idea of what just happened outside of the entrance doors. "Malu got stabbed!"

"WHAT?! What are you talking about?" Ashley exclaims. She gets out from behind the front desk and runs outside. Once outside, she sees Malu, with his arm around Sam's neck, trying to stand up as he bleeds through his black shirt., "OH SHIT!" She screams. "Babe, are you ok?! WHAT THE FUCK HAPPENED!!??"

"He needs to go to the E.R.!" Sam says to Ashley, while holding Malu up.

"He needs to go NOW!" Ryan necessitates.

Ashley nods and runs back inside. She grabs her purse from behind the front desk and runs back out. She pulls out her keys and unlocks their SUV that's sitting right outside of the club. "Sam, put him in, put him in!" She says trying to hurry him. She gets into the driver's seat and starts the car. Once Malu is in the passenger's seat, she reverses the car to the main street and speeds off. She grabs Malu's hand and says with tears in her eyes, "Babe, stay with me ok."

At the same time that all of that is happening, Kaleo, Jimmy and Jimmy's parents make their way to Robin's office. With the door still closed, Kaleo knocks to see if they may enter. He knocks a second time, but with the music blasting from the Fish y Chicks performance, he figures that she probably can't hear him. He opens the door slowly making sure he's not intruding on anything, but doesn't see Robin at her desk. He opens the door a little further, however, the door hits something and doesn't open all the way. He looks down to see what's blocking the doorway and realizes it's Robin. She's passed out on the floor on the backside of the door. "HOLY SHIT!"

Jimmy looks down and sees what Kaleo is reacting to, "Oh my God!"

Kaleo creeps his way into the office through the crack of the door and moves Robin away, so the others can enter. "Robin, are you ok?! ROBIN!" He taps her face slightly before checking her pulse.

"Does she have a pulse?" Jimmy asks.

"Uh, I don't know. I think so," Kaleo panics.

Jimmy drops down and feels for a pulse in Robin's neck. "Yeah, she's got one. It's faint, though." He looks to his mom and dad who are standing and watching in shock, "Mom, call 911. Hurry!"

Jimmy's mom quickly grabs her cell phone from her purse and calls 911. "Yes, amburance. Violet Nightcrub. A woman fainted. Yes. Yes. Barery breathing. Please hurry!"

Kaleo looks to Jimmy with desperation in his eyes, "What do I do?"

Jimmy grabs Kaleo's shoulder and looks him dead in the eyes, "I got this, ok? Do you trust me?" Kaleo nods and moves out of the way. Jimmy takes off his suit jacket and positions himself to start CPR. He begins to pump Robin's chest, "One, two, three, four, five, six…"

Watching from the side of the stage, Chyna notices a bunch of commotion going on in Robin's office and decides to head over. Once she gets near, she asks "What's going on in h—, OH MY GOD!" She immediately sees her best friend on the floor unconscious with Jimmy working on her. "Oh my God, what's happening?!"

"I don't know! We came in and she was passed out on the floor," Kaleo explains. "Do you know if she's allergic to anything or if she took something?"

"No, I don't thi—" Chyna stops herself and then quickly makes her way to Robin's purse, she just might have a clue what the problem is. She reaches in and takes out Robin's ARV pills that treat her HIV; it's completely full. "Shit!"

"What? What are those?" Kaleo asks as Jimmy still continues to give Robin CPR.

"It's her HIV pills," Chyna informs, "She hasn't been taking them."

"WHAT?! Why would she do that? And why wouldn't she tell anyone that she's battling with HIV?" Kaleo is shocked and upset.

"It doesn't matter. Did you call an ambulance?" Chyna redirects Kaleo's focus.

"Yes. I did. Zey on Zeir way," Jimmy's mom chimes in.

Chyna looks at the older asian couple, then back at Kaleo, "Who's this?"

"These are the Wongs," Kaleo replies staring into Chyna's eyes trying to telepathically tell her that they are the owners of the building.

Chyna receives Kaleo's eye contact, but doesn't know what he means. "The Wongs?" Then almost instantly, as soon as their names leave her lips, it hits her. "Oh my God, the Wongs!" She walks over to them and shakes their hands. "Hi, pleasure to meet you. I love the club, I love the space." Trying to make a good impression for the building owners, Chyna almost forgets that her best friend is lying on the floor. She looks down and then back at the Wongs, "Sorry we have to meet under these conditions."

"Chyna!" Kaleo yells. Chyna looks back. "You have to distract the audience. Can you do that?"

"What do you mean?" Chyna panics. Her mind is all over the place.

"The ambulance is coming and they're probably gonna have to take her out on a stretcher," Kaleo explains his plan, "I'm gonna have them take her through the back door, but they still need to take her out of the office and into the main part of the club to get there. So, I need you to keep the audience looking the other way. We don't need them to start panicking. Can you do that for me?"

"Ok, yeah. I can do that," Chyna responds half-heartedly. She leaves the room and goes back to watching the drag show from side-stage. Only this time, she's watching the audience and starts thinking of possible ways to get the entire crowd to look the other way.

Not even a minute later, Ryan runs into the office. Kaleo doesn't look up, his focus is on Jimmy, who is working hard on Robin.

"Kaleo!" Ryan says to get Kaleo's attention, only then does he notice Robin on the floor. "Oh my God."

"Ryan?" Kaleo is confused as to why he, of all people, is standing at the door to Robin's office. "Don't worry, Ryan, we got this under control."

"No," Ryan deflects, "Malu just got stabbed."

"WHAT?!!" Kaleo shrieks.

The Wongs look at Ryan with faces that say *What is going*

on at this club?

"Yeah, there was some gang that rushed him outside," Ryan explains.

"Did you call an ambulance?" Kaleo asks frantically, but then realizes they already have one ambulance on the way for Robin. His mind starts racing, *Shit, did we call them twice? Are they sending two ambulances or did they think that two people called for the same situation and they are only sending one? Can they fit Robin and Malu in the same ambulance? Will they even allow that?*

Before Kaleo's head explodes with unanswerable questions, Ryan informs, "No, Ashley rushed him to the ER. They're on their way there now."

Slightly relieved that there would be no mix up or confusion of ambulances, Kaleo snaps back into reality. He quickly registers that instead of one emergency, he now has two situations on his hands. Amidst his millions of thoughts, he suddenly realizes that with Ashley and Malu gone, no one is working the front desk and Sam is the only door man.

Things start to move in a strange, slow-motion sort of way. Kaleo looks at the Wongs, who watch their son try to save their tenant. He follows their gazes down to Jimmy giving CPR to Robin, then back up to Ryan, who's staring at him for what to do next. At that very moment, it all became clear. Kaleo has a rude awakening. Understanding that there's no one else to take the lead in this situation, Kaleo realizes it has to be him.

He changes his tone to a man who means business and begins to give orders, "Ryan, there's an ambulance on the way to the club right now. I need you to go outside and wait for them. When they get here, you take them around the back to this door and you make sure none of these guests in here notice."

"Ok, got it," Ryan understands his duty.

"Go," Kaleo relieves him. He looks to Jimmy's parents and

knows he needs their help as well. "Mr. and Mrs. Wong, I am so sorry for you to see us like this. I have no idea what's going on tonight, but I promise you that it's not usually like this. I need your help. Please," Kaleo begs with desperation in his voice. The Wongs nod in agreement.

Kaleo divulges his plan, "Mr. Wong, I need you to open the back door and wait there until you see Ryan and the paramedics coming. Mrs. Wong, I need you stand right outside this office, so you can see your husband and you can see Chyna on stage at the same time. Mr. Wong, as soon as you see the paramedics heading toward you, you let your wife know they're coming and, Mrs. Wong, as soon as you see his signal, you cue Chyna to let her know that it's time for her to distract the audience. Got it?"

"Understand," Mrs. Wong says calmly, while Mr. Wong just bows in comprehension. They leave the room and man their posts.

Jimmy looks up at Kaleo while still giving chest compressions, "Go. I got this."

They look into each other's eyes and share a quick second of intimate silence. "Thank you," Kaleo says with a tender tone.

Jimmy nods and encourages his crush, "Go!"

Kaleo makes his way out of the office, leaving Jimmy alone with Robin. Passing by the back bar and without stopping his cadence, he fires commands, "Momi, I need you at the front bar."

"Why?" Momi asks confusedly.

"I just need you at the front bar please," Kaleo directs.

Momi realizes that Kaleo is on some sort of serious mission and just complies, "Ok." She grabs her bar key and heads over to the front bar.

Kaleo looks over at Tisha and Beau, "You guys got this?"

"We got it," Tisha responds feeling his intense energy.

"What's going on?" Beau asks cluelessly. Kaleo ignores him and make his way toward the front.

At the front bar, Momi passes Parker without saying a word and settles into Kaleo's spot. Parker gets thrown off. *What is she doing here?* Following just behind her, Parker notices Kaleo coming at him with a purpose. Worried about his distressed friend, Parker asks, "You ok?"

Kaleo stands on the customer's side of the bar, in the middle of Parker and Momi, so they both can hear. He shouts over the music playing, but not loud enough for the guests to hear, "I need you both to run the club for me."

"What do you mean?" Parker asks.

"Malu got stabbed," Kaleo reveals.

"What?! Is he ok?" Momi is terrified at the news.

"I don't know, but Ashley took him to the hospital, so I hope so," Kaleo replies. "Listen, I'm gonna have to shift everyone around since they're gone, ok?"

"Yeah, do what you need to do," Parker encourages.

"Also, there's an ambulance coming, so as much as possible, I need you guys to keep the paramedics out of sight," Kaleo instructs.

"Wait. Didn't you just say that Ashley already took Malu to the ER?" Momi asks.

"Yeah, why don't you just cancel the ambulance?" Parker suggests.

"No, the ambulance is for Robin," Kaleo discloses.

"WHAT?!" They say is unison.

"What's wrong with Robin?" Parker questions.

"I don't know. We went to her office and she was passed out on the floor," Kaleo responds trying to leave his emotions out of it.

"Oh my God, is she ok?" Momi is concerned.

"She's barely breathing, but Jimmy's giving her CPR right

now, until the paramedics arrive," Kaleo informs his two friends.

"Jimmy?" Parker's never heard of a Jimmy.

"I'll explain later," Kaleo knows there's no time to explain the whole Jimmy situation. "When they come, I'm gonna hop in the ambulance and go with Robin to the hospital. So, if anything happens... I mean shit, I don't know what else could happen tonight, but if something does... just deal with it ok?"

"We got it," The say in unison and look at each other.

"Don't worry about the club, you just do whatever you gotta do. We'll keep everything under control," Parker consoles.

"I'll text Ash and find out how Malu's doing," Momi offers.

"Cool. Thanks guys." Kaleo looks at his two friends with sincerity.

Kaleo leaves the awkward exes and heads around the back of the bar. "CHICO! YUKI! Come here," he yells. "Listen, Ashley and Malu had to leave, so I need you guys to fill in for them." He decides there's no time to explain why.

"Ok, papi," Chico says with a smile and asks no questions.

"Sweet! I like change," Yuki gets excited.

"Yuki, I need you to work the front desk. It's forty-five dollars per person, even if they're a regular. No exceptions! It's a fundraiser, so everybody pays," Kaleo mandates.

"Hai!" Yuki responds with a *Yes!* in Japanese.

"Chico, I need you to be a doorman and help Sam out," Kaleo directs.

"Yaaasss! Come on, doorman!" Chico responds with glee.

"Work the door, make a couple rounds inside... just protect the guests, yeah?" Kaleo instructs.

"Gotcha boss," Chico agrees.

Kaleo walks outside the club to check out the aftermath. There are a few people smoking outside, but otherwise the streets are calm. It's as if nothing ever happened. The air is still and there's a looming feeling approaching. Feeling a drop of water fall on his cheek, he looks up and notices the heavy clouds in the night sky. *Of course it's gonna rain.* Through the dark clouds, the full moon peeks its head out. *AND IT'S A FULL MOON?! No fucking wonder!* He looks to his left and notices Sam staring out in front of him blankly and mumbling under his breath.

"I should've been there. I wasn't there," Sam mutters.

"Sam! Are you ok?" Kaleo tries to get Sam's attention.

Sam looks at Kaleo. "I wasn't there. I couldn't protect him. I went to the bathroom at the wrong time. Why did I have to go to the bathroom? That's my best friend and I wasn't there for him." Sam tries to make sense of the situation and his guilt.

"Sam, it's ok. You couldn't have known."

"But he's my best friend and I didn't have his back. He always has my back."

"It's ok, Sam. He's my baby brother and I wasn't there for him too, but he's gonna be ok. Alright?" Kaleo grabs Sam's big broad shoulders to get him to focus, "Listen, I know what happened is fucked up and Momi is gonna keep us updated on how he's doing, but right now I need you to be here… mentally and physically here, and protect everyone else that's still in this club ok? Can you do that for me?" Sam nods. "Chico's gonna help you."

"Hola!" Chico comes walking in their direction innocently. He still hasn't heard the news.

Now that Chico has arrived, Kaleo explains the game plan to the both of them. "Ok guys, so there's an ambulance on its way. It's for Robin."

"WHAT?!" Chico and Sam say in unison. There eyes widen with hearing such shocking news.

"Don't worry, she'll be fine. I'll explain it all later." Kaleo points at Ryan who's out on the main street waiting for the ambulance, "Ryan is gonna intercept them and guide them to the back door. Just keep the path out here clear ok? And, as much as possible, try not to let the guests see. I mean, if they're out here smoking, then whatever, but just try to keep the craziness out of sight. Yeah?"

"Yup," Sam says with a melancholy tone.

"Gotcha boss," Chico says with his naturally cheery demeanor.

"Thanks guys, I owe you one," Kaleo thanks his co-workers and heads back toward the entrance.

Chico looks at Sam, "Wow, what an eventful night, huh?"

"Man, you have no idea," Sam responds.

Just before Kaleo enters the club, he looks back and points at Sam, "Sam… it's not your fault!" He gives him one last reassurance before going back in.

Chico, not knowing what Kaleo meant, looks at Sam with skepticism, "Did you poison Robin?"

Sam laughs and defends himself, "No! I don't know what happened to Robin."

Back in the office, Jimmy continues to give Robin CPR. Sweat drips from his forehead as he speaks to her almost lifeless body, "Come on, don't give up on me now." He looks up and notices Kaleo sneaking back into the office and closing the door quickly, so that none of the guests can see what's going on.

"How's she doing?" Kaleo asks.

"I don't know, but I'm doing everything I can," Jimmy answers.

"Thank you," Kaleo says genuinely.

"Don't thank me yet," Jimmy remarks. "Are they almost here?" He asks, referring to the ambulance.

"They should be. Everybody is in place. Let's just hope this all works out," Kaleo breathes heavily.

"It will," Jimmy assures.

Outside the club, the ambulance has just arrived. Having come to the club many times before, the paramedics are familiar with Violet. They pull up right outside the front doors and start heading for the entrance, but Ryan catches them in their tracks.

"This way, guys!" Ryan redirects. "We're gonna use the back door."

Sam holds the entrance shut, leaning his 300 pound body against the front doors.

At this point, there are only two guests outside smoking, so Chico decides to befriend them and get them to believe a fake story. "Hey girls!"

"What's with the ambulance? What's going on?" One of the girls asks.

"Oh, it's the thai food place just around the corner," Chico lies. "There was a guy that was allergic to peanuts."

"What! Why would he even go there? Isn't there like peanuts in almost every thai dish?" the other girl asks confoundedly as she takes another drag from her cigarette.

Chico shrugs and the three of them watch Ryan and the paramedics disappear around the corner. "I guess he just couldn't resist dem nuts," Chico jokes to lighten the mood. The three new friends share a laugh.

Back inside, The Fish y Chicks have just finished a few dance numbers. They corral back in their dressing room, taking a moment to breathe, drink water and change into their next costumes.

Onstage, Chyna is talking to the audience to stall for time. She's a natural on the mic. That is, she used to be. Having hosted many shows back in the day, her quick-wit serves her well, especially in high pressure situations. However, this time, knowing that her best friend is lying on the floor close to death, her thoughts are scrambled.

"Let's give it up for the Fish y Chicks one more time ladies and gentlemen," Chyna starts. "What a night, huh?" She pauses for a second and tries to think of something to say, but her mind is so caught up on the image of Robin on the floor that she's at a loss of words. "Uh..." She looks at the audience, who's looking straight back at her and for the first time in her life, she understands what everyone is talking about when they say 'stage fright.'

Now silent onstage for almost an awkward amount of time, Chyna looks around the room for something to talk about. Grasping at straws, she finally spots the buffet line in the back of the club. "How's the food?" She says into the mic. "I haven't had a chance to try everything. Oh, you know, just being the host and all." The audience chuckles politely. "Let's give it up for our catering company, you guys. Yes, thank you!"

Holding the back door open, Mr. Wong sees Ryan and the paramedics running toward him with a stretcher. He looks into the club and signals his wife to let her know that they have arrived.

Mrs. Wong nods and starts waving her hands in the air to get Chyna's attention, but it doesn't work. Chyna continues rambling on.

"You know what I noticed?" Chyna starts to get her groove back, "Have you ever noticed how local people are not shame to go back for seconds?" She looks down at her friend Derek who is now sitting at a table close to the stage. "That's you, yeah Derek?" The audience laughs. "How many plates you had already?"

Derek laughs, "This is my first one!"

"No lie!" Chyna pokes fun at her old friend, "And more worse, he think just because he played music earlier tonight that

162

he can eat for free. Too good, yeah? This is a fundraiser braddah, not even I can eat for free!" The audience starts to crack up. "Nah, nah, nah."

Just then, Chyna notices Mrs. Wong flapping her arms like a bird on the side of the stage. *Oh shit! They're here. Ok, ok, keep your cool, Chyna. Don't let the audience know anything is up.* Just when she felt she was winning the audience over, she gets slapped in the face with reality again. She knows she has to get the entire crowd to look away from the stage and toward the entrance of the club, but how? *What do I do?*

She quickly has an internal chat with herself, *Ok. Food, food. I already talked about the food. Shit, what else? What goes with food? DRINKS!* "Well, you can't enjoy all the food without a good drink, am I right?" Chyna quickly blurts out, "Let's give it up for our bartenders, ladies and gentlemen. First, here at the back bar, we have the beautiful Tisha. Not only can she make an amazing cocktail, but she's a dancer, baby.'" Tisha sticks her tongue out and teases the audience with a light 'twerk,' but then stops and waves her finger 'no-no.' "Yaaasss! Oh nope, you gotta pay for the full twerk. Come on, somebody give that girl a dollar! Remember this is all for the fundraiser."

"Next to her, we have the beautiful... and cocky, Beau." The audience laughs. Beau flexes his arms as if he's in a bodybuilding competition, showing off and loving the attention. "Can you tell he's straight?" Chyna makes fun of his poses. "Maybe one of you thirsty mahus can pop his cherry."

As she finishes poking fun at Beau, the paramedics enter the building with a stretcher and open Robin's office door. Chyna knows she has to get the attention to the front of the club NOW! "And at our front bar, ladies and gentlemen, please give it up for the resident couple of the club, our very own Mr. and Mrs. Violet, Parker and Momi!" Chyna has yet to hear the news that they broke up.

The entire audience turns around to look at Parker and Momi at the front bar as the spotlight shines on them. They wave and smile as the audience applauds. Knowing that the audience will soon look back at her and also knowing that the paramedics have not yet left the building, Chyna starts motioning to Parker and Momi to distract the audience. She makes big gestures with her body and she lips the words "DO SOMETHING!"

Momi, understanding Chyna's message loud and clear, tries to quickly think of something to keep and hold the audience's attention. She looks at Parker, who's looking back at her. Without any ideas, he shrugs his shoulders. Momi looks back at the audience, she knows what she needs to do.

She jumps onto the bar top with a bottle of whisky in her hand and pours a shot straight into her mouth. She continues pouring the whisky over her head and then over her tits. She even pours some over Parker's head from above him. She puts down the bottle and starts to slowly move and dance sexually. The audience is hooked.

"YAAAASSS!!! Give her some music, DJ!" Chyna yells into the mic. She looks at the audience, who are now locked in on Momi. With everyone looking the other way, Chyna knows this would be the perfect time for the paramedics to remove Robin from the club. She looks over at the office, but the door is still closed and they haven't made a move yet.

At the front bar, Momi continues to give the audience a show. What started off as a alcohol-soaked wet T-shirt contest has quickly become a striptease. Momi dances to the music and slowly starts to take off her clothing, piece by piece. The audience goes nuts! A lot of the guests get up out of their seats and head up to Momi to tip her. Sticking dollar bills in whatever clothing she has left, the audience cheers and dance around the front bar.

With nothing left on, except her bra, her thong and a pair of work boots, she looks at Parker and extends her hand. The audience hollers with encouragement for Parker to join her on the bar top. Momi looks down at her ex-boyfriend. She knows she hasn't been the kindest to him recently, but she hopes that for the sake of Robin, he will play along. She smiles at him and then winks her infamous wink.

Parker smiles and then jumps up on the bar top. The audience screams with excitement. Joining in on the fun, he grabs the bottle of whisky, takes a shot and then starts pouring free shots into the guests' open mouths. Looking like a bunch of fish gasping for oxygen, Parker starts laughing.

From behind, Momi reaches for the bottom of Parker's tank top and quickly pulls it over his head. Revealing his chiseled body, the audience shouts and starts throwing dollar bills at him. He looks back at Momi, who's looking at him with a sassy face saying, *Yeah, I did it. What you gonna do about it?*

Parker puts the bottle down and chases after Momi playfully. She runs on the bar top as far away as she can go, but Parker catches her. She struggles to get free, but then concedes. Now face-to-face, Parker holds Momi in a bear hug. Having this feel all too familiar, time starts to slow for a second as the old couple share a brief moment of what once was. They smile at each other and without words, they both know that everything is going to be alright between the two of them.

While Momi savors the moment a second longer than Parker, Parker reaches for the back of Momi's bra and unhooks it with one swift maneuver. Having done it a million times before, he's happy he's still got the magic touch.

Momi's face cracks and she immediately grabs the front side of her bra, so that the bra doesn't come off completely. With one free hand, she smacks Parker's arm as he runs to the other side of the bar. Now frozen in a state of shock, she looks down at the guests who are now chanting, "Take it off! Take it off! Take it off!"

Being caught in the moment and believing in the 'Free the Nipple' campaign anyway, Momi thinks to herself, *Oh, what the hell*, and throws her bra into the audience and reveals her beautiful set of tits. Now topless, she dances to the music as the guests tip her even more!

As Momi and Parker dance on the bar up front, Chyna looks over and sees the office door open. With Robin completely strapped onto a gurney, the paramedics wheel her out of the building without any of the guests noticing. *OH MY GOD! WE DID IT!*

In the office, Kaleo does a quick glance around the room to see what he might need. He grabs Robin's purse and pills, just in case. He looks Jimmy straight in his eyes and says, "Thank you so much!" Kaleo kisses him on the cheek and walks out quickly.

Once out of the office, he looks over to make sure that the audience is occupied. To his surprise, Momi and Parker are on the bar top dancing together. He doesn't know what exactly is happening out there, but he doesn't care because all that matters is that no one is looking in his direction. He looks over at Chyna onstage, who's looking back at him and flashing two thumbs up. He nods and lips, "I'm gonna go with her."

Chyna nods and gestures, "I'll call you."

Kaleo runs out the back door to make sure the ambulance doesn't leave without him.

23. Cherry Bomb

- 1 oz Cherry Vodka
- 1/2 Pint Energy Drink
- Splash Grenadine

At the hospital, Malu is hooked up to an IV. His pain, while still present, has subsided thanks to the medication he was given. Having had doctors in and out since he got there, Malu decides to take a rest. With his eyes closed and his mind drifting off into the dream world, he lies there completely unaware of the doctor that is in the room talking to Ashley.

"He's going to be ok, but I want to hold him here until we get the test results back. We have to make sure the knife didn't puncture his lung," the doctor informs.

Ashley exhales a deep sigh of relief, "Thank God! Thank you."

"Of course. I'll be back when I receive his results." The doctor turns around and walks out.

When they first arrived at the hospital, Ashley pulled right up to the emergency entrance and put the car in 'park' without waiting for permission. Seeing her struggle to get her boyfriend inside the lobby, the hospital staff quickly came running out to help. They rushed Malu to the front of the line after seeing his bloody ribs.

Now sitting by his side, Ashley wishes smoking were allowed in hospitals. Feeling every urge in her body to run outside and take a quick hit, she refuses to leave Malu's side. She holds his hand and looks at him; she knows she's been extra hard on him recently. As much shit as she gives him, tonight has really put things into perspective for her. She imagines a life without him, a life without a father for her children, *God damnit*

Malu, what would I do without you? What would WE do without you? She kisses his hand and pets his forehead. She leans in and whispers in his ear, "I love you."

In the same hospital, but on the other side of the emergency ward, Robin is being worked on by multiple doctors. Still unconscious, Robin's breathing is now hooked up to a ventilator to calm her body down. With tubes coming out of almost every orifice and bright lights gleaming on her body, she looks like a scene out of a sci-fi movie.

Up until now, Kaleo has been by Robin's side. However, with no one being allowed in the operating room except for the medical staff, Kaleo stands by the swinging doors letting the chaotic sea of people pass. As Robin gets further and further away from him, he says a little prayer internally, *Please God, don't take her yet. Please.*

Too antsy and anxious to sit down, Kaleo paces the halls waiting to hear any information from any of the hospital staff. As a nurse comes out from one of the doors, Kaleo stops him, "Is she ok? How is she? Is she breathing?"

Not sure of who Kaleo is or who he is speaking of, the nurse turns to him and says diplomatically, "Sir, I'm sure she'll be fine, but for now, I need you to take a seat back in the lobby, ok?" The nurse walks away and carries on with his original task. Not feeling satisfied with that answer, Kaleo decides not to listen and continues to pace the halls, waiting for another hospital worker.

Knowing that this could be serious, he takes out his phone and calls his older brother, Lopaka. The phone rings and rings and rings, then goes to voicemail. *Fucking Lopaka!* He hangs up and calls again, but the same thing happens. He tries a third time and this time decides to leave a voicemail, "Call me as soon as you get this. Robin's in the hospital." He hangs up and opens up

168

a text to Lopaka, hoping that texting him will somehow reach him faster. *Call me. NOW!*

He goes to call his younger brother, Malu, instead and suddenly remembers, *Oh shit! Malu!* Having been so caught up with Robin's situation, he completely forgot about Malu getting stabbed. Knowing that this is the closest hospital to Violet, he's almost sure that Ashley brought him here and that they're somewhere in the building. Needing to do something other than worry and walk in circles, he decides to go find his younger brother.

Back in Malu's hospital room, Malu is still in the paper gown that was given to him. Now wide awake and sitting upright on the hospital bed, he and Ashley share an intimate moment, staring into each other's eyes. Realizing that they've been on two different pages for awhile now, the couple begin to apologize.

"I'm sorry, babe," Malu starts, "I've been neglecting you and the kids."

"No. *I'm* sorry!" Ashley cuts in. "I've been so hard on you. I know you work hard. I just get scared that you're gonna get fed up one day and leave us. That's why I get mad when you're not around. I know, it's stupid..."

"Yeah, it is stupid," Malu scolds in a playful manner. "Babe... I work hard for *us*. I hate being away from you and the kids, you know that! You guys are my life!"

"I know. I just miss you a lot of the time, you know?" Ashley admits.

"And I miss you too. I know things have been a bit off between us recently, but... we can work it out." Malu gets sentimental, "I love you, Ash. I'll do whatever it takes to make this work."

"Me too," Ashley says with teary eyes.

"Happy wife, Happy life, right?" Malu jokes.

"Uh, do you see a ring on this finger?" Ashley comes back with playfully.

"Eh, ring or no ring, you're mine! You heard? Don't you ever forget it!" He commands.

Ashley throws her arms around Malu and hugs him tightly.

"OW!" Malu holds his side and screams in pain.

"OH MY GOD! I'm so sorry babe, I didn't mean to—"

"Nah, nah, nah. Just playing, babe." Ever the prankster, Malu jokes even on a hospital bed.

"You son of a bitch!" Ashley slaps him hard on his arm.

"OW!" This time Malu means it.

"Good for you!" Ashley says with a smile.

Just then, there's a knock at the door. The door is already open, but they figure the person is trying to be courteous. The couple stop play-fighting and look to the door.

"Kaleo!" Ashley says surprised. She was not expecting him. She gets up and gives him a hug to say hello.

"Hi guys," Kaleo greets in a mild tone. He walks up to his brother and touches him on the shoulder, "You ok?"

"Yeah, I'm good," Malu replies.

"He got lucky. The knife didn't puncture his lung, thank God! So, he just has to let his body heal now," Ashley informs Kaleo.

"Good, good…" Kaleo responds in a half-hearted way.

"You ok?" Ashley asks. She thought he'd be more excited to hear the news that Malu is going to be fine.

"Yeah, you look a little out of it," Malu adds.

"Yeah… yeah… um…" Kaleo stutters.

Trying to help him out, Ashley decides to take the lead, "What did Robin say when she heard that Malu got stabbed?"

"She's here," Kaleo replies quickly.

"Where? Oh shit, am I in trouble?" Malu starts to freak out

thinking that Robin is on her way into the room.

Never wanting to look weak in front of anyone, Kaleo always keep his feelings deep down inside. As the lead bartender of the club, his goal is to remain unbiased and diplomatic when dealing with co-workers and guests' issues alike. However, there's a limit for how much any one person can withstand no matter how hard they try.

Without being able to hold in his emotions anymore, Kaleo bursts into tears. He tries to look away and hides his face, but it's no use.

"Oh my God!" Ashley runs over to Kaleo and starts hugging him. Not having a clue what's on his mind, she asks, "What's the matter, babe?"

Unable to get up from his hospital bed, Malu knows something is really bothering Kaleo. "Talk to us, brother. I know you have a lot on your mind. Let it out."

Having not allowed himself to cry for months, possibly even a year, Kaleo's tears come flooding out like water bursting through the Hoover Dam. All the frustration of being 30 and not having a direction in his life to his confusing feelings over Parker and now to Robin, Kaleo can't hold back any longer. He physically feels a release within himself happening as he starts to catch his breath and calm down.

Knowing that Kaleo has been struggling internally and putting on a front for awhile, Malu and Ashley sit silently and let him get it all out. Malu just watches while Ashley has her right hand on Kaleo's lap trying to comfort him. They wait patiently letting him speak when he's ready.

After a brief moment, Kaleo looks to his brother and sister-in-law and says, "Sorry."

"For what?" Malu counters.

Finally collecting himself and feeling a bit better, Kaleo's mind instantly recalls images of Robin lying on the floor, passed out in her office. He looks down, shakes his head and starts to tear up again. He knows he definitely can't handle this situation on his own.

Needing strength and encouragement, Kaleo looks his brother right in his eyes and finally speaks, "I think Dad is dying."

"What do you mean 'Dad is dying?'" Malu tries to comprehend Kaleo's last statement.

"I don't know. I went to her office and she was passed out on the floor." Kaleo starts to cry again, "She was barely breathing… I didn't know what to do, so I called 911 and rushed her here."

* * *

In the late 80s, long before Robin transitioned into a woman, the gender-confused teenager experienced a lot in a little amount of time. Having just graduated high school and finally feeling free, Robin found herself at a lot of parties. At the time, being known by her birth name, Robert, or Robbie for short, Robbie always knew he was different than the other boys in the party scene.

Although he never truly came out of the closet, Robbie knew he was always attracted to men. With no real knowledge of transgender people at the time and thinking that there were only two options of 'straight' and 'gay,' Robbie figured he was gay by default. That is, until one summer party.

While at a house party one warm summer night, Robbie met his destiny… Rowena. Rowena was the most beautiful girl that Robbie had ever laid eyes on. She had long curly hair that was as brown as her smooth, tanned skin. She had a nice pair of boobs, a thin waist and a big butt that made the boys go wild. She was a local boy's dream and Robbie was that local boy.

Rowena was a party girl and loved going out. She was a lot of fun, but got into a lot of trouble. You never knew what was going to happen when Rowena was around. For some reason, that sort of spontaneity and danger, mixed with her gorgeous looks really attracted Robbie to her. He was enamored with her, but this confused Robbie completely. At an age where hormones are raging and everyone is trying to figure out their sexual identity, Robbie decided that maybe his 'gay-ness' was just a phase.

Looking like a young Duke Kahanamoku, Robbie was a good-looking guy and Rowena quickly took notice. They started to hang around each other, partying together, getting into trouble, fooling around and before they knew it, they were a couple.

Four short years and three sons later, the couple had rapidly become a family of five. Now in their early twenties and suddenly parents of three beautifully brown baby boys, reality set in. They had no money and no life to call their own.

With their fun careless nights having long faded away and Robbie starting to feel attracted to men again, it was then that Robbie realized that he didn't want to be with Rowena, but instead, he wanted to *be* her; not Rowena specifically, but he now understood that he longed to be a woman. His obsession with Rowena's curvy body was because he wanted female curves of his own. He wanted long curly hair and feminine facial features. He always knew he was different than the other boys and having never really felt right in his body, he finally knew why.

After doing the hard task of confessing his truth to Rowena, Robbie began his journey toward becoming a female. Rowena tried her best to handle the predicament, but the weight of motherhood and having a partner come out as transgender sent her into a downward spiral. Being too much for her at such a young age, Rowena started to party again to drown the pain of reality. Little by little, Rowena got into harder and harder drugs. She would go missing for a day or two at a time and soon enough, she completely ran away.

Now being a single parent with three young sons to take care of, Robbie knew he couldn't do it alone. With the help of his mom, who raised Robbie as a single parent herself, Robbie was able to provide for his sons and complete his transition toward becoming female. However, knowing that he was the biggest factor in Rowena's disappearance, Robbie has always harbored a feeling of guilt.

* * *

"Wait, where is she? Is she here?" Malu asks in reference to Robin.

"Yeah, they took her into the operating room," Kaleo responds. "I wasn't allowed in there, so I've been waiting until I was given the green light."

"Well, let's go see her." Malu takes out his IVs and gets out of his hospital bed.

"Malu, what are you doing?!" Ashley shrieks.

"I just said they wouldn't let me in. They're not gonna let you in either," Kaleo tries to reason with his brother.

"Listen to yourself! Our dad might die. That's what you just said, right? I'm not gonna just sit around until she does. I'm gonna see her, whether they let me or not." Malu turns around and walks out of the room.

Knowing that Malu is right, Kaleo and Ashley look at each other and then quickly head out of the room trying to catch up to him.

24. Liquid Marijuana

- 3/4 oz Spiced Rum
- 3/4 oz Midori Melon Liqueur
- 3/4 oz Malibu Coconut Rum
- 3/4 oz Blue Curaçao
- 1 oz Sweet & Sour
- 1 oz Pineapple Juice

Back at Violet, the fundraiser is over and the night has come to an end. The guests have left and the staff clean up the aftermath.

"What a night, huh?" Parker initiates conversation with Momi.

Being the only two at the front bar, Momi knows he's speaking to her. Even after all of the hype from just a few hours ago, she still doesn't know how to talk to him normally. Trying to keep conversation at a minimum and not knowing exactly what to say, she continues cleaning and responds with a mere, "Yeah, it was."

Parker expected the short answer, but didn't expect the lack of eye contact. Having not had a real conversation with his now ex-girlfriend in weeks, he decides to take this time to do just that.

"Hey," he says gently to get her to look in his direction.

Momi looks over her shoulder and awaits nervously for the next few words to come out of his mouth. *Please don't tell me you still love me*, she thinks to herself. *I can't handle that right now.*

However, instead of saying anything, he just stares at her. His face isn't exactly expressionless. It isn't happy, mad or sad either. There's a familiar calm in his eyes that Momi starts to remember. They stare right into each other's eyes, both not saying a word. It's as if time has frozen around them. As Parker looks into Momi's dark brown eyes, he notices her face change as she fights to hold back tears.

"I'm sorry, Parker. I'm so sorry." Momi can't hold it in any longer. She breaks the silence with tears falling down her face.

Parker smirks and gets closer to her. He grabs her and hugs her tightly. It wasn't his intention to make her cry, but he's happy that they're making progress. Anything is better than the silent treatment.

Momi cries into Parker's chest and wipes her tears on his T-shirt. "I never meant to hurt you. I swear. I don't even think I fully realized what was going on. I didn't realize I was that *in* to girls until that one incident with the ice cream girl."

"Simone," Parker interrupts.

"Yeah, her. I was devastated when she left. I don't even know why." Momi wipes away her tears and pulls away from the hug. "I blamed it on you and ran away. After that, I started to hang out with Tisha and well… one thing lead to another. And please don't be mad at her. I was the one who initiated everything. I had to convince her that we were in an open relationship, which we were, but…"

"…not with close friends," they both say in unison.

"I know… and that's where I have to apologize." She pauses and then picks up, "I love you, Parker. You've given me the best three years of my life. You've been there for me every single time, you've seen me at my worst, but most of all, you've been my best friend," her eyes fill up with tears again, "and I'm really scared I'm gonna lose that."

Parker starts to tear up too. They look at each other, then hug again. "I fell in love with you from the first time we hung out. We all went bowling, remember?" Parker reminds Momi. "There was something so different about you, so confident and carefree, but… caring, in an ironic way. That hasn't changed. You're still that spicy Hawaiian-Latina girl, but you're just not my spicy girl anymore… and I'm coming to terms with that." Parker exhales hard and quickly rubs his eyes to make it seem like he wasn't crying in a very straight guy way.

"I want you to know that I'm not mad. I'm not mad at Tisha, either. I mean, I was at first, but it was mostly because I was in shock and it hurt my pride. Oh, and the lies. The lies didn't help," Parker jokes to lighten the mood, "but I'm not mad. I'm happy that you're happy and that you're finding who you really are because that's all I care about.

"You know, I fell in love with you quickly, but I don't think falling out of love with you will be as fast, so I ask that you just let me love you from afar for now. I won't intervene and I won't make it awkward, I promise, but if you ever catch me looking your way… just give me a signal to know that you've received it, alright?" Momi smiles and winks her signature wink. Without any words needed, Parker understands that her wink will be that signal.

"Or you could just flash me your tits," Parker jokes to do away with all the sad sentimentality. Momi's jaw drops and scoffs. She slaps him on his arm like she used to when they were together. "What? You showed everyone else your tits tonight."

"Yeah, that was your fault!" Momi says in a jokingly angry way. "You unhooked my bra!"

"Still got it!" Parker says smugly and flashes his eyebrows.

From the back bar, Beau and Tisha watch Parker and Momi interact.

"Seems like they've made up, huh?" Beau comments.

"Yeah… I'm happy for them." Tisha smiles, not taking her eyes off the two, who are now playfully fighting.

178

"Maybe she's turning straight again," Beau tries to stir up some shit.

"Well, she's straighter than you'll ever be." Tisha walks away and leaves Beau by himself.

"I'm not gay!" Beau yells, but Tisha pretends not to hear.

Just then, the Fish y Chicks pass the backbar with all of their luggage in tow. Alexus leads the group with Arita and Matt following closely behind. Bringing up the rear, with her big derrière, is Karmen. As she passes Beau, she blows him a kiss and says, "Good night."

Beau clears his throat and tries to make his voice deeper than it usually is, to sound more masculine and straight, "Ahem. Good night, yeah, uh, good night." He looks around to see if anyone is watching. With no one in sight, Beau's eyes follow Karmen's butt bouncing on the way out of the club. He starts to imagine what he would do to that ass.

"I see you." Tisha comes out of nowhere catching Beau red-handed.

"What? I was just saying bye," Beau tries to defend himself.

"Mmhmm, sure. And I'm the first black pope," Tisha says sarcastically.

Outside the club, the Fish y Chicks pass Chico and Sam who are sitting on the ground, leaning up against the club. "Good night!" the queens chant in unison.

"Good night, chicas!" Chico yells back. Sam just waves.

"I can't believe I wasn't there," Sam speaks to himself, but out loud.

"It's ok, brother. Nobody knew it was gonna happen," Chico comforts. "You can't beat yourself up over it." He takes a hit of his vape pen full of his finest weed extract and exhales a small cloud of smoke. He offers his pen to Sam, but Sam declines.

"I know, it's just that... he's my best friend. He always has my back, but the one time that he needed me to have his, I wasn't there." Sam can't seem to release his guilt. "I don't even know if he's ok."

"Hey. Remember my cousin, José? The one that got shot the day of his graduation?" Chico tries to jog Sam's memory, "I beat myself up over it for a long time. 'Why wasn't I there?' 'I should've been there.' 'I shouldn't have joined the military.' 'I shouldn't have left in the first place.'"

"How did you get over it?" Sam asks genuinely.

"Truthfully, it's not something you ever really get over… but you learn how to live with it in a healthy way. Time has a way of healing things and you just have to believe that everything happens for a reason."

"There's no good reason for someone to get stabbed," Sam responds.

"You would think that, but God works in mysterious ways. If I didn't go to the military, I probably would've been with my cousin that day he got shot and I probably would've got shot myself. We'd both be dead and then who would've taken care of my abuela? You know what I mean? It doesn't always make sense, but somehow, someway, you have to make it make sense." Sam nods and starts to understand.

"When my abuela first passed away, she came to me in my dreams. She smiled because she wasn't sick anymore. She told me that she was happy because my mom, my dad and José were there to greet her. Some people may say it's just a dream, but I know, in my heart, that it was her. Ever since that day, I've felt peace knowing that my family is together in heaven, or wherever they are, and that one day, when it's my time to go, they'll be there to greet me too."

Sam wipes away a tear from his left eye. "Damn, man. You didn't have to get me all emotional and shit."

As Sam tries to collect himself, the door to the club opens.

180

Momi, Parker, Tisha, Beau and Yuki all walk out with their bags ready to go.

Momi looks over to her left and notices Chico and Sam sitting on the ground. "You ready, boys?" Momi asks.

"Oh shit, sorry." Sam gets up quickly. "Did you guys finish cleaning already?"

"Yeah, no thanks to you!" Beau says sarcastically.

Sam jerks forward quickly with a clenched fist. He pretends as if he's going to punch Beau in the face. Beau flinches and then cowers behind Tisha.

"Boy, get your wimpy ass away from me," Tisha delivers.

"Everything's all good," Momi brings the conversation back. "We're all heading to the hospital, so grab your stuff and let's go."

"Why? Is he ok? Is Malu ok?" Sam asks and anxiously awaits the verdict.

"Ashley texted—" Momi starts.

"Is he ok?" Sam interrupts, too nervous to wait for the rest of her sentence.

"She said Malu is fine. He'll be back to normal in no time," Momi reveals.

Sam exhales the biggest breath of his life. "Oh thank God! Thank you, God!" He looks up to the sky with his hands clasped together.

Chico walks up to Sam and puts his arm around him, "See brother, you gotta believe!"

"We gotta hurry though," Momi interrupts the tender moment to try and get the boys to move a little faster.

"Why? I thought you said Malu was gonna be alright?" Sam asks.

"We're not going to the hospital for him," Parker suddenly joins the conversation.

"We're going to see Robin," Momi informs.

"Oh shit, Robin! That's right." Sam quickly remembers and puts a spring in his step. The two boys run back inside to grab their belongings before heading to the hospital with the rest of the group.

25. Hawaiian Iced Tea

- 1/2 oz Vodka
- 1/2 oz Light Rum
- 1/2 oz Tequila
- 1/2 oz Gin
- 1/2 oz Triple Sec
- 1 oz Sweet and Sour
- 2 oz Pineapple Juice

In the lobby of the emergency room, Chyna comes running in and heads straight to the check-in counter. Completely out of breath as if she just ran a marathon, she begins frantically asking the receptionist about Robin. Panting in between each word, she asks, "Excuse me… Hi…. yeah… sorry… gotta catch my breath… Woman… tall… Hawaiian… Robin Kāmaka," she uses Robin's real last name, "Is she here?"

"Chyna!" A voice yells from behind her. She turns around and sees Ashley walking toward her with Malu and Kaleo.

"Kids! Oh my God." Chyna notices her best friend's children. She turns and walks away from the receptionist abruptly. Still out of breath, she runs up to the group, but then dramatically plops herself down onto a random seat nearby. "Oh my God… I came… as fast… as I could," she manages to get out between breaths.

"Breathe," Ashley encourages. She hands Chyna a water bottle that she's been carrying around. Chyna grabs the bottle swiftly and downs the whole thing in a matter of seconds.

Finally calming herself down, she asks, "How's everything going? How is she?" She looks at Malu, who's still in his hospital gown. "Malu! Oh my God, I totally forgot about you! Sorry baby. Are you ok? How're you doing?"

"I'm good," Malu responds strongly. "We gotta find Robin."

"What do you mean? Where is she? Can we see her?" Chyna is filled with concern.

"She's in the operating room," Kaleo starts. "They won't let us in to see her."

"Like hell they won't," Malu says under his breath.

"But she's breathing, right?" Chyna asks Kaleo, desperately waiting to hear good news. Malu and Ashley also look at Kaleo awaiting his response.

"She had a pulse when they took her in, but I don't know about now. I can only hope," Kaleo informs the group of what he knows.

"Yes, she *is* breathing!" Malu says strongly trying to convince himself. The image of Robin not breathing is too much for him to handle. "And we're gonna see her right now." He storms off.

"How are we gonna do that?" Chyna asks. Kaleo and Ashley shrug and shake their heads not having any clue. They both know that once Malu is determined to do something, he'll find a way to do it one way or another. They walk briskly through the lobby to catch up with Malu.

At the receptionist desk, Malu asks the heavy set receptionist woman, "Excuse me. Hi, where can I find Robin Kāmaka?" The other three stand behind him looking at each other kind of shocked. Knowing Malu's past, they thought he would have gone for a more radical approach of getting to Robin.

As the receptionist starts searching Robin's name in the computer, a doctor from just behind her overhears the conversation. He's a tall white man, wearing the standard white coat. He walks up to the front and puts his hands on the receptionist's shoulders, as to signal her with, *I'll take it from here.*

" Hi there. I'm Doctor Pike. Who is it that you're looking for?" The doctor asks kindly.

"My da—" Malu interrupts himself, "My mom. Robin Kāmaka." He figures it would be too much hassle to explain in detail how Robin is his dad and technically, Robin played both their mom and dad growing up.

"Yes, yes." Doctor Pike, having dealt with many transgender people in the past, understands exactly why Malu hesitated when answering. "I'm afraid she's in critical condition. If you'd like to see her, I can take you to her."

"Yes!" Chyna jumps into the conversation hastily. "Please take us."

"I'm sorry, ma'am. We can only take blood relatives at this time. Are you related?" Dr. Pike asks.

There's a brief pause in the conversation before Kaleo takes the lead, "Yes, this is her sister. She's my aunty." He lies trying to get Chyna to see her best friend. "I'm also Robin's son."

Dr. Pike looks at Chyna, who looks nothing like Robin or the two boys. He knows they are probably lying, but lets it slide. These situations can be very sensitive. He turns his focus now to Ashley, "And you, miss?"

Now that they got Chyna in, Ash doesn't want to push it any further. She looks at the group and then to Dr. Pike, "Um, I'm not related." Malu's eyes widen trying to say, *Why didn't you just lie?*

"It's ok. Go guys. Hurry! I'll be fine, I promise. I'll be out here," Ashley reassures. The group each take their turn hugging Ash to say sorry for leaving her behind. Last in line is Malu.

"I love you." Malu grabs her face.

"I know, babe. Go. She needs you," Ashley directs. The couple kiss, then break away.

"Shall we?" Dr. Pike asks. The group nods and they hurry quickly to see Robin. Being left behind, Ashley finds a comfortable seat in the lobby and sits in a trance trying to take in all that has happened in one night.

About fifteen minutes go by and Ashley hasn't moved from her spot. Still staring off into space, she doesn't notice the entire Violet gang walk into the lobby. With Momi leading the pack, she spots Ashley like a hawk to a prey and heads in her direction.

"Ash!" Momi says as loud as she can without yelling. She doesn't want to be rude to the others in the lobby. However, Ashley doesn't notice and continues in her daydream. Thinking she probably didn't hear her, Momi walks right up to her cousin. Now with the entire Violet gang standing right in front of her, Ashley still doesn't notice them and looks right past them as if she's been hypnotized.

"ASH!" Momi says standing right in front of her. Finally being awoken from her spell, Ashley looks up from her seat and sees her cousin and all of her friends.

"Oh my God. Hey! Where did you guys come from?" Ashley is still half-dazed. She gets up and starts hugging everyone hello.

"How's Malu?" Momi asks.

"He's good. He'll be ok," Ashley answers.

"Where is he?" Sam jumps into the conversation wanting to see his best friend.

"Uh, they just went in to see Robin," Ashley replies.

"Why didn't you go with them? You didn't have to wait for us," Momi scolds.

"I can't. I mean... we all can't." Ashley pauses knowing that she's not being very clear. She tries to find the best way to explain, "They won't let any of us in unless we're blood-related."

"Aw man, that sucks," Parker comments.

Lowering her voice so that none of the workers can hear her, Ashley admits, "Well, we managed to get Chyna in, but I didn't want to push it."

"That's right! Chyna left the club as soon as the show ended," Momi fills her cousin in on the details. "Well, I'm glad she's in there. I think she would've been a nervous wreck if she had to wait out here."

"You should've seen her run in. I've never seen her move so fast in my life," Ashley jokes. "Well, thanks for coming guys. I know Robin will really appreciate it, but truthfully as for right now, there's not much else we can do except wait."

The group understands and slowly disperses. Some of them find a seat, while others go outside for some fresh air. Momi and Ashley take a seat next to each other and continue in their own private conversation.

"I'm sorry I just left you guys," Ashley apologizes.

"Girl, shut up!" Momi responds. "You're apologizing for taking your boyfriend, who was stabbed, to go get help? Don't be stupid. You did what any sane person would've."

Ashley looks at her hands and reimagines what they looked like with Malu's blood on them. "I was so scared, cousin." She starts to tear up, "I never thought about what would happen if I ever lost him." Momi puts her arm around her cousin and rubs her back trying to comfort her. "There was blood everywhere. It's probably still all over my car."

"It's ok, babe," Momi consoles. "All of that doesn't matter now. He's ok, right?" Ashley nods. "Then that's all that matters. You did everything you were supposed to and because of you, he's going to be fine. I'm proud of you." Ashley looks up and into Momi's eyes. They share a smile before embracing each other. "Let's just hope for the same with Robin."

26. Dark and Stormy

- 2 oz Black Rum
- 4 oz Ginger Beer

"Here she is," Dr. Pike says as he finishes ushering Kaleo, Malu and Chyna to a random hospital room. "Remember, she's not in great shape. I'll give you a moment with her." He turns around and walks away.

At the door to the room, the three 'blood-relatives' share a brief moment. They are unsure of what they are about to see. Chyna takes a big breath for the group and exhales audibly. "Let's go, boys."

As they enter, they see Robin on a hospital bed completely incapacitated. She's pale and still. There's numerous tubes going in and out of her body, her heart beats on the monitor and even with everything helping her, they can tell she's having a hard time breathing. Completely deprived of strength and energy, she closes her eyes and drifts in and out of consciousness. The trio walk up to her bedside and gently try to get her to open her eyes.

"Hey sis," Chyna starts. "We're here." She pulls up a chair next to the bed and touches her arm softly to try to wake her up.

"Hi Robin," Kaleo takes his turn from the other side of the bed. "Are you awake?"

At an early age, the boys saw their father physically turn into a female. But being so young, they barely have any memories of it. Knowing that she didn't want them to continue calling her 'Dad' after or during her transition, Robin thought it best that the boys would simply call her by her name. So, that's what they did. When speaking about her or to her, 'Robin' was the selected proper noun. Robin did think of having her sons call her 'Mom', but she didn't want to disrespect Rowena. *They have a mother*, she thought, *she's just not present.*

At the foot of the bed, but keeping his distance, Malu is silent. He's unsure of what he's feeling and what to say. Leaning with his back up against the wall and arms crossed, he decides to let Chyna and Kaleo do the talking.

"Robin, we're here," Kaleo tries again. "Wake up."

Struggling to open her eyes, Robin slowly opens one eye and then the other. She looks straight ahead and notices Malu first, "My son…" She musters enough energy to say those two words. That one line alone causes her to lose her breath and start into a violent coughing fit.

That's all it takes, Malu's backseat approach quickly dissolves. He bursts into tears and runs to her side, kneeling right next to Kaleo.

"I'm sorry, Robin," Malu says with tears streaming down his face. Kaleo hugs his brother tight and starts to cry himself. "I'm so sorry. I'm sorry. I'm sorry, Robin." He's not sure what he's saying, but it's all that he can manage to get out.

Finally catching her breath, Robin moves her right hand and touches Malu's face. "Ssshh." She smiles weakly and looks at her two boys. She looks over at Chyna and her face immediately breaks as if she's gonna cry, but she doesn't have enough energy to actually do so.

"Rest, sis. It's ok," Chyna says trying to comfort her best friend. Now with tears in her eyes as well, she pets Robin's forehead and continues saying, "Rest, babe."

After gathering enough breath, Robin weakly asks, "Lopaka?"

None of them know exactly how to answer, so Chyna takes the lead, "He's in LA, babe. Remember?" Robin nods, having had her memory jogged. She wishes all three of her sons were there, but doesn't harp on it.

Kaleo takes out his phone and quickly texts Lopaka again, *GET YOUR ASS HOME NOW!*

"This is just like him, always missing when something important happens, when we need him!" Kaleo says with contempt. His frustration with always having to act like the oldest brother has reached its peak.

"Ssshhh," Robin hushes her son. "It's ok. Love him. Take care of him. Take care of each other. Promise me." Kaleo and Malu both nod in assurance. She looks to Chyna and touches her chest, "Thank you. Thank you, my friend." She pauses as tears fall from her face. "Take care of my boys, ok? I love you." Chyna nods while crying and trying to put on a smile for her friend.

With barely any breath left in her body, she looks back to her sons and smiles weakly, "Find your mom... Tell her I'm sorry." The boys look at each other in confusion. They were always told that their mother was a deadbeat drug addict not worth knowing, but wanting to give Robin whatever she wants, they nod in agreement. "I love you... with all my heart..."

Her eyes roll back and shut. Her head plops back heavily against the pillow and her heart monitor flat lines. The moment they were all fearing had finally arrived.

Chyna immediately runs out into the hallway and yells, "HELP! PLEASE SOMEONE HELP!"

A couple of nurses nearby run into the room and start working on Robin right away. "I'm going to need you to step back please," one of the nurses asks of Kaleo and Malu. Malu, who has been holding Robin's hand, doesn't want to let go. "I'm sorry sir, I'm going to need you step back please," the nurse reiterates. Knowing that this is their only chance at reviving their father, Kaleo grabs his brother and pulls him back. He bears hugs him from behind and they both watch the nurses go to work.

Dr. Pike finally walks in and starts speaking to the nurses in medical lingo. "Is the defibrillator ready?" They hook Robin up to the machine and send an electrical current through her body to get her heart to start up again.

With everything feeling like it's going in slow-motion, Kaleo looks over at Chyna, who has also stepped back and watches with her hands over her mouth. He looks at his brother, who is crying in his arms and then looks at Robin. He notices her body and face is lifeless and realizes... she's gone.

The group of medical professionals continue this routine for what seems like hours, but in actuality has only been a few minutes. The nurses continue to perform, but look to Dr. Pike for the next orders. Dr. Pike looks down and realizes there's no use continuing. "Damn it," he whispers under his breath, then to one of the nurses says, "Call it."

"Calling it. Time of Death, 1:32am."

Having been restricted to the lobby of the hospital, the group of Violet employees have run out of things to talk about. All sitting quietly and staring at their phones, they wait for any sort of news; good or bad.

Ashley texts Malu for the sixth time, "How's she doing?" but again there's no reply. *He must've left his phone in his hospital room.* She's been resisting the urge to text Kaleo to give him space, but her need to know how Robin is doing has finally taken over. She opens up a text to him, but just as she does, Kaleo, Malu and Chyna come walking out into the lobby.

Ashley and Momi are the first to notice. They get up out of their seats and run to the trio. The other employees get up a second later and start heading in that direction as well.

"What happened? Is she ok? Can we go see her?" Ashley spits a million questions a minute. Malu looks at his girlfriend and without saying anything, shakes his head.

"She's gone." Kaleo delivers the bad news, then begins to cry heavily. Having held it together until that moment, he covers his face and begins to shake. Chyna grabs him and hugs him tight. She tries to console him, but starts to cry herself.

"It's ok, baby. It's ok. Let it out," Chyna whispers to him.

Parker walks up to the two of them and silently lips the words "I got it," to Chyna. He motions to hand Kaleo over to him and she does. Kaleo looks up and sees his best friend with open arms. He quickly latches on to him hugging him tight and crying into his chest. Parker hugs him back, kisses his forehead and lets him get it all out. Being much taller than Kaleo, Parker rests his chin on the top of Kaleo's head. "Sshh, it's ok."

Ashley immediately hugs Malu and thinks about how she could've lost him tonight as well. "I'm so sorry baby, I'm so so sorry," she sniffles. Malu nods, but doesn't say anything. He does his best not to cry in front of everybody.

Sam walks up to the couple and let them have their moment of intimacy. Once Ashley breaks away, Sam swoops in and hugs Malu, picking him up off the floor.

"Ow! Ow!" Malu shouts out. His puncture from getting stabbed is still sensitive.

"Oh shit! Sorry bro." Sam puts him down and goes for the bro-hug instead. "I'm sorry, man. I wasn't there for you. That's messed up."

"Nah, it's not like that," Malu reassures his friend. "There were like five guys acting all dumb, so I let 'em. I told them just to move along, you know how we do, try and keep calm, but then they tried to go in the club. I stopped them and then they got all nuts. Brah, I would've had all of those guys too if it wasn't for that one guy with the knife. It was a cheap shot, sneak attack."

"Brah, I'm sorry. For real," Sam continues to apologize.

"Sam, stop. It's not your fault. K?" Malu looks his friend right in the eyes. Sam nods in agreement.

"I'm sorry about Robin."

"Me too, man. Me too."

27. Bay Breeze

- 1 1/2 oz Vodka
- 2 oz Cranberry Juice
- 2 oz Pineapple Juice

About a month goes by and while things have settled, keeping Violet open and running is still a high point of stress. With the fundraiser having been a mediocre success, they were still able to come up with enough money to pay off all the past debts and cover three more months of rent; this month and the next two months. However, still needing money for the future, Kaleo wonders how he's supposed to pay the Wongs once these next two months are over.

"What are we gonna do? Have a fundraiser every month?! That's gonna look so suspicious, especially when nothing changes at the club. Everybody's gonna wonder where their fundraising money is going to," Kaleo asks Chyna all stressed out.

"Don't worry about that now, babe," Chyna consoles, but knows that she has no clue either. "Let's just focus on this and enjoy today. Let's not let it pass us by because that would be unfair to her."

Today is Robin's funeral or a celebration of Robin's life, as they would prefer it to be called. Different than most funerals, Kaleo, Malu and Chyna decided to hold the commemoration at her favorite beach on the west side of O`ahu named Yokohama. Seeing that Yokohama, or Yokes to the locals, was where Robin basically grew up and brought her sons when they were growing up, they knew it had to be her final resting place.

"Do you have the ashes?" Kaleo asks Malu.

"Yeah, I set it up on the table, next to her photo," Malu

answers.

For her ceremony, there's two large tents made of silver pipes with gray tarp roofing and there's tables and chairs by the many. Toward the center of the two tents, a smaller table is placed with a photo of Robin smiling and an urn of her ashes. With more flower leis than can fit the tiny table, Malu starts dressing the ground around the table with flowers as a next best option.

"How many people do we expect to come out?" Malu looks to his brother and Chyna as he continues to set up.

Kaleo shrugs, "I don't know."

"I put the word out there in the newspaper and on every social media platform, so we'll see. She knows a lot of people," Chyna informs.

"Thanks for doing that, by the way," Kaleo thanks.

"Of course. Anything for my best friend," Chyna responds. She looks over to the photo and smiles. "Love you, sis," she whispers to herself. She blows a kiss to the photo and goes back to work.

Having come down to the beach early to reserve the best spot, Kaleo, Malu and Chyna are the only three setting up. Wanting this celebration to be less formal and more casual, like a picnic with friends, they figured they wouldn't need that much help getting everything arranged, but now they wish they had a few other hands.

"Sup bitches!"A voice comes from behind them. It's Yuki walking toward them with his arms full of paper plates, cups and utensils. "Oh, shit, sorry. Am I not supposed to swear at this kind of thing. Oh shit, I said shit." Almost like instant karma, and in true Yuki fashion, he trips and falls, throwing everything he is holding into the air. "I'm ok. I'm ok."

Behind him, Parker and Sam follow Yuki carrying trays of food and other decorations. "We come bearing gifts," Parker announces from a few feet away.

Kaleo's face lights up when he sees his best friend. He didn't expect to see them 'til much later. "Hey!" Kaleo greets Parker and they do their secret handshake from high school.

"We made it!" Sam says and bro-hugs his best friend, Malu.

"Sup Samoan," Malu says

"Sup Hawaiian. How's the ribs?" Sam asks.

Malu lifts up his shirt and shows his scar that's still healing. "Brah, cherry! Ready for round two!"

"Das right! And I'll be there this time! We goin' lick those fuckahs!" Sam eggs his friend on. They both scream, "CHEEEEE-HOOOOOOO!"

"Alright, calm down you two bozos," Chyna interjects.

"Malu, how are you gonna beat anybody up when you cannot even get in the ocean? The salt water would kick your ass," Kaleo makes fun of his brother.

"I'm melting, I'm melting," Yuki teases with a reference from *The Wizard of Oz*.

"Shut up, Yuki!" Malu flexes and fake advances at Yuki. Yuki cowers to the other side of the tent.

"Anyway, thank you guys for coming. I know it's early," Kaleo says to the three who just arrived, but mostly to Parker. "Is it only the three of you?"

"Well, I picked the two of them up and we carpooled it here. Chico and his boyfriend were following me in their own car, but I think I lost them. You know how they are… 'slower.'" Parker puts and imaginary doobie to his lips and implies that they probably smoked a bunch of weed and got sidetracked. He looks back to where his car is parked and sees another car parking right behind him. "Actually, I think that's them pulling up now." Parker changes gears, "Ok, what needs to be done?"

"Well, if you guys want to start setting up the food table, that would really help."

"I'm on it." Parker heads over to the far side of the tent and puts his trays of food down.

With their eyes all red and walking at a leisurely pace, Chico and his boyfriend Riley finally reach the tents. In one hand, chico holds a bouquet of flowers and in the other, he holds a tiny chihuahua-fox terrier.

"Oh my God! He's so cute!" Chyna puts her face right up to the puppy and he licks her on the nose. "Awww, can I carry him?"

"Sure." Chico hands the dog over to her.

"He's so small. What's his name? Is it even a boy?" Chyna flips the dog on his back to check if he has a penis.

Chico laughs, "Yes, he's a boy."

"A *gay* boy!" Riley adds. The whole group laughs.

"Yes, our little gay baby boy," Chico corrects himself. "We named him José, after my cousin."

"Awww, that's so sweet," Chyna comments. José starts to squirm, so she puts him down on the ground. He runs right up to Sam and stops. He looks up and just stares.

"Look guys, David and Goliath," Yuki jokes looking at the huge size difference between Sam and the puppy.

"He likes you," Chico says to Sam.

"Oh yeah?" Sam picks up the dog and places him on his left shoulder. José doesn't get scared. In fact, he looks comfortable as if he's been up there a million times before. "I like him too."

"Makes sense," Chico starts, "If José were still with us, the both of you would've gotten along really well."

Sam looks at the puppy on his shoulder and smiles. He starts talking to him quietly. "Sup José. You wanna help us set up this table?"

An hour goes by and the rest of the Violet employees start to filter in. Momi and Tisha arrive together, Beau drives himself and the four Fish y Chicks show up crammed in Alexus' beat up Toyota Camry. Ashley is the last of the employees to show up, but with her kids and parents in tow, it came as no surprise to anyone.

"Hey cuz!" Momi says to Ashley as she and her family arrive.

"Hi cousin!" Ashley responds. "Sorry we're late. Had to wrangle these kolohes (*kolohe* is a hawaiian word meaning 'rascal')!" She motions to her kids.

"Hi Uncle! Hi Aunty!" Momi says to Ashley's parents as they walk up. She kisses them both on the cheek.

"Eh behbeh girl! How you?" Ashley's dad, Bruce, greets his niece. Nearby and hearing a familiar voice, Chyna turns around and notices her old friends.

"Eh Bruce! Oh my God, Grace! I haven't seen you guys in forever." Chyna heads over to greet Ashley's parents.

"You guys know each other?" Ashley and Momi say in unison. They didn't know Ashley's parents knew Chyna.

"Oh we go way back when! From high school time," Ashley's mom, Grace, enlightens the two girls.

"Back when she was Chuckie," Ashley's dad says nonchalantly.

"Bruce!" Grace whacks her husband on the arm.

"What? She was." Bruce is confused. He questions himself, *That is Chuckie, right?*

"Sorry. He doesn't know any better," Grace apologizes for her husband.

Chyna drops her voice low to a male's bass level, "Oh you mean, when I would talk like this?" The three old friends crack up.

"I'm sorry for your loss," Grace offers, "We came to pay our respects. I know how close you two were."

"Yeah, we were. We had a good run, though." Chyna looks

over at Robin's photo and talks to it as if Robin were standing there herself, "Yeah, you old bitch?" The three old friends share a laugh again.

A few more hours go by and the group gets larger and larger, expanding past the two tents that were originally set up. Thankfully, in true Hawaiian style, a lot of people brought their own tents and umbrellas and set up on the beach around the site respectfully. Friends and family from all over come to celebrate Robin's life; people who haven't seen each other in years. Kaleo, Malu and Chyna stand near each other and take a look around.

"Wow, there's a lot of people here," Malu says to the other two.

"The entire LGBT community is here," Chyna says with her eyes watering with how happy she is to see the support of her people. Malu rubs her back to comfort her.

Kaleo looks around at everyone laughing, drinking and having a good time. "Yeah, everyone, except her own son."

"Lopaka isn't coming?" Chyna asks.

"I wouldn't know," Kaleo responds, "I've tried calling him, texting him… I don't even know if he knows that Robin's dead. Fuck, for all I know, he could be dead too."

"Don't say that, Leo!" Malu scolds his brother, but knows that he could be right. "Screw him. This day is about Robin. That's all that matters right now. We'll deal with the rest later, k?" Kaleo nods his head in agreement.

"Alright, well, I guess we should get this ceremony started, huh?" Chyna suggests. She and the two boys head up to the middle of the tent, next to Robin's photo.

"Hi guys! Can we gather round please. We're gonna start the ceremony," Chyna announces loudly to get everyone's attention. The numerous amount of small groups quickly combine

199

together and make one big group facing Robin's altar.

"Aloha everyone! God, it makes my heart so warm to see so many people here. I know Robin is thankful for all of you showing up." She clears her throat, "I know a lot of you here, but… I'm Chyna and these are her two sons, Kaleo and Malu." The two boys wave to greet the crowd of people. "Lopaka, her oldest son, couldn't be with us today, but that's ok, he's with us in spirit.

"Robin was my best friend. She was my rock. She was my husband before I had a husband." The group shares a laugh as Chyna looks over at her actual husband and smiles. "She was everything that I wasn't, you know? Smart, poised… she could sing, she could dance, she could cheer. Boy could she cheer! We were cheerleaders back in high school, you know! Well, I mean, we weren't on the team, but that didn't stop us." The group laugh amongst themselves again.

"I remember this one time, a long time ago, I was dating this guy; a real jealous type. You know the kind, the kind that gets real hot-headed and physical too. He would lose his temper about God knows what and then he would hit me. Of course, he would always blame it on me, tell me he was doing it because he loved me… and I believed him. So, I wouldn't tell anyone and I would hide the bruises… until, one day, he gave me a black eye. There was no hiding that, you know? I remember running to Robin's house, not knowing what to do. She took me in, took care of me as she always did and I slept over that night.

"The next morning, I woke up and went home. There were a bunch of messages on my answering machine like he always would, 'I'm sorry babe. Please come back,' blah blah blah. Next thing I know, there's a knock at my door. I open it and it's him… with *two* black eyes. I started to crack up in his face because I knew those were from Robin. She went to his house while I was sleeping and cracked him two good ones. I slammed

200

the door in his face and never saw him again." The audience starts clapping and cheering.

"That's just the kind of person Robin was. She wasn't afraid of anything or anyone. She was always so confident, she was even my confidence when I didn't have any. So, sis…" She looks over to her picture, "Thank you for everything you've ever done for me. You've been my number one fan my entire life and I know you're still cheering me on from heaven." Chyna's voice breaks and she begins to tear up. "I love you and this world will never be the same without you." She steps back to signal that she's finished speaking.

Kaleo steps forward and pulls Malu forward as well, "Hi everyone. Well, first of all, my brother and I just want to thank all of you for coming out today. It really means a lot to us to see you all here." *If only Lopaka could have made the same effort*, he thinks. Just as Kaleo has that thought, a red car pulls up behind his truck. In the distance, he watches as a familiar looking guy gets out of the driver's seat and starts to make his way over to the tents.

Being completely consumed with trying to make out who he is, Kaleo is oblivious to the fact that he's standing in front of the crowd silent. Not having spoken for an awkward amount of time, Malu elbows him to get him to focus.

"Ahem, sorry. Um— Like I was saying, my brother and I—" He looks up again and realizes the familiar looking guy is none other than his older brother, Lopaka. He stops mid-sentence and looks at Malu.

Malu looks back at his brother confused and then looks over in the direction that Kaleo was staring. He sees Lopaka for himself and finally puts the pieces together.

"I'm sorry. Will you excuse me for a second?" Kaleo leaves in the middle of his speech and heads off quickly. Only a couple steps behind him, Malu follows Kaleo, who is now walking with a stern stride. Some of the guests follow the brothers with their eyes, while others look at each other with confusion.

Chyna realizing exactly what's happening, but not wanting to take anything away from Robin's reception decides to take the lead. "Well, it's been quite an emotional time for all of us and I think the boys just need to take a moment right now, so let's just take a small break and we'll start back up in a few minutes. Please everyone, go eat! There's tons of food. Don't be shy!"

Ashley and Momi, who are now aware that Lopaka has just showed up, quickly get up and stand next to Chyna. Speaking quietly, trying to keep the guests unaware of the situation, Momi asks, "Should we go over there?"

"No, let them go," Chyna suggests. "Let them hash it out."

 Halfway to the tents, Lopaka walks toward his brothers in his nice black button up shirt, black slacks and slippers. His sunglasses hide his eyes and he holds a lei in his left hand. As his brothers get closer, he opens his arms to initiate a hug.

Finally getting close enough to Lopaka, Kaleo shoves him backward forcefully. "Where the FUCK were you?" Lopaka falls on his ass and the entire group of guests gasp and watch the drama unfold.

"WHAT THE FUCK, KALEO?!" Lopaka yells from the ground. He picks himself back up and darts toward Kaleo, shoving his brother this time. Kaleo falls back, but doesn't fall down. The two boys head at each other like two bulls seeing red. Being completely taken over by his pent up rage, Kaleo tackles Lopaka to the ground. The two brothers wrestle on the beach kicking up sand everywhere.

Ashley's dad, Bruce, and a couple of the older uncles start heading in the boys direction to try and break it up, but Chyna stops them, "Let them go! Let 'em go, Bruce."

Being completely unready for this fight, Lopaka is at a disadvantage. He knew his brothers were probably going to be angry with him, but he didn't expect this. "What's your fucking problem, Leo?!" Lopaka yells while they're still rolling around in the sand.

"What's MY problem? FUCK YOU, PAKA!"

Malu, who was standing back for a second, now gets in between the two brothers. Being the youngest, but the only one who wrestled back in high school, he easily pulls them apart and pushes them in different directions. He looks to Lopaka first and points a finger at him, "Wait there." He quickly walks up to Kaleo and tries to reason with him.

"I know you're pissed. I'm pissed too, but look..." Malu motions toward the tents where everyone is watching. "This is not the way, Leo. This is not the way Robin would have wanted it. Especially not today. Take a lap and calm yourself down. I'll go talk to Paka." Kaleo turns around and walks toward his truck.

Malu heads back toward Lopaka. He throws up his hands and shakes his head. Calmly he starts, "Brah... what the fuck? Where you been?" Lopaka is hesitant and braces himself as Malu approaches. He's not sure if he's about to get another surprise attack. This time, Malu opens his arms and initiates the hug. Lopaka drops his guard and accepts his brother's hug. They hold each other tightly for a good ten seconds before letting go.

"I'm sorry. I'm sorry, brother. I'm sorry I wasn't here," Lopaka apologizes with tears in his eyes.

"Come." Malu pats Lopaka's back and ushers him toward Kaleo's truck. Trying to cool off, Kaleo sits on the tailgate of his truck smoking a cigarette.

"I thought you quit," Lopaka remarks regarding Kaleo smoking again.

"And I thought you were a decent human being, but I guess

we were both wrong," Kaleo comes back sarcastically.

"Alright, alright," Malu cuts the two off from cutting each other down. "Look Paka… truth is, a lot of shit went down and we could've used your help. That's why Leo's so mad and, honestly, I'm pissed too. You got a lot of explaining to do."

"I know and I'm sorry. I'm sorry, guys. I'm sorry I wasn't there. I'm sorry you guys had to carry the burden of everything on your own. I really am. I know you're mad and you have every right to be, but I promise you it's not what it seems." Lopaka takes a deep breath before he continues.

"I know I went to LA in a hurry. I didn't even say bye to you Malu and I'm sorry about that too. I didn't say goodbye to Robin either, but you know…" He looks up to the sky to try and keep his tears from falling, "Add it to my list of regrets, I guess." Kaleo and Malu listen quietly, but still wait for Lopaka to explain why he never called."I know I ran away to LA, but I never ignored your calls. I promise you that."

"Then what the fuck happened? Huh? Lost your phone? You could've found other ways, Paka," Kaleo says with heat still in his tone.

"No, they took away my phone," Lopaka reveals.

"What? Who's 'they?'" Malu asks, thinking Lopaka was in prison or something.

"You're never gonna believe this, but… I was on a TV show," Lopaka confesses.

"What?! Which one?" Malu asks half-amused, half-skeptical.

"I got on 'America's Next Top Drag Queen.'"

"Shut up, Lopaka. You're such a liar," Kaleo says angrily.

"I'm not lying. I promise."

"But weren't you only a drag queen for one night? That one night of the competition thing?" Malu asks.

"Yeah, well, when I was in LA, I saw that they were casting

for the show, so I figured 'Shit, why not?' So, I dressed up in full drag and waited in line with a billion other drag queens. When I got inside, one of the producers said 'Hey, I know you. You're that queen from that video.' Apparently, someone filmed my Fish y Chicks Drag competition piece, put it online and it went all over the internet. The producer liked how weird I was so he put me on the show."

"You're fucking kidding!" Malu is now totally into this story.

"I swear to God. I swear to you guys, I promise. That's why I didn't call. When you're on a reality TV show like that, they take away all of your outside communication. You can't call anyone, text, FaceTime or even use social media. They don't want you letting your friends back home know the rundown of the show like who went home first and who's in the lead. If you're not filming the show, they basically keep you trapped in a hotel room every night with about six channels on the TV and your own thoughts. They want us to all go a little stir-crazy so they can get more drama for the cameras."

"That's nuts," Malu adds.

"Yup and you can imagine how nuts it was when I finally got my phone back filled with texts and voicemails saying that Robin passed away." He breaks down and starts to cry. "I can't believe it. I didn't even know she was sick."

Malu hugs his oldest brother. "Neither did we."

Still trying to catch his breath, "I know you guys have known for awhile, but I just found out yesterday, so I'm still in shock. I booked the first flight I could to get home. I'm trying to process everything, but it's all happening so fast. I'm just happy that I didn't miss this funeral."

Lopaka looks to Kaleo and addresses him personally, "I'm sorry, Kaleo. I really am. I'm sorry you had to carry the burden of everything on your own. That's not your responsibility. I'm the oldest and I should've been the one making all the arrangements."

Kaleo, still sitting on his tailgate with his arms crossed over his chest, starts to cry. Lopaka grabs his brother and hugs him tightly. Malu bear hugs the two of them and the three brothers embrace and cry together.

After they all calm down, the brothers pull apart. "I promise I would've been here earlier if I knew," Lopaka adds as he wipes the snot from his nose. "But I didn't have my phone for the longest time because… guess what…" Kaleo and Malu look at him, not knowing where he's going with it.

Lopaka whispers, "I won."

"SHUT THE FUCK UP!" Malu's jaw drops.

"Are you serious?" Kaleo asks in amazement.

"Yeah, but I'm not supposed to tell anyone, so…" He motions as if he's zipping his lips shut.

"Oh shit, sorry," Malu apologizes.

Now trying to keep it down so that no one hears, Kaleo loudly whispers, "That's crazy, Paka! That's frickin' amazing!"

"I know! And you know what's even more amazing… I won a hundred thousand dollars."

"SHUT THE FUCK UP!" Malu's jaw drops even further.

"Yup, and I'm giving it all to the club," Lopaka springs this information on his brothers.

"Are you serious?" Kaleo asks.

"I got your messages about how the club isn't doing too well, so… now it will. And I've already lined up all my friends from my season, all the other contestants, to come and perform at different times throughout the year too, so that should bring in the crowds."

With tears streaming down his face again, Kaleo throws his arms around Lopaka once more. "Thank you so much, brother. You really don't understand how much this is gonna change everything."

"It's for Dad. Violet was her heart and joy," Lopaka explains. "Oh! There is one catch though... I don't actually have the money yet. When the finale episode airs on TV, which should be in like two months, the producers said they'll wire the hundred grand to my account."

"Wait 'til we tell Chyna!" Kaleo declares.

28. Sex on the Beach

- 1 oz Vodka
- 1/2 oz Peach Schnapps
- 1 oz Orange Juice
- 1 oz Cranberry Juice

Finally finding common ground, the three brothers head to the tents to join the rest of the party. Excited to tell Chyna the good news, Kaleo looks around trying to find her.

"Remember now, I have to keep it a secret," Lopaka reminds his brothers. "If the producers of the show find out that I told anyone, I could lose the win and lose the money. They made me sign a contract, an NDA, so technically, I wasn't even supposed to tell you guys."

"Yeah, no worries," Malu replies.

"So, should we even tell Chyna?" Kaleo asks his brother. "I mean, we gotta tell her, right?"

"Well…" Lopaka thinks it over for a second, "maybe we can let her know that I came up with the cash, but we won't tell her how… at least, not yet." Kaleo and Malu nod in agreement.

"Where is she anyway?" Kaleo wonders out loud. "I'm sure she's dying to see you. You always were her favorite." Lopaka smiles smugly knowing it's the truth.

"There she is," Malu points out. Chyna stands near the food tables having a conversation with three women. The three brothers walk up to her and interrupt.

"Chyna, guess what!" Kaleo says with excitement.

"Oh, boys!" Chyna seems caught off guard, "I see you've made up."

"Yeah, we worked it out," Kaleo quickly gets back to the point, "but you won't believe what Lopaka just told us." Chyna disregards Kaleo's last remark and looks back at the three women and then back at the three boys.

Kaleo stands in confusion. *Don't you want to know what I'm about to tell you?* He notices Chyna's slight awkwardness. *Who are these three women? Chyna doesn't get intimidated easily.*

Kaleo sizes up the three women. He notices that one of the women is older than the other two; a very pretty local aunty type. Although gorgeous for her age, her face shows that she's been through some rough times in the past. Kaleo realizes that the other two women are not women at all, but instead a couple of teenagers. They're the same height and look very similar, *Sisters, for sure. Possibly even twins*, Kaleo thinks, but can't be too sure. Their tanned complexion matches that of the older aunty and they all have the same dark brown eyes. Kaleo puts a story together in his brain, *Oh, these two girls must be her daughters.*

Chyna starts back up with a little hesitation in her voice, "Umm… Boys… This is Rowena…. Your mother." The three brothers stare blankly at her in silence. After having nothing but choice words for each other for the past twenty minutes, they are finally at a loss of words.

"Hi boys," Rowena starts tentatively. The three brothers continue to stare silently as if they've just seen a ghost. "Gosh, you've all grown up to be so handsome. Just like your dad. I'm not sure if you remember me. You were so young." She pauses briefly, "How have you been?"

With the boys still standing silent, Chyna tries to wake the brothers out of their trance. "Well, say hello boys."

"Uh— Hi Aunty. Sorry. I mean, Mom." Malu breaks the silence with his awkward exchange of words. He goes in and kisses her on the cheek out of respect. Kaleo follows and then, Lopaka.

"Sorry. We just never thought we'd ever meet you," Kaleo

tries to explain the reasoning for their shock.

"Yeah, we thought you might be dead," Lopaka says smugly as he throws a jab at Rowena's expense. Having not been by Robin's side when she was passing, Lopaka didn't hear Robin's last words of *Find your mom… Tell her I'm sorry.*

Kaleo elbows Lopaka in the ribs and gives him a stern look that says *Cut it out!* "What he means to say is… we were told that you got hooked on drugs, ran away and no one ever heard from you again."

Rowena pauses and looks at the ground. After a brief moment, she looks back up at the boys and says, "It's true. It is. All of that did happen and I don't know what else to say except I'm sorry." The boys nod, but don't say anything. They await, wanting to hear more.

"It's not like I planned on abandoning you kids. It just sort of happened. I know that doesn't make any sense…" Rowena stops to collect herself. She realizes that she needs to explain in deeper detail.

"I was 23 and I already had three children. I panicked. I wasn't ready to be a mom. I couldn't take care of three kids, I could barely even take care of myself! I tried to suck it up and accept my fate, but when your father told me he was going to turn into a woman, I… I lost it. I freaked out." Rowena breathes heavily. She always knew this day would come.

"It was selfish and I know that now, but I was young and dumb and… I just wanted to escape reality for a bit. I started partying a little again and then a little turned into a lot. I went out with some of my old friends and then got mixed up with the wrong crowds. Pretty soon, I found myself away from you boys for so long, that I felt embarrassed to come home. I don't know how to explain it, but… I was too ashamed to come back. I didn't know how to come back. So, I just didn't… and there's no excuse for that." Rowena covers her face as she starts to cry.

"I live with that guilt every day of my life, I do, but after being out of your lives for so long, I figured it would be easier for you guys if I just stayed out, since I was the one, who left in the first place." She continues to wipe away tears from her eyes, "I hope you boys can find it somewhere in your heart to forgive me. Maybe not right away, but eventually."

Malu, with the toughest exterior, but softest heart, goes up to Rowena and gives her a huge hug. Kaleo and Lopaka stand back and let their brother have his moment.

Curious, Kaleo asks, "How did you hear about Robin's passing?"

"Well, Robbie and I were friends on Facebook and someone posted on her page that they were holding a funeral service here at the beach, so—"

"That was me," Chyna cuts in. "I'm glad to see that my posts were worth it." She looks around at all the guests that are present.

"Who knew? All we would've had to do was search on Facebook and we would've found our mom," Lopaka chimes in slightly sarcastically. He's still unconvinced as to why he should get to know her or even care that she's here.

All of a sudden, Robin's voice echoes through Kaleo's head, *Find your mom...Tell her I'm sorry.* His mind quickly flashes back to Robin laying on a hospital bed and then snaps back to the present moment. With Rowena standing right in front of him and without seconding guessing himself, he blurts out, "Robin says she's sorry."

"What?" Rowena is completely caught off guard.

"She wanted us to find you and say sorry," Kaleo explains, sounding like he just spoke to Robin's spirit.

"What are you talking about, Leo?" Lopaka, having not heard Robin's dying wish, asks in confusion.

"It's true," Chyna cuts in. "On her deathbed, she asked the

boys to find you and apologize for her. I'm not exactly sure why, but I know she's always felt responsible for your disappearance."

Rowena covers her face and bursts into tears, she never thought anyone would understand why she left. However, knowing that Robin, the main person she abandoned, ultimately understood, there's a feeling of relief that starts to unlock within her.

While Rowena gathers herself and calms her breathing, the two girls that she came with step forward and start to console her. Up until now, they have been standing back a few steps and letting Rowena and the boys figure things out.

"And who are they?" Lopaka motions to the two girls. He's still confused as to what exactly is going on.

"Oh, I'm so sorry," Rowena apologizes, still wiping away a few tears, "These are my daughters, Kaimana and Kehau."

"Wait. What?" Lopaka is stunned.

"Daughters?" Kaleo wants to make sure he heard correctly.

"You mean to say that, all of sudden, we now have a mom AND sisters?" Lopaka can't seem to believe the situation.

"Half-sisters," Rowena clarifies, "but yes."

"Look at that boys, a three for one deal," Chyna tries to joke and keep the mood light-hearted. She hopes the boys can stay distracted enough, so they don't realize that she knew Kaimana and Kehau existed this whole time.

"Damn, she does look like you, Kaleo," Malu mentions the resemblance between Kaleo and Kaimana. The two girls wave kindly at the three brothers.

"I'm sorry, but this is way too much for me right now." Having just found out that Robin died yesterday and now having his long lost mother standing right in front of him, Lopaka's mind is on overload. Needing a moment to decompress and comprehend the reality of the situation at hand, he turns and walks away.

"Lopaka!" Kaleo yells for his brother, but Lopaka continues to walk further away. "I'm sorry. It was nice meeting you all," Kaleo addresses Rowena and his two newly found half-sisters. He turns around and chases after Lopaka, leaving Malu as the last brother standing.

Malu looks at Kaimana and Kehau, "So... I have sisters, huh? Right on!" He walks up to them and gives them each a hug. "I don't care what my brothers say, I think it's pretty cool. And don't worry. They'll come around."

Malu smiles, then has a quick change of thought, "Hey, do you guys wanna meet my kids? They'll be stoked to know that they finally have aunties and not just uncles." Malu takes Rowena and his two sisters over to where Ashley and his kids are playing.

On his way trying to catch up to Lopaka, Kaleo runs into Parker.

"Yo!" Parker says jumping in his path. He's holding Chico's dog, José.

"Hey!" Kaleo is slightly startled. Being too focused on catching his brother, he didn't see Parker coming. He notices José in Parker's arm and talks to him, "Hi José. Hey little buddy!"

"You wanna hold him?" Parker offers.

"Sure!" Needing a little warm cuddly love on such a heavy day, Kaleo takes José from Parker and snuggles him tight to his chest.

"Everything ok? I saw you and Lopaka beefing earlier," Parker inquires.

"Yeah, we're all good, but now we have another situation on our hands," Kaleo confesses.

"What do you mean?" Parker questions.

"You see those girls that Malu is walking with over there?" Kaleo tilts his head over and looks in Rowena's direction. He doesn't want to point directly to avoid being too obvious.

"Yeah, I saw Chyna talking to them earlier. Who's that?" Parker asks.

"Well... the older lady is my mom and the other two girls are my sisters that I didn't even know I had," Kaleo discloses matter-of-factly.

"WHAT?!" Parker's eyes widen with sheer shock.

"Yup. Just when I thought this day couldn't get any crazier, BAM! I was wrong." Still holding José, Kaleo shakes his head and shrugs his shoulders.

"I thought you said your mom was some sort of crack head and maybe died on the street or something." Parker repeats what was told to him awhile ago.

"Yeah, that's what we thought too," Kaleo nods his head in agreement.

"She doesn't look like a crackhead," Parker states.

"She's not. I mean, I don't think she is. Maybe she was, but yeah... I don't know." Kaleo's mind races trying to piece together the puzzle of Rowena's life, but having too much on his mind, he can't think clearly.

"Shit, that's crazy, Leo! How are they? How's your mom. Is she cool? Jeez, that sounds so weird coming out of my mouth... your *mom*."

"Trust me, I know. Her name is Rowena. I never even heard Robin mention her name before, but apparently they still kind of kept in contact over Facebook. Leave it to Robin to keep secrets," Kaleo says sarcastically, implying that she kept her health a secret from everyone. "I mean, she's cool, I guess. She apologized for abandoning us and started crying, but I don't know. It's hard to feel anything cause we've lived without her for so long. It's just something that's gonna take time I think."

214

Just as Kaleo finishes his last sentence, José jumps out of his arms and starts running away from them. "Shit!"

"José come back!" Parker yells.

"I'll get him." Kaleo starts running after him feeling like it was his fault.

"No no no, you've got enough on your plate. I'll go get him." Parker stops Kaleo and then runs past him. "I'll catch up with you later." Parker runs after José and Kaleo continues his chase for Lopaka.

"Damn, he's a speedy little fucker," Parker says to himself under breath as he runs after José. He thinks to himself, *I better catch this dog or Chico and Riley are gonna be pissed.* Parker continues in pursuit of José, always trailing just far enough behind him, until he sees José and another dog collide. The two dogs pounce on each other and tumble around on the sand while their tails wag joyfully. *Ah! He probably smelled or heard this dog and wanted to play.* Now knowing that the dogs are playing just a few feet away, Parker stops running and walks up to the two dogs easily.

"José! Come here," Parker commands. Finally paying attention, José turns around and runs up to Parker's legs. Parker kneels down and picks him up and holds him tight, making sure he doesn't run away again. While on one knee, the other dog comes up to Parker and licks him on the hand. It's a small, cute, white Yorkshire Terrier.

Parker pets the other dog and speaks to him kindly, "Hey buddy. Where's your owner, huh?" As he's petting the dog, he realizes that he's seen this dog before. "Wait, I know you." He grabs the the dog's collar and reads the dog tag that's attached.

"Casper! Casper! Come here, Casper!" A female's voice yells in the distance.

Parker looks up and sees Simone, the girl from the ice cream shop, looking around for her dog. "That's how I know!" Parker picks up Casper. Now with José in his left arm and Casper in his right, he walks over to a slightly distressed Simone.

"Hey!" Parker yells while walking in her direction. "I found your dog."

Not noticing that it's Parker yet, Simone comes running over in her Brazilian cut Bikini. "Oh my God! Thank you so much. I was looking all over for him. One minute he was there and then the next—" Finally reaching Parker and the dogs, she realizes who exactly is holding her dog. "Uh— Hi."

"Hey," Parker says with a smile, knowing by her reaction that she remembers him. "Haven't seen you in awhile. How you been?"

"Yeah, I... I've been good... busy," Simone stutters.

"Oh, here's Casper." He hands Casper over to Simone. "I think they like each other. I had to chase this little one all the way over here."

"Yeah, he tends to like other dogs. Male dogs specifically," Simone confesses.

"Yeah, this guy too. Apparently, he's a little charmer and brings all the boys to the yard," Parker jokes. They both put their dogs down and let them play around with each other while they catch up.

"Is he yours?" Simone asks.

"No. He belongs to a friend of mine. He's a bartender too. Oh, Chico! The latino guy, who works the front bar with me. You probably saw him." Parker tries to jog her memory.

Simone shakes her head. "Sorry. I only went that one time and that night is kind of a blur." She looks away awkwardly, trying to avoid eye contact with Parker.

"Yeah, what happened that night?" The details of that night are still a bit of a mystery to Parker.

"Oh, nothing. I just had to go. In fact, I should probably be getting back to my party." Feeling uncomfortable, Simone tries to back out of the conversation.

"Yeah, right. Sorry to keep you." Parker realizes he probably pushed too far. "Well, it was nice seeing you again."

"Yeah, you too. Come on, Casper." She turns around and walks back to her party, kindly scolding Casper as he walks alongside her.

"Hey wait!" He runs up to her. José runs up too. He starts up in conversation again, "Hey, look… I know this is probably a long shot, but… do you wanna go out some time?"

Completely confused, Simone asks, "Don't you have a girlfriend?"

"Oh, Momi? Yeah, she was my girlfriend, until she realized that she's a lesbian, so… that's how that worked out," Parker discloses what happened between him and Momi in a short and sweet manner.

"You think?" Simone says strongly and sarcastically. "She basically had her hands down my pants at your club."

"Oh so you do remember what happened that night?" Parker catches her in her lie.

Simone scoffs playfully and smiles. Knowing that she's been caught. "I might have some memories," she admits.

"I really don't know what happened between the two of you that night, but I'm sorry for putting you in that situation," Parker apologizes sincerely.

"It wasn't your fault. I was the one that decided to come." Simone takes the blame.

"I promise Violet's not always like that." Parker does his best at convincing her. "And, if it makes you feel any better, Momi is happily with another woman."

"And you?" Not wanting to play any more games, Simone asks Parker what his relationship status is outright.

"Me? Nah, I'm still waiting for the right woman to come

along. Hopefully one that loves dogs and ice cream, too..."
Parker plays her game, but in his own way. Simone rolls her
eyes playfully. "We have a lot of food back over there." He
points toward the tents. "You should come by. We're celebrating
my friend's parent passing."

"A funeral?" She scrunches up her face, "Nah, I'd feel too
awkward."

"What about tomorrow then?" Parker comes back with
quickly, not wanting to give up on this fate-placed opportunity.
"Can I take you out? Maybe some ice cream. I know you like
ice cream."

"You know what..." Simone pauses, looks at Casper and
José playing and having a good time, then answers, "Sure. Why
not?"

"Uh, I don't have my phone on me," Parker just realizes.

"Yeah, neither do I." They both ran to find their dogs
leaving their phones behind.

"Alright, well, let's do this..." Parker comes with a plan,
"Let's meet up at the ice cream place just around the corner
from Violet at 6pm. We'll get dessert first and then get some
dinner."

"At the place where we first met?" Simone raises one
eyebrow. "You think you're so sly, huh?"

"I didn't even realize that. I promise!" Parker pleads.

"Alright, fine, but don't be late or I'm leaving." Simone
finally realizes that the ball is in her court now.

"Ok. Yeah, I won't," Parker obeys.

"Come on, Casper. Let's go."

"I'll see you tomorrow!" Parker says with a huge grin. She
looks back at him, smiles and then runs back to her party.

Back at the tents, everyone is drinking, getting loose and
having a good time. Music plays loudly over the big portable

speaker that Sam brought and the guests socialize, recalling their best memories of Robin.

Parker hands José back to Chico, but Chico just puts him down and lets him roam freely. Malu and Ashley are joking back and forth with Kaimana and Kehau, while Chyna and Rowena talk about old times. Momi, Tisha, Sam and Yuki swim in the shore break as the Fish y Chicks stand in a circle, trying to keep the volleyball up as long as they can.

Beau, having had one too many beers, notices the Fish y Chicks and decides he wants to play too. Stumbling in their direction, he trips and faceplants, spilling his beer everywhere. The Fish y chicks crack up at Beau's expense, all except Karmen Sense.

Karmen runs over to check on him, "Oh my God! Are you ok?"

Beau hops up quickly and dusts himself off, "I'm good. I did that on purpose."

Karmen chuckles, "No, you didn't. You ate it."

"Not!" Beau has no other come back.

"Oh my God! Look at your knee!" Karmen gets Beau to look down at his knee which he managed to scrape when he fell. A tiny little cut, with the smallest amount of blood, starts to bleed out. Beau sees this minuscule amount of blood and immediately faints.

Karmen slaps his face, but Beau is out cold. Having done a lot of weight lifting before she transitioned, Karmen gets herself into a proper stance and picks Beau up. Hoisting him over her shoulder, Beau's dead weight doesn't phase Karmen in the slightest.

She looks back at the Fish y Chicks and tells them, "I'll be back." Not knowing what just happened or why Karmen is wasting her time on him, the Fish y Chicks go back to lofting the volleyball back and forth.

Karmen carries him all the way to Alexus' Toyota Camry. Figuring the car would be within sight distance, the Fish y Chicks left the doors unlocked. Karmen opens the door to the back seat and plops him down inside. As he hits the cushion of the back seat, he starts to come back to his senses.

Still drunk and only half conscious, Beau looks up at Karmen, who is standing at the open back door looking down at him. With the sun shining from Karmen's back, it makes her look as if she's glowing.

"Wow, I must be in heaven," Beau slurs.

"What?" Karmen can't make out what Beau just said.

"This must be my reward for being such a good person on Earth." In his delirious state, Beau thinks he died and is now in heaven. "Come here, angel. Beau's got a big *present* for you." Already shirtless and just in his surf shorts, he pulls down his shorts and exposes his dick.

Karmen, having seen a lot dicks in her days, looks at Beau's and tilts her head, *I thought it would be bigger*. She shrugs her shoulders and smiles, she never passes up a fun time. She hops in the back seat with him, closes the door and the two of them go at it like two horned up jack rabbits.

The Fish y Chicks look back at Alexus' Toyota Camry that's now bouncing up and down.

"Ew!" Arita yells.

"Not in the car!" Alexus shouts, but knows it's too late.

"So, that's why she went to help him." Matt finally catches on to the situation.

29. Blue Hawaii

- 1 1/2 oz Rum
- 3/4 oz Blue Curaçao Liqueur
- 3/4 oz Coconut Cream
- 2 oz Pineapple Juice

A few hours later with the sun slowly making its exit, Chyna gathers the remaining guests. With Robin's celebration being an all day thing, some of the guests have left, while some others have just arrived. Chyna assembles Robin's friends and family and herds them toward the far end of Yokohama Beach.

"Hi everyone. We're about to spread Robin's ashes, so if we could all make our way toward the rocky area over there. You'll see Robin's sons on the rocks, that's where we'll be scattering her ashes."

As the guests slowly start to filter in, the three brothers share a tender moment before the loads of guests make their way over. With Malu holding the base of the urn of ashes, Kaleo holding the sides and Lopaka placing his hands on the top, the three brothers face each other with Robin at the center. They take a big breath in and exhale together. They close their eyes and Kaleo begins a little prayer just between the three of them.

"Dear God, Dear Universe, Dear Higher Power… Thank you for all that you've given us. Thank you for giving us life. Thank you for giving us breath. Thank you for giving us each other. Thank you for giving us Robin." Kaleo pauses trying to stop himself from crying, "Thank you for Robin, Lord. Thank you for blessing us with such a beautiful soul, who we were lucky to call our parent. Take care of her on the other side and let her spirit fly. Let her be with us in everything that we do, in every moment that we succeed and especially when we fall.

Give us the strength to move forward without her in this life, but keep her near our hearts always. Take care of our health and let us take care of each other, just as Robin always took care of us." Kaleo looks at his brothers to see if they want to say anything.

"We love you, Robin. Thank you for everything you've ever done for us. We love you so much," Lopaka adds to the prayer with tears in his eyes.

"We love you, Dad," Malu expresses simply.

"Amen," Kaleo concludes the prayer.

"Amen," Lopaka and Malu follow suit.

The three brothers wipe away their tears, look up at each other and smile. Malu kisses the urn, then cradles it as the other two remove their hands. They look back at the group of guests, who have now fully collected and have been watching them silently.

In the front of the group, standing in a line side by side, the Violet staff hold hands and wipe away tears as they watch the brothers finish their prayer. At the front and center of the entire crowd, Chyna stands there with a bouquet of violet-colored roses in her hands. With tears in her eyes, but a smile on her face, she looks at the boys and nods to begin.

Kaleo motions for Chyna to join them at the top of the rocks, but she shakes her head no. She waves her hand as to shoo the boys and continue without her, but Kaleo jumps off the rocks and physically grabs her to join them at the top. He looks her dead in her eyes and says, "We're not doing this without you." Chyna finally concedes and stands next to the three brothers as they begin.

"Knowing Robin, she would've hated all of this attention. She loved the attention when she was performing on stage, but when it came to her personal life, she would've rather kept it private. But today, it's all about you Robin, whether you like it or not." The crowd laughs quietly. "You were so many things to so many people, but most of all, you were a rock. You were our rock and a pillar to the gay community. You kept us going, you pushed us forward and you're going to continue to do that from the other side, whether *we* like it or not." The guests laugh again. "We love you, Robin, from now until forever. Thank you for everything."

The three brothers and Chyna turn around and face the ocean. Chyna starts singing the old Hawaiian song "Aloha Oe" and the rest of the guests slowly join in. Now with the entire group singing, Malu walks to the edge, opens the urn and starts pouring Robin's ashes into the ocean. Some of the ashes get swept away in the wind, but most land where the water meets the rocks and creates the reef.

Just as the song comes to an end and Malu pours out the last of Robin's ashes, a butterfly comes flying by. The entire crowd of guests notice this random butterfly as it flaps it wings near the brothers and then toward Chyna. With the bouquet of roses still in her hand, Chyna follows this butterfly's path heading straight toward her. The butterfly flaps its last flap and rests itself right on one of Chyna's violet-colored roses.

The crowd gasps and the three brothers watch in amazement. They knew how much Robin loved butterflies. Chyna breaks down and starts to cry. "It's her, it's her!" She holds out the bouquet for everyone to see and those who were not already crying, begin to shed tears.

She holds the bouquet close to her mouth and with the butterfly still resting on the flower, she whispers, "I love you, sis." The butterfly takes off with the last breath of Chyna's affirmation and flies happily into the sunset. Chyna smells the bouquet one last time and throws it into the ocean.

After a few minutes, the crowd disperses. Some walk back to the tents while others stay and watch the sunset. Chyna stands alone and stares off into the distance, trying to take in all that just happened. The three brothers hop off the rocks and into the arms of the Violet employees. Single hugs, turn into double hugs and eventually a big group hug is formed amongst all the friends. After separating, the friends pair up and slowly head back to the tents chatting the whole way. Kaleo and Parker are the last left behind and trail the rest of the group.

"That was beautiful," Parker admits to his best friend.

"Thanks," Kaleo responds. He takes a breath and turns to his best friend, "Thank you, Parker, for everything. We've been through so much and you're still by my side."

"And I always will be." Parker smiles and assures any doubts that Kaleo might have. Kaleo jumps into Parker's arms and hugs him tightly. As they hug, Parker notices a good-looking asian guy, standing on the side and smiling at Kaleo. "Looks like you have a visitor." Kaleo turns around and sees Jimmy standing there in a T-shirt, surf shorts and slippers. "He's hot! Go talk to him."

Kaleo pushes his best friend playfully. "What do you know about hot guys?"

"Well, I am one, so…" Parker jokes.

As the two friends walk toward Jimmy, Jimmy's eyes never break from Kaleo.

"Hey," Jimmy greets as they get near.

"Hi… I didn't know you were here," Kaleo admits.

"Yeah, I came when Chyna was ushering everyone over," Jimmy explains. "Just in time."

"Hey, I'm Parker," Parker butts in, wanting to know who this guy is.

"Oh sorry. This is my best friend, Parker. He's a bartender at Violet too," Kaleo introduces.

"Yeah, I've seen you. You work at the front bar, right?" Jimmy asks. Parker nods in confirmation. The two boys shake hands and Jimmy introduces himself, "Jimmy. It's nice to meet you."

"Ohhh, so you're the Jimmy that Kaleo told me about," Parker says with an accusatory tone in his voice.

"Oh he has, has he?" Jimmy looks back at Kaleo with a smile.

"That's enough, Parker," Kaleo says mildly to get his friend to be quiet.

"Yup, he was just telling me how he met this handsome guy named Jimmy and how he wants to see where it will go, but he's too afraid."

"That's enough, Parker!" Kaleo yells to stop Parker from disclosing anything else.

"I'll let you guys catch up." Parker starts to walk away, but then turns back and looks Kaleo in the eyes, "Finish what you started!" He spouts their old friendship motto with a smile, then heads back to the tents.

"Wow, you had some nice things to say about me," Jimmy acknowledges what Parker just confessed.

"I didn't say all of that," Kaleo defends himself.

"But you did say some of it though, right?" Jimmy pursues. Kaleo smiles and avoids eye contact knowing that he's been check-mated. "Hopefully the handsome part and the part about how you want to see where it will go…"

"Thanks for coming," Kaleo quickly tries to change the subject.

"I wouldn't miss it for the world." Jimmy stops playing and looks Kaleo right in his eyes. "My mom and dad couldn't make it, but they said they were gonna send over some Chinese food."

"Some?! They sent a feast for a whole village!" Kaleo exaggerates. "Tell them I said thank you."

"Maybe you can tell them yourself, when we all go out to dinner one night?" Jimmy casually slips into conversation.

"I told you, I don't play that in the closet, 'I'm just a friend' bullshit," Kaleo reminds him.

Jimmy chuckles, "And you won't have to."

"What do you mean?"

"Well… seeing Robin pass away made me realize how short life is and how unhappy I've been. I've been playing so many different roles to so many different people and when you said you didn't date guys, who were in the closet, it made me really think. It made me think about if I was living my life for me or if I was living my life the way everyone else wanted me to live it. So… I grew some balls and I told my parents. I told them that I was gay."

"Seriously?" Kaleo's eyes widen and his jaw drops agape.

"As serious as I can be," Jimmy says with a confident smile, "And funny enough, they took it pretty well too. My dad didn't want to hear it at first, but my mom talked him into it. They basically told me that they don't care that I'm gay as long as I have a good job and make good money. I mean, they are Chinese after all." The two boys share a laugh.

"Wow. I must say, I'm impressed," Kaleo admits.

"And it's all because you gave me the 'Gayest drink you have!'" Kaleo rolls his eyes, remembering the first time Jimmy ever ordered from him. "So, thank you."

"You're welcome," Kaleo says smugly.

"So… can I have that date now?" Jimmy gets right back to the point.

"You just won't give up, huh?"

"I'm consistent." Jimmy flashes his eyebrows. "Why don't we just start with a walk on the beach. Can I at least have that?" Jimmy asks kindly. Kaleo smiles and nods. "Come on." Jimmy offers his arm like an escort and Kaleo links his arm in his. The two boys walk along the shoreline as the sun sets, joking and laughing the entire time.

30. Li Hing Mui Margarita

- 1 oz Tequila
- 1/2 oz Triple Sec
- 1 oz Sweet and Sour
- 1/2 tsp Li Hing Mui Powder
- 1 dash lime juice

Almost two months have passed and things have calmed down since Robin's passing. Lopaka has gone from a no-named go-go boy to a reality TV star with his appearance as 'Jenna Talia' on 'America's Next Top Drag Queen.' With the show airing every Friday and Violet throwing a viewing party every week, the local LGBT+ community have come together to support 'Jenna' and watch as she takes down her competitors week by week.

With only three contestants left, tonight is the night where the finale episode will be aired and the whole world will find out (what the three brothers already know) that Lopaka takes the win.

Sitting at a table in *Taco Hell*, the Mexican restaurant a couple blocks away from Violet, Chyna and Lopaka finish up the rest of their early dinner.

"I'm so proud of you," Chyna says and touches his cheek with her hand.

"Thank you," Lopaka replies.

"You've come so far in such a short amount of time and I'm just so happy that you've come into your own. Some people never do," Chyna admits.

"I know and it wouldn't have happened if you never gave me that speech that one day," Lopaka confesses.

"What speech?" Chyna questions.

"You don't remember?" Lopaka looks at Chyna with offense. "We were sitting right here, at this exact table with Robin. I was upset about Ryan not calling me for the billionth time and you let me have it. You said 'If he wanted to be with you, he would be with you' and then you said something like 'You're settling and you know what the saddest part is… you know you are.' And the truth was, I did know that, but no one ever had the courage to say it to my face. Shit, I didn't have the courage to say it to myself! You really made me think."

"I said all that?" Chyna is impressed with herself.

"You don't remember?!" Lopaka can't believe that something that has changed his life isn't at all memorable to the one person who said it.

"Boy, I am too old to be held accountable for all that I say… but I do give some good advice, huh?" She winks at him and the two of them share a laugh. "Everything happens for a reason, babe."

"You know, you always hear people saying that, but you never really understand it's meaning until something big happens to you."

Just as he finishes his sentence, the three little gay boys with matching outfits walk up to Lopaka excitedly. Once obsessed with the Fish y Chicks, they have now transitioned into die-hard 'Jenna Talia' fans.

"Oh my God! Hi! Sorry, we don't want to interrupt, but we just want to say how much we love you on America's Next Top Drag Queen!" The little gay in red can't help, but speak to his idol.

"You're, for sure, gonna win tonight!" The little gay in yellow says without a doubt.

"Aww, thanks guys," Lopaka, who is completely out of drag, expresses his gratitude toward these three fans.

"Do you mind if we get a photo with you?" The little gay in

blue asks apologetically.

"No, of course not. Here." Lopaka takes the little gay in blue's phone and hands it to Chyna.

"And what am I? Chopped Liver?" Chyna jokes. "I"m just kidding boys, get in there." She snaps a photo of Lopaka with the three little gays and hands the phone back to them.

"Thank you so much!" The little gay in blue thanks Lopaka and immediately begins posting the photo to his Instagram.

"Are you guys coming to Violet tonight?" Lopaka asks the boys.

"We wouldn't miss it for the world!" The little gay in yellow says with conviction.

"Thank you again!" The little gay in red puts his hands together in a prayer position to thank Lopaka. They take off jumping and giggling as if they just met Beyoncé.

"You see what I mean? I'm just so proud of you." Chyna smiles at Lopaka like he is her own son. "Let's go see if they need help setting up for your big finale."

"Don't you wanna know if I won or not?" Lopaka asks.

"Nope! Don't even care in the slightest," Chyna declares.

"What!"

"Because to me, you've already won. You're *my* winner," Chyna confesses.

"Awww, so corny," Lopaka ruins the tender moment.

"Shut up, boy! You might be a celebrity to the youngin's, but you remember who changed your diapers when you were little." Chyna snaps right back into Aunty mode. "I will whoop your ass harder than Robin used to!" Chyna pretends as if she's going to spank Lopaka. He laughs and scurries away. "Get back here and clean up your mess!"

31. Four Horsemen

- 1/2 oz Jack Daniel's Tennessee Whiskey
- 1/2 oz Jim Beam Bourbon Whiskey
- 1/2 oz Johnny Walker Scotch Whiskey
- 1/2 oz Jameson Irish Whiskey

Outside of Violet, the staff congregate and wait until Kaleo shows up with the key. The entrance doors to Violet have been painted over with a huge butterfly in tribute to Robin. Malu and Sam shoot the shit right outside the doors alongside Chico, Yuki and Tisha. Momi and Ashley stand further away and have one of their private cousin chats.

"How are you and Malu?" Momi asks.

"Oh, we're great. Things really took a turn that night he got hurt," Ashley reveals.

"Yeah, that was a scary time," Momi affirms.

"You're telling me! Funny enough though, it really brought us closer together," Ashley confesses. "I think when you're truly faced with not knowing if the person you love is going to make it or not, you realize a lot. We don't take each other for granted anymore and we just take things less seriously. Well, we take the dumb shit less seriously. We've learned how to just let the unimportant things go."

"The key to life: 'Let it Go,'" Momi summarizes.

"Shit, for real though," Ashley confirms.

"Do you miss working here?" Momi asks her cousin.

"Nah, not really. I mean, I miss working with all of you guys, but it's better for our relationship and better that I stay with the kids."

A few weeks after Robin's funeral, Malu and Ashley decided that it was more important to have at least one of them be at home with the kids every night. With the club basically being a part of Malu's DNA, they agreed that Malu would continue to work at Violet with his brothers and Ashley would take care of the kids.

"Yeah, I know what you mean," Momi supports her decision.

"It's better for all the boys that walk through that door too," Ashley states while in her sweatpants and no make-up. Just coming to drop off Malu, she figures what's the point of dressing up.

"What do you mean?" Momi asks needing clarification.

"No one will get head-butted because of Malu's jealous rages over me anymore." The two girls share a laugh, knowing it's the truth.

"Nah, but he's been getting better at his temper," Ashley discloses. "I guess, it helps that he's been taking MMA classes and getting all his aggression out over there."

"Yeah, I saw that on his Instagram," Momi admits.

"Yup. And he's good too! I guess I shouldn't be so surprised. He's always watching UFC on TV." Ashley changes the subject, "How's Yuki working the door?"

"You know what? He's actually pretty good," Momi reveals. "I think carrying buckets of ice or a stack of cups was not his forte. Now he sits behind a register all night and collects entrance fees. It's perfect for him. Nothing for him to trip over."

"Good, I was worried about who would take over my position, but it seems like it's all working out." Ashley's guilt of leaving subsides.

"Yeah, it is," Momi reassures her.

"Speaking of which, how are you and Tisha working out?" Ashley presses her cousin. She wants to know the 4-1-1.

"Oh we're not together anymore," Momi responds without hesitation.

"Really?!"

"Yeah, I mean we still fuck around every once in awhile, but it's casual," Momi explains.

"Wow, I thought you guys were in it for the long haul," Ashley admits.

"Yeah, we tried it, but we decided it was better if we were just friends," Momi clarifies.

"Is it awkward that you guys still have to work right next to each other?" Ashley presses further.

"No, not at all. If anything, it makes it easier 'cause now we're free to flirt with whoever we want. Whether it's for a tip or for a phone number, we're free to do as we please. We even help each other sometimes." Momi chuckles to herself.

"Really?" Ashley's having a hard time believing the situation.

"Yup. I mean, I'm freshly out of the closet. It's time for me to explore my *lesbianism*." Momi says the last word in her sentence like a soap opera actress.

"Oh god, here she goes." Ashley rolls her eyes playfully.

"What? It's true," Momi defends her statement.

"Bitch, you've *been* exploring your lesbianism for years now," Ashley corrects her cousin.

"You're not wrong," Momi concurs.

From around the corner, Parker and Simone come walking hand in hand toward the club. In their other hand, they each have their own ice cream cone from the shop just a block away. They wave hello to the two cousins and head straight to the bigger group of employees.

"Good morning!" Momi and Ashley say in unison as the couple passes by. The couple wave back politely. However, knowing that it's early evening, Simone is confused. She looks to Parker, who explains to her that 'Good Morning' is just Violet lingo for 'hello.' She quickly catches on.

232

"She's a ditz, huh?" Ashley starts back up in a private conversation with Momi.

"Nah, she's actually really sweet," Momi defends Simone.

"How do you know? Have you tasted her?" Ashley twists.

"I tried." The cousins laugh remembering the infamous night that she actually did try.

"How are you and Parker anyway?" Ashley digs in.

"Fine. Like we were before, except now we're not dating," Momi describes their current status.

"That's great!"

"Yeah, it really is. I mean, he's such a good guy, you know. He could've been bitter and held onto a grudge and all of it would've been completely understandable, but he didn't." Momi looks at Parker chatting and laughing with the rest of the Violet employees. He randomly looks over at Momi and Momi winks one of her infamous winks at him. He smiles and goes back to conversing. "He chose not to hold onto any of that and now we're both happier and happy for each other."

"He *Let it go*," Ashley works in the saying.

"He sure as fuck did! And quick, too! Man, we gotta put that on a shirt. 'L.I.G.' Let it go."

As Momi imagines creating a shirt with the letters L.I.G. printed across the front, Alexus' Toyota Camry pulls right up next to Ashley and Malu's SUV. When it stops, one of the doors to the back seat is the first to open and Beau exits the car promptly.

After Beau and Karmen's drunken hook-up, Beau realized that it was the best sex that he's ever had. Being a hedonistic hormonal male, he eventually went back for seconds (and thirds) and now he and Karmen have developed a weird unofficial relationship. Seeing how Karmen is a transgender *woman*, Beau found this as a loophole to justify sleeping with her in his small mind.

The rest of the Fish y Chicks get out of the car a second later. Alexus' pops the trunk and Beau immediately starts taking out their luggage.

"Looks like Karmen got Beau to be their bag boy," Ashley narrates as she watches Beau lift the Fish y Chicks' bags out one by one.

"More like *bitch* boy. I still can't stand him," Momi remarks.

"Hey, I give him credit for being open enough to be with Karmen," Ashley admits.

"No, don't give him any credit. He's a male chauvinistic pig," Momi comes back with immediately.

"Wow, you really have turned lesbian," Ashley jokes. "No, I meant I give him credit for being with Karmen because she's dumb as a rock.

"Well… like attracts like, right?" Momi convinces.

From around another corner, Chyna and Lopaka pop out of nowhere and walk toward the two cousins. They join the two girls in their conversation.

"Who would've thought, huh? Beau and Karmen," Lopaka starts off with.

"That's what we were just talking about!" Ashley reveals.

"I knew!" Chyna admits, "I knew it was only a matter of time with that one." She lifts her head and motions toward Beau.

"Really?" Ashley asks.

"Girl, I've met many men in my time… if you know what I mean," Chyna implies that she's been a hooker for a long time. "He's a classic Craigslist type. You know the ones: they swear up and down that they're straight, but hitting my ad up left and right when they're home alone."

Lopaka looks back at Beau and Karmen, who are now making out like animals. With a disgusted look on his face, he says, "Well, good for them, I guess." He then looks over to the group of Violet workers and notices his ex-boyfriend, Ryan, among the others.

"What is Ryan doing here?" Lopaka asks hastily.

"He's new security," Ashley informs. "He's gonna work the door with Malu and Sam."

"Since when?" Lopaka is shocked to hear this news.

"Since tonight. Tonight's his first night, I think," Momi responds.

"Malu said they needed help monitoring the entire club, so he asked Ryan and Ryan said 'yes,'" Ashley delivers as stoically as possible, trying to inform Lopaka without triggering him.

"Why him of all people?" Lopaka is completely thrown off.

"Did you know that Ryan was the one that threw the guys off of Malu when he got stabbed," Ashley enlightens her friend.

"No." Lopaka thought Malu took care of his attackers himself, but just got stabbed in the process.

"Yeah, if Ryan hadn't been there at that time, Malu might be dead right now," Ashley paints out the horrible possibility. "Look, I'm not saying that that excuses him for everything he did to you in the past, but look at you now, you're on TV! Who cares about all that old shit? He's probably regretting he ever treated you like that."

"L.I.G. Paka," Momi asserts.

"What?" Lopaka has no idea what Momi is talking about.

"*Let it go*," Momi explains the acronym.

"You know, if it wasn't for him breaking your heart, you might never have even tried drag. Everything happens for a reason. Remember I said that earlier?" Chyna voices the hard truth. Lopaka nods his head reluctantly. "Go talk to him. Squash it and move on."

Lopaka walks over to the rest of the group. Everyone's there: his brother Malu, Sam, Parker and Simone, Chico, Tisha,

Yuki, Beau, the four Fish y Chicks and Ryan.

"What's up guys," Lopaka says mildly.

"Oh la la! Here he is! America's Next Top Drag Queen!" Chico shouts and everyone starts applauding and cheering.

"No, we don't know that yet!" Lopaka stops his friends from assuming that he won, even though he already knows he has.

"Well, you might be!" Tisha encourages. The Fish y Chicks rolls their eyes out of jealousy.

"Yeah, tonight's the big night!" Malu tries to hype his brother up.

"Are you nervous?" Yuki asks innocently.

"Nah, it's already all recorded and set. All I have to do now is watch," Lopaka downplays.

"Oh, so, are you admitting that you won?" Sam plays detective.

"Nice try! and I'm not admitting anything." Lopaka isn't falling for any traps. "You'll just have to wait and find out like everyone else. It's just a couple more hours. Jeez."

Malu walks up to Lopaka and gives him a hug. He pulls him aside to have a private conversation of their own. "Hey, I just want you to know how proud I am of you and I can't wait for everybody else to find out because number one, this secret is killing me and number two, there's never been anyone more deserving."

"Aww thank you, Malu." Lopaka is touched by his brother's kind words.

"I mean that. You've been through a lot of shit and it's about time for you to catch a break." Malu continues in a quieter tone, "A hundred thousand dollar break at that. Shit." The brothers share a laugh.

"I noticed that you put Ryan on the team," Lopaka confronts head on.

"Oh," Malu is caught off guard, "Yeah, I meant to talk to

you about that first, sorry. He's really—"

"It's cool," Lopaka cuts him off. "I heard he saved you."

"Yup. He's pretty strong cause the guy that got me with the knife was a bigger guy," Malu describes.

"Thank God he was there," Lopaka expresses.

"Yessah!"

"How are you doing anyway?" Lopaka asks. Malu lifts up his shirt to reveal his scar of where he got stabbed.

"All healed!" Malu says in a cocky manner. "And now I get one fancy doodle mark on my body. I let the kids color around it with their markers."

"Maybe I should thank Ryan," Lopaka jokes, but Malu takes him seriously.

"Really? I'll call him over. You want me to?"

"Shit, why not?" Lopaka figures he has to talk to his ex sooner or later.

"Ryan! Try come," Malu yells. Ryan walks over and joins the two brothers.

Ryan walks up to Malu and asks, "What's up?" He looks over at Lopaka and gives a cordial, "Hey," trying to test the waters.

"Lopaka wanted to talk to you." Malu turns around quickly and walks back to the group leaving the two exes to speak privately.

"Hey," Ryan starts.

"Hey," Lopaka responds. For a brief moment, there's an awkward silence between the two of them.

"Congratulations on tonight. I mean, if you win... But even if you don't win, still congratulations. I mean, that's pretty cool that you—"

"Ryan, shut up," Lopaka cuts him off. "I want to say thank you."

"Really?" Ryan is confused and isn't sure where this is

going.

"Yes. I want to say thank you for saving my brother and…" Lopaka pauses, "Also, for saving me in a way." Ryan decides to stay silent and let him finish. "Honestly, Ryan, you really hurt me."

"I know and I'm sorry," Ryan apologizes.

"But that hurt turned into anger and that anger turned into passion. Passion that took me all the way to the top, to the finale, to tonight. This crazy gay fame thing wouldn't be happening if I never met you. So, I want to say thank you."

"Ok, my turn," Ryan turns the tables, "I'm sorry, Paka. I was a dick. I stood you up on more than one occasion and I played with your emotions. I knew what I was doing to you the whole time, but… I was dumb. There's no excuse. Hey, look, I know you're gonna be busy now that you're a hotshot celebrity and all…"

"Shut up," Lopaka says through a smile.

"But maybe, if you ever have some free time, we should go out to dinner," Ryan offers.

"HELL NO!" Lopaka comes back with immediately. "I'm never waiting for your ass at a restaurant ever again!" Ryan laughs, knowing his attempt was a longshot.

"Fair enough," Ryan states unhurt.

"But maybe if it's a group thing and we all go as friends," Lopaka tweaks the conditions.

"Deal."

Parker's phone buzzes. He reaches into his pocket to check it. On the lock screen, there's a text from Kaleo. "Oh here it is ladies and gentlemen. Let's see what the problem is this time," Parker announces to the group of Violet employees.

The entire group congregates. Momi, Ashley and Chyna join in from the left and Lopaka and Ryan rejoin from the right.

Finally getting his phone situated, Parker reads the text out loud, "I'm running late."

"Yeah, no shit," Momi expresses.

"We figured that much out," Ashley backs up her cousin.

"Tell him I said to get his ass over here," Lopaka instructs.

"Yeah, her highness is getting a blister standing around so long," Beau says sarcastically. Lopaka shoots him a sharp look.

"Oh wait, he's typing…" Parker adds to the conversation. Three dots flash in his text to Kaleo, indicating that Kaleo is typing and about to send something through. "'But I'm just around the corner.'" Kaleo's text comes through and Parker reads it aloud.

"Yeah, we'll see about that," Alexus, of the Fish y Chicks, says under her breath.

Without as much as a beat passing, a Prius turns the corner and pulls up to the entrance of Violet. On both sides of the car, there's an advertisement that reads "Jimmy Wong, Wong Realty" with a picture of Jimmy smiling. Matching the photo on the side of his car, Jimmy drives up to the group of friends with the same huge smile and Kaleo in the passenger seat. He puts it in park and both of them get out.

The entire staff clap for Kaleo as he gets out of the car. Thinking it's funny, Jimmy laughs, gets out of the car and bows a grand bow.

"Alright, alright. That's enough." Kaleo tries to get his group of friends to calm down.

"And I thought I was gonna be the one receiving the applause tonight," Lopaka jests.

"Sorry to keep him guys," Jimmy apologizes. "We were having dinner with my parents."

"Ooo, dinner with the parentals," Momi says with a grin on her face. "Intimate."

"Shut up! It was for business," Kaleo explains. "I was actually gonna tell everyone this later, but since we are all here… we did it! With the help of Jimmy's power of persuasion, we got the papers signed over to us and we still own the club." The group erupts with real cheers this time. "After Robin passed, we needed to assign someone as the new owner and today, I'm happy to say that, instead of one owner, you now have four part-owners."

"Four?" Ashley asks.

"Yup. Me, Lopaka, Malu and Chyna," Kaleo divulges.

"ME?!" Chyna says completely shocked. The group cheers again.

"Yes, you! Chyna, my brothers and I wouldn't be anywhere in this world if it weren't for you. So, this is our gift to you."

Chyna bursts into tears. "Oh my God. I don't know what to say. Thank you, boys! So much."

"We talked it over and agreed that this is what Robin would've wanted," Lopaka declares.

"I'm speechless." Chyna can't find the words to express how she's feeling.

"Alright, alright. Now, everybody get inside and get to work. You're all late!" Kaleo unlocks the entrance doors and swings both doors wide open. The butterfly painting on the door splits in half and looks as if its wings are flapping.

"Yeah because of you!" Sam accuses.

"You're the one who's late!" Beau confronts. All of the employees playfully throw jabs at Kaleo.

"Yeah, yeah, yeah. Get it in there you buncha hoodrats!" Kaleo comes back with.

"You sound just like Robin!" Lopaka admits and then steps to the side to have a conversation with Malu and Chyna. Kaleo walks Jimmy back to his car door, so they can speak in private.

"Ok babe, I better get in there. You made me late!" Kaleo playfully blames Jimmy.

"Not as late as you used to be!" Jimmy justifies.

"True." Kaleo smiles and places himself an inch from Jimmy's face. Jimmy grabs him and kisses him a sweet kiss goodbye.

"I'll come by a little later, k?" Jimmy reassures Kaleo that he'll be back.

"Ok. Thank you again."

Jimmy gets back in his car, flashes his eyebrows at his boyfriend and, with a big smile still on, he pulls out and drives away.

Kaleo walks back toward the entrance of the club. With everyone else inside, the three brothers and Chyna are the only ones left outside.

"So… club owners, huh?" Malu double checks that it's a hundred percent true.

"Yeah, do you believe it?" Kaleo confirms.

"Boys, I don't know what to say. Thank you so much," Chyna starts. "This club has been just as much a part of my life as it has been yours. Thank you for continuing to have me be a part of it."

"We wouldn't have it any other way," Kaleo assures.

"You're family," Malu states.

"Yeah and now you're stuck with us whether you like it or not!" Lopaka jokes. The four of them share a laugh.

"Well, I guess the only thing we have to worry about now is coming up with the rent every month," Chyna thinks logically.

"I think we got that covered," Lopaka convinces. He smiles and winks at Chyna.

Chyna's eyes widen with surprise. With no words exchanged, she instantly realizes that Lopaka has won 'America's Next Top Drag Queen.' With tears in her eyes, she hugs Lopaka and whispers in his ear, "Congratulations, love!"

32. Tequila Sunrise

- 2 oz Tequila
- 4 oz Orange Juice
- 1/2 oz Grenadine

A few hours later, Violet is packed with a long line of people still outside, waiting to enter. Everyone's eyes are on Lopaka in full drag, who's standing on the stage watching his own image projected on the big screen. Standing patiently to the side, he awaits anxiously as the host of the show is about to announce him as the winner.

Even though he knows he's already won, Lopaka is filled to the brim with nervous energy. *What if I'm not the winner? What if at the last minute they chose to go with someone else? You just never know in Hollywood. I don't actually have the money yet. They said they would wire my bank account as soon as I was publicly announced as the winner.*

With the entire club silent and everyone holding onto each other, the host begins her final speech. "The winner of America's Next Top Drag Queen and the winner of one hundred thousand dollars is…" The TV show pauses for dramatic effect and the entire crowd does an almost synchronized inhale.

Things start to move in slow-motion for Lopaka as he looks around the room. He looks at the hundreds of guests that are packed in Violet just to see him. He looks at his brother, Kaleo, who is serving drinks to a long line of people. He looks down at his hands with purple fingernail polish and also at his beautifully beaded dress with a small butterfly pin just over his heart. Finally, he looks at the door to Robin's office. *I hope you're proud of me, Daddy.*

"…Jenna Talia!" The host announces on the big screen

waking Lopaka up out of his little trance and bringing him back to the present moment. The entire crowd erupts with cheers. Applause, shouts and screams of praise fill the entire room. *I did it. I actually won!*

Lopaka starts to cry tears of joy. He steps forward and waves to the large group of fans cheering for him.

As he starts to walk toward the audience, someone from behind taps him on his shoulder. He turns around and sees Chyna standing there with a large rope pikake lei. She smiles, leis him with the beautiful fragrant lei and hugs him tight.

"I'm so proud of you, babe," she whispers in Lopaka's ear. She finishes her hug and looks him straight in his eyes, "This is just the beginning for you." With a mic in one of her hands, Chyna steps to the front of the stage and starts to MC. "Ladies and Gentlemen, I present to you, the newest winner of America's Next Top Drag Queen, your Hawaii girl and Violet's very own... Miss Jenna Talia!"

The crowd erupts once again and a chant soon begins, "JEN-NA! JEN-NA! JEN-NA!" Lopaka steps next to Chyna and waves to the audience. Someone in the audience yells "SPEECH!"

"Yes, yes! Do you have any words for us?" Chyna hands the mic to Lopaka and takes a step back.

Lopaka exhales. He puts the mic to his mouth, but before he can say any words, he chokes up and gets teary-eyed. He puts the mic back down and puts his free hand over his heart. The audience cheers louder to encourage him.

After a brief moment, he exhales again and puts the mic back to his mouth. "Thank you so much! Thank you! Can you believe it?!" The audience screams again. "First of all, this win would not have been possible without so many people... To my brothers, Kaleo and Malu, you are everything that I'm not... responsible, stable and you are the machine that keeps this club operating. Thank you for all that you are and all that you do."

He looks over his shoulder at Chyna, "To you, Miss, sorry... MRS. Chyna Make Love, you are the glue that keeps, not only our little Violet family together, but this entire community together. Thank you for your leadership.

"To all my Hawaiians," The crowd goes nuts, "We may be small in number, but we are the strongest at heart. This win is for all the Hawaiians, who have ever felt overlooked or have felt less than. It's our time now, time to show the world who we are!

"And lastly," Lopaka looks down at his butterfly pin, "this win is for Robin. Many of you were lucky enough to know her, I was lucky enough to call her 'Dad.' This win is for you! Thank you for everything you've done for all of us. We love you!"

Lopaka bows and takes a step back to signal that he is finished. He hands the mic to Chyna, who steps forward and takes over. "America's Next Top Drag Queen everyone! Let's give it up for her. Thank you, Jenna." The audience continues to applaud.

"Ok, Jenna will be doing a meet and greet right here on this stage in about twenty minutes, so feel free to come and meet your local sistah, take a photo and buy one of her brand new T-shirts. At midnight, Jenna will be performing for the first time as your newly crowned winner, so don't go anywhere! But for now, grab a drink from your favorite bartender, make a new friend and dance the night away! Hit it, DJ!"

The music starts and Lopaka heads directly to Kaleo at the front bar. Fans stop him along the way for selfies and to tell him how much they love him. Once to the bar, he gets Kaleo's attention. "Excuse me! Excuse me! Bartender! Somebody spilled my shot. I need another one for free," Lopaka jokes.

"Shut up, Lopaka. I mean, your *highness*." Kaleo makes fun of his brother.

"It's Jenna Talia, thank you very much. Don't blow my

cover," Lopaka requests.

"Cover? Looks like you need a little more foundation to cover that stubble over there." Kaleo starts to feel Lopaka's cheek with his hand.

Lopaka slaps his brother's hand away. "Shut up, Leo!"

"What do you want?" Kaleo tries to hurry his brother.

"Jeez, so rude," Lopaka scoffs.

"Well, I'm busy. Look at how long my line is," Kaleo asserts. Lopaka looks back at all the people waiting for a drink.

"Yeah, you're welcome," Lopaka insinuates that the club is only busy because of him and Kaleo rolls his eyes.

"Alexus, I need more ice!" Kaleo yells without looking. Alexus takes her turn at rolling her eyes behind Kaleo's back.

"What is Alexus doing behind the bar?" Lopaka asks.

"She's our new barback," Kaleo informs.

"WHAT?!" Lopaka is shocked.

"Yup, all of the Fish y Chicks are. They gotta start contributing to this club too!" Kaleo reveals his first plan of action as a new part-owner of the club.

"Speaking of contributing… I wanted to give you this." Lopaka reaches in his bra, pulls out a check and hands it to Kaleo.

"Ew. It's damp," Kaleo pinches the check with his thumb and index finger, trying not to touch anymore of it than he needs to.

"Just take a look at it, would you!" Lopaka yells. Kaleo takes a look at the check and his eyes widen. "I just checked, they wired the money into my bank account once I was announced as the winner."

"Fifty thousand dollars?!" Kaleo questions. Lopaka stands smugly, knowing how happy his brother is about to be. "I thought it was supposed to be a hundred thousand?"

"So ungrateful! Give me that back!" Lopaka is fed up with

his brother's lack of gratitude and tries to grab the check back, but Kaleo retracts it.

"Nah, nah. Thank you, brother. For real," Kaleo quickly shapes up.

"I did win a hundred thousand, but I gotta pay taxes on it. Everybody knows that," Lopaka explains.

"This is really gonna help. You saved this club. Thank you, Paka and Congratulations!" Kaleo finally commends his brother and Lopaka smiles. "Now, get out of the way! You're holding up my line!"

"God, you really are like Robin!" Lopaka proclaims.

Lopaka steps to the side and is immediately met up with his other brother, Malu.

"Paka!" Malu yells over the music to get his attention. He hugs his brother to congratulate him, "You did it! How does it feel?"

"Surreal," Lopaka confesses, "and amazing!"

"Hey, Rowena and the girls are here. They wanted to congratulate you." Malu looks back to make sure Rowena, Kaimana and Kehau were still following him. Waiting patiently behind him, Malu steps to the side and let's his birth mother have a moment with his older brother.

"Hi *Jenna*!" Rowena laughs, "Congratulations! How exciting!" She leis him with a beautiful ginger lei and hugs him.

"We've been watching every week," Kaimana admits.

"You really were the best," Kehau assures.

"Thank you," Lopaka graciously accepts the compliment. Kaimana and Kehau each give him a lei as well. "Hey, listen… I'm sorry for walking away at the funeral. It was just a lot to process at one time and—"

"Don't be," Rowena stops him before he goes any further. "I walked away from you boys for your entire life, so you don't owe me or anybody else an apology." Lopaka nods in silence. "I

246

just hope that maybe we can start anew."

"I'd like that," Lopaka affirms.

"We all would!" Malu jumps back into the conversation and puts his arms around Rowena and Lopaka.

"Oh God! Malu you smell like mildew!" Lopaka says with a sour face on.

"No I don't." Malu sniffs his armpits to make sure.

"Do you guys want to see where I get ready?" Lopaka offers Rowena and his two half-sisters.

"Sure!" The girls respond emphatically. Malu heads back outside and Lopaka starts escorting the girls to his dressing room giving them a tour of Violet on the way.

Near the restrooms, the Fish y Chicks congregate. As the new barbacks, they've been carrying buckets of ice back and forth to the bartenders wells, collecting dirty cups from the dance floor and washing those cups in the sink.

"Ugh, I no can believe I gotta touch all dese cups dat everybody's mouths have been all ovah. So gross!" Arita Bitch expresses her disgust, in her pidgin accent.

"It's so embarrassing," Matt Makeup sides with his older brother.

"At least you guys aren't behind the bar the whole time, where Hitler can see your every move," Alexus Convertible implies that Kaleo is a dictator.

"I think it's kind of fun actually," Karmen Sense says with a smile. The other girls shoot her a sharp look.

"And the worst part of all is that we can't be in drag!" Alexus pouts.

"Oh my God, is that Jamba Nay?!" Karmen says as she looks toward the entrance of the club.

"It is!" Arita yells. The girls run over to greet her!

"OH MY GOD! JAMBA!" The Fish y Chicks hug and jump

up and down screaming.

"Jamba dis is my braddah, Matt. Matt, dis is Jamba," Arita introduces. "Dis is who you replaced."

"Ahh, so you're the infamous Jamba Nay Transy," Matt finally has a face to put to the name.

"That's me! It's nice to meet you." Jamba and Matt kiss each other on the cheek.

"We held a drag competition once you left to find your replacement," Alexus informs.

"Yeah, I heard," Jamba reveals. "But there's no replacing Jamba Nay, Honey!" She jokes, but is mostly serious.

"Wait, I thought you died and went to heaven?" Karmen says scratching her head.

"No Karmen, *Haven*. New Haven, Connecticut. My husband got restationed, remember?" Jamba reminds her Fish y Chick sister.

"Ooohhh!" Karmen doesn't remember, but pretends she does.

"I see not much has changed," Jamba hints that Karmen is still a clueless bimbo. "Wait, why aren't you girls in drag?" The girls look at each other, but don't say anything.

"Don't ask," Alexus asserts.

"Did you see dat Lopaka is doing drag now?" Arita questions her friend.

"Yeah and he just won ANTDQ! Ugh, I can't believe it." Alexus stomps her foot. She thought she was going to be the first queen from Hawaii on the show.

"HO HER GAWWD!" Jamba screams with disgust. Reunited, the Fish y Chicks gossip and chat, while completely ignoring their duties as barbacks.

Back at the front bar, Kaleo finally catches a break. He wipes the sweat from his forehead and takes a sip from his water bottle. He sees Parker finishing up with his last customer and heads over in his direction.

"Man, this is crazy, huh?" Kaleo expresses.

"Shit, you're telling me! And it ain't over yet," Parker admits.

"Yeah, I know." Kaleo pretends to be overwhelmed, but secretly loves the rush and the revenue that it's bringing.

"I'm proud of you, Leo," Parker delivers from out of the blue.

"For what?" Kaleo responds.

"You did it. You're a club owner. I know that's what you've always wanted," Parker commends his best friend.

"*Part*-owner," Kaleo clarifies. "But I kind of feel like I cheated, like I just got grandfathered into it."

Parker shakes his head, "That doesn't matter! I promise you no one is thinking that, except you. Be happy, man. Today is a day of celebration! In fact, we need to celebrate. You want a shot?"

"You know what…" Kaleo looks around the room at everyone drunk and dancing, "I'm actually good." For the first time in possibly years, Kaleo has declined a shot. Parker looks over at his friend with a shocked look on his face and then nods his head in approval.

A split second later, Jimmy walks up to the bar from the left and Simone walks up from the right. Meeting in the middle and not noticing each other, they both say "Hey!" to Kaleo in unplanned unison

"Hi babe, I didn't even see you walk in," Kaleo greets his boyfriend first.

"I'm Chinese, I'm stealthy," Jimmy jokes.

"Hi Simone. You look like you're having a lot of fun out there," Kaleo turns his attention to his best friend's girlfriend.

"Yeah, I love it here. The music is so good!" Simone says,

still bopping along to the beat. She's been dancing with her friends for at least a good hour.

"Yeah, it's a good playlist tonight!" Kaleo concurs. "Hey, have you two met?" He gets Simone and Jimmy to realize that they're standing right next to each other.

"Oh Simone!" Jimmy says feeling dumb for not having noticed her. "Yeah, of course we have!"

"Oh my God! Jimmy! Sorry, I didn't even know that was you!" Simone admits. The two friends hug and kiss each other hello.

"You want a shot?" Jimmy asks Simone.

"Sure!" Simone replies.

Jimmy looks back to his boyfriend on the other side of the bar, "Can I have two of the 'gayest drinks you have,' please?

"Oh, I'm not really drinking tonight, babe," Kaleo responds.

"Who said they were for you?" Jimmy says sarcastically.

"Oooop!" Simone looks away, trying not to laugh.

"I like him!" Parker comes forward and shakes Jimmy's hand over the counter. "What's up Jimmy!"

"Sup Parker! I want to buy Simone a shot. Is that cool with you?" Jimmy asks Parker.

"Yeah, of course, man," Parker replies.

Kaleo puts down two shot glasses and pours two shots of the finest whisky they have. "It's on the house," he informs.

"Aww, thanks babe." Jimmy leans in and kisses Kaleo over the bar counter.

"GAY!" Beau shouts as he walks by and ruins the moment. A bunch of large, buff men in leather turn around and give him a death glare wanting to hurt him for making fun of someone for being homosexual. "I was joking, I was joking! I know them! I promise. Don't hurt me!" Beau cowers and runs away.

"Cheers!" Jimmy holds up his shot glass to toast Simone.

"Cheers!" Simone clinks her glass to his and the two of

them swallow the whisky in one fast gulp.

"Let's go dance!" Simone pulls Jimmy to the dance floor without a choice. From the dance floor Jimmy looks back at Kaleo and shrugs his shoulders. He smiles at his boyfriend and then starts dancing with Simone.

"Looks like we got trouble on our hands, huh?" Parker says as he stands next to Kaleo. They watch their other halves dancing and having a great time together.

Kaleo's focus goes from his boyfriend dancing with Simone to noticing how crowded and full Violet is. He glances over at the stage where Lopaka is signing autographs and taking photos. On the screen behind Lopaka, a projection of a big butterfly flaps its wings in time with the music.

Kaleo looks back at his best friend and smiles, "Looks like we finally finished what we started."

Jared Paakaula is a hungry Hawaiian. He's in a deep, intimate relationship with food... it's about compromise. Born in Honolulu, he grew up in a mix of places on the island of O`ahu: Ewa Beach, Village Park and often Waianae. He is a part-time performer, a part-time recreational surfer and a part-time stepmom of two. "On The Rocks" is his first novel.

IG: @jaredkainoa

Made in the USA
Las Vegas, NV
01 December 2021

35755060R00152